I0740554

Sydney Dobell

The Poems of Sydney Dobell

Sydney Dobell

The Poems of Sydney Dobell

ISBN/EAN: 9783337401443

Printed in Europe, USA, Canada, Australia, Japan

Cover: Foto ©Andreas Hilbeck / pixelio.de

More available books at **www.hansebooks.com**

The Canterbury Poets.

EDITED BY WILLIAM SHARP.

SYDNEY DOBELL.

.˙. FOR FULL LIST OF THE VOLUMES IN THIS SERIES,
SEE CATALOGUE AT END OF BOOK.

The Poems of Sydney Dobell: Selected, with an Introductory Memoir, by Mrs. Dobell.

LONDON:

WALTER SCOTT, LIMITED,

PATERNOSTER SQUARE.

NEW YORK: 3 EAST FOURTEENTH STREET.

CONTENTS.

CONTENTS.

Introductory Memoir.

Introductory Memoir.

YDNEY DOBELL was born at Cranbrook, in Kent, on the 5th of April 1824. He died at Barton End House, Nailsworth, Gloucestershire, August 22nd, 1874.

Though he lived into his fifty-first year, his literary fame was achieved before he was thirty, and his literary labours well-nigh closed with his thirty-fifth. What he has left of completed work is, therefore, the product of comparative youth. But the mass of memoranda contained in his note-books testifies to the amount and to the importance of work planned for that future of restored health to which he always hopefully looked forward.

From both father and mother Sydney Dobell

[The biographical portion of this Introductory Note is chiefly extracted from the Memorial Notice preceding the collected edition of Sydney Dobell's Poems, edited by John Nichol, M.A., Oxon, LL.D., in 1875.]

inherited literary and speculative tastes. His father, John Dobell, the descendant of a younger branch of an old Sussex family, was the author of a remarkable book, entitled " Man unfit to govern Man." His mother, a woman of great force and originality of character, between whom and Sydney, her eldest-born, the attachment was of singular intensity, was a daughter of Samuel Thompson, well known in the earlier part of this century as a leader of political reform in the city of London, and as the founder of a " Church" intended to be on the primitive Christian model.

Both parents had strong prepossessions in favour of home education, and not one of their ten children was sent to school or college.

In 1835 John Dobell removed with his family to Cheltenham, where, till his death, he carried on the business of a wine-merchant. From the time he was twelve, Sydney was an energetic and indefatigable help to his father—a man of delicate health and nervous temperament. At the same time, the boy, with some assistance from tutors, pursued his own studies with a zeal greatly in excess of his physical strength. Later on, to these studies was added that of the law, there being at that time some idea of his qualifying for the bar.

His attempts at verse date from his fifth year; but after he had entered his teens these efforts were ambitious. A number of his early pieces were published in the local papers, he was encouraged by the favourable notice of the poet Campbell, and in his eighteenth year completed a drama entitled " Napoleon."

In the early summer of 1839 he became engaged to Emily Fordham, daughter of George Fordham, of Sandon-Bury, Cambridgeshire. The engagement was, of course, a long one, and the enchanted times of his youth were those seasons when, visiting Miss Fordham's home, the old Manor-House of the village, he left town and business behind him, and plunged into the pure pleasures of a thorough country life.

In 1844 he married, and, for the thirty years that followed till his death, his wife was his inseparable companion, intimately sharing his thoughts, hopes, and aspirations. After his marriage—(and it is well to note that the income on which the young people began was very slender, and their installation of the most modest)—Sydney Dobell continued for some years an active superintendence of his father's business.

At the beginning of 1847 he was laid aside by long and severe illness—rheumatic fever—from the effects of which he never completely recovered, though all his important literary work was done afterwards.

In 1848—his father having given up to him a branch business lately established in Gloucester—he went to live at the village of Hucclecote, two or three miles from that city, on the old Roman road ; and here, in a little study, looking over fields and orchards to the hills, great part of " The Roman " was written. Another change of residence was, however, soon necessary, and, late in this same year, he moved to Coxhorne House, Charlton

Kings, near Cheltenham—which house he held for five years.

"The Roman" was the outcome of the poet's enthusiasm for Italy and the Italian cause. This enthusiasm always remained, among many modifications and changes of opinion, a link between his earlier and later politics. One of the latest fragments found in his handwriting, "Mentana,"* bears witness to his undiminished and even passionate sympathy with the Italian struggle. It breaks off with these lines :—

> "That Italy who, tho' she hath been hewn
> In pieces,—as when the demons hew
> An Angel, whose immortal substance, true
> To his Eternal Image, is not slain,
> But from a thousand falchions rears again,
> Still undivided by division,
> His everlasting beauty, whole and one,—
> When sounds the trump at which the nations rise
> Shall lift her unseamed body to the skies,
> And in her flesh see God—" . . .

In 1850, with the publication of "The Roman" —the success of which was rapid and unmistakable—a new phase of life seemed to open before Sydney Dobell. The book, doubtless, owed something of its popularity to its subject. It is not too much to say that, since Byron "woke one morning to find himself famous," no young poet of this century had achieved so great and so unexpected a success.

If this sudden notoriety had no disturbing effect upon him, it was not that he cared for none of these

* Page 419, Collected Edition.

things. He greatly valued and desired power over the minds of other men. But he was pre-eminently one of those for whom this life is inseparable from the life hereafter ; weighted, therefore, with such a sense of deep and wide responsibilities as precludes danger of any "intoxication of success." For him, to use his own words,

> " To-day
> Washed Adam's feet and streams away
> Far into yon Eternity."

It was about this time that he published in *The Palladium* an article on " Currer Bell," which led to an interesting correspondence between him and Miss Brontë.*

In August of this year a visit to North Wales afforded him his first experience of anything wild or grand in nature, and, in the following year, he made a tour in Switzerland. For evidence of how he was impressed by the Alps and Alpine valleys the reader can turn to the description of Chamouni, extracted from " Balder," in the present volume.

The earlier part of 1852 was spent at Malvern : during his stay there he had some pleasant walks and talks with Tennyson, Carlyle, and Dr. Westland Marston, whose acquaintance he had previously made. The later part of this year and the first three months of 1853 were passed in London, where he met, and had more or less intercourse with, Robert

---

* This article, and the correspondence to which it gave rise, is printed in *The Life and Letters of Sydney Dobell.*

Browning, Ruskin, Holman Hunt, Emmanuel Deutsch, Mazzini, and other men of eminence in literature or art.

In April he returned to Coxhorne, but only for a brief rest. Coxhorne had to be given up. "Balder" was finished in a cottage-lodging on Amberley Hill, and soon after its completion he went to Scotland, where the three next years were spent ; the winters chiefly in Edinburgh, the summers in various parts of the Highlands.*

At the close of 1853, "Balder," part 1st, was published. Of the scheme of this book its author had written to a friend that he felt, at last, to have found scope for all his powers. Standing, as it does, alone, when, in the writer's mind, it was little more than an introduction to the Great Epic he hoped to write, it is not difficult to perceive why, though containing his deepest thought and noblest poetry, it failed to achieve popularity, or even to be generally understood. The plan of the book was unfortunate. It was pitched on too great a scale, and demanded more than the energy of one life for its accomplishment.

During the years passed in Scotland, he came into contact with most of the best and brightest spirits of the time and place, and formed many life-long friendships. In 1855 he issued, in conjunction with Alexander Smith, a small volume of sonnets on the Crimean War, and, in 1856, stirred by the same

---

* It should, perhaps, be said, that these frequent changes of residence had, almost invariably, for their object, the search of fresh advice or fresh treatment for his wife, always an invalid.

theme, he published the collection of lyrics, entitled
" England in time of War."

Before finally leaving Edinburgh, in April 1857,
he delivered a lecture " On the Nature of Poetry "
at the Philosophical Institution. But his health
had now begun seriously to give way, and symp-
toms of chest delicacy made residence in a milder
climate desirable. The four following winters were
spent at Niton, in the Isle of Wight, the summers
in Gloucestershire, at Cleeve Tower, Birdlip, and
other beautiful and elevated spots among the
Cotswolds.

From this time, regular literary work being for-
bidden by his physicians, he found himself cut off
from his most cherished and congenial occupation.
It was characteristic of Sydney Dobell that he
immediately turned his energies into other channels
of usefulness. He had always wished to prove that a
poet might be a thoroughly capable " man of affairs,"
and that the poetic or ideal faculty, rightly cultivated
and employed, should assist instead of impeding
practical life. It was one of the articles of his
creed, not merely that a good man of business *may*
be a gentleman, but that in order to be the one, in
any thorough sense of the word, he *must* be the
other. He now planned and superintended the
organisation of a new and ultimately extensive
branch of the business in which, for so many years
of his youth, he had actively taken part. In doing
this he was one of the first in England to introduce
and apply the system of Co-operation which has
since been widely extended. He held that every
mercantile firm should be a kind of Commonwealth,

in which the advancement of one ensures the advancement of all, and his efforts were always directed towards the realisation of this idea. These years, therefore, during which he was withheld from any continuous imaginative or philosophical writing, were fruitful of good work in other ways. All who knew Gloucester at that time knew Sydney Dobell as, in every sense of the word, a good citizen, warmly seconding every movement for the promotion of the best interests of the town.

With 1862 increased stress of ill-health made it needful for him to spend the winters abroad—in the south of France, in Italy, and in Spain—but the summers of these years were still spent in Gloucestershire.

His letters of this period show the vivid interest with which he studied the characteristic life, the social and political aspects, of the countries he visited. He acquired new languages rapidly, and soon found it possible to converse easily with the people among whom he was living. It is scarcely necessary to say how well the author of "The Roman" loved Italy, and he must have exulted in seeing, as achieved facts, the freedom and unity of which, in the enthusiasm of youth, he had sung. For Spain he had a profound admiration, and he always expressed the strongest faith in some future revival of her ancient glories. Meanwhile there was no weakening of his concern in all that affected his own country. In addition to many smaller contributions, in prose and verse, to various periodicals, he published, in 1865, a pamphlet on the then burning question of Parliamentary Reform—a pamphlet written in the spirit of the Liberal-Conservatism to which he latterly adhered. In this he advocated a system of graduated suffrage and plurality of votes in proportion to the status and responsibilities of each voter—a view to which the majority of our great thinkers have inclined.

After 1866 the consequences of an accident met with in Italy made further foreign travel impossible. Rest from all brain-work was more and more insisted on by his physicians as an absolutely indispensable condition of recovery. But it need hardly be said, that, in his, as in all similar cases, to live without breathing would have been as easy as to live without strenuous thinking. Among the writings of this time are many letters to the current journals on various questions of the hour, besides the pamphlet, "Consequential Damages," suggested by the American difficulty, and the "War Saga"—"England's Day."

In the summer of 1869, when trying a recently purchased horse, the animal reared and fell over with and on him. The indirect effects of this second accident were peculiarly disastrous, as he was never again able to resume the constant outdoor exercise which had hitherto been the chief means towards his restoration.

In 1871 he went to live at Barton End House, in a beautiful district above the Stroud Valley. The last three years of his life were spent there, under the almost constant pressure of disabling illness. With the spring of 1874 came a train of circumstances involving for him more than one shock of peculiar pain, and necessitating mental wear and tear of a kind for which he was absolutely unfit: the constitution, which had gallantly struggled through so much, was thus vanquished at last. The illness, long held in abeyance, assumed an acute form, and before the end of August he had passed to his rest.

The story of a life thus prematurely closed, of powers thus fettered from their due exercise, would seem to be incomplete without some additional detail as to the character of a man who, by those who knew him best, was held to be greater than any work he was permitted to complete. This may be the more needful because, at the time of the publication of " Balder," many of the critics persisted in identifying its author with his morbid and dreamy hero. This was a singularly perverse mistake—for Sydney Dobell was one of the most healthy-minded and sagaciously practical of men. Far from being a cynic, or misanthrope, he "loved his kind " in no mere theoretic sense, his instincts were pre-eminently social, he encouraged every opportunity of intercourse with his fellows of whatever class ; and whether it was a labourer breaking stones by the road-side, or a cultured fellow-passenger on a journey, with whom occasion led to some brief converse, he never departed from these chance encounters without leaving an impression of brightness and sympathetic kindliness not soon to be forgotten. His sense of humour, of which little or no trace appears in his writings, was nevertheless always keen, and remained so to the last. His almost boyish delight in hearing or telling a "good story" is remembered with something of pathos by those who were with him in his later days of hopeless illness. He was too genial, in spite of his own simplicity of taste, to be an ascetic; and "plain living and high thinking" did not hinder him from exercising towards others a refined and generous hospitality. His charities might, without exaggeration, be called, in proportion to his means, munificent. His practice accorded with the theory expressed in "Balder":—

> "Charitable they
> Who, be their having more or less, *so* have
> That less is more than need, and more is less
> Than the great heart's good-will."

Simple to the verge of austerity in his own life, charity, in its various forms, was his one extravagance. Not only of pecuniary aid, but of his scanty leisure and scantier strength he was always lavish. He was a most careful critic, keenly perceiving defects of imagination or faults of style, but at once penetrating with sometimes over-generous recognition to the essential excellence of book, picture, political creed, or popular enthusiasm. As to his political views, many dicta of his so-called Toryism are now accepted by acknowledged Liberals; but his philosophy, political as well as religious, started from a loftier standpoint and took an ampler range than that commonly appreciated by the ordinary newspaper reader or writer.

A thinker pre-eminently, he, nevertheless, keenly relished all manly exercises and country sports—seldom so valued by one whose resources are so independent of them.   He was loved to enthusiasm by all children and young people with whom he came in contact ; he had a rare power of not only amusing, but of insensibly arousing and elevating them. The gentleness of his counsel and the kindness of his sympathy will not be forgotten by those who were privileged to know him in this relation.   He was brilliant in conversation—having at his command not only acute reasoning power, but endless variety of unexpected illustration, and it was to be noted that he was never niggardly of his resources, but poured out of his treasures, new and old, without weighing the importance of the recipient When his life had become limited to a monotony that most men would have found unbearable, he still breathed an atmosphere of fresh and vital thought and feeling—of undiminished interest in all that was transacting itself in the outer world—of vivid sympathy in everything affecting the welfare of his fellows. To the last nothing could blunt the edge of his delight in the natural loveliness surrounding him—the changing phases of which he never tired of watching from his windows, when he was no longer able to go out doors.

Of the resources of the intellect so mysteriously held back from what seemed its fitting work, perhaps only a few, even of those who knew him best, can judge ; but his life evidenced, as no words or work could have done, the vitality of his faith, at once enlightened and deeply reverent—faith that was never shaken by the temptations of the intellect, nor weakened by years of disappointment and deprivation. No pressure of suffering was able to exhaust his cheerfulness, nor to wear out the sweetness of his patience. In him innate brightness and elasticity had been strengthened and elevated by spiritual culture into something beyond and above the result of mere temperament. To the last moment of his conscious life he remained bravely submissive, "trusting not God the less for an unanswered prayer."

Some critical estimate of Sydney Dobell as a poet seems to be called for in introducing a selection of his poems to a wider public.

"Mr. Dobell's true place among the English poets of this century," says Professor Nichol, "seems to us, in spite of manifest faults which critics will variously estimate, to be a high and permanent one. He belonged to the spasmodic* school, with which he was, during his residence in Edinburgh, topographically associated, in virtue of defects shared with men indefinitely his inferiors. Of these the chief were occasional violencies and frequent involutions of expression, recalling the conceits of Donne and others of the so-called metaphysical school of the seventeenth century ; a

* This epithet "spasmodic," originally applied by Carlyle to Byron, was, afterwards, used by Professor Aytoun to describe the school of younger poets among whom Sydney Dobell, Philip Bailey, and Alexander Smith were prominent.

tantalising excess of metaphor, a deficient sense of artistic proportion, and a weakness, latterly outgrown, for *outrés* 'fine things.' . . . Though unequal, his verse at its best is in strength and delicacy seldom surpassed by that of any of his contemporaries ; his imagery, though redundant, is remarkably clear and incisive. But the great merit of his work is that it is steeped in that higher atmosphere towards which it is the aim of all enduring literature to raise our spirits. . . .

" ' Balder ' is not likely to become popular in our generation ; to most readers it will remain a portent ; but, in spite of flagrant defects, it has stamina for permanence, and will keep its place in our literature as a mine for poets."

The following remarks are by Dr. Westland Marston*:—

". . . 'The Roman,' with its noble fervour of tone and wealth of illustration, proved that we had amongst us a new poet, whose genius was dedicated, not chiefly to the expression of personal feeling, or to the treatment of domestic themes, but to the worship of liberty and the defence of a glorious but enslaved country. The sympathy which, in the first poem, he showed with the larger interests of human life, is indeed discernible in all the more important works that subsequently proceeded from his pen.

"His patriotism and love of orderly freedom, are,

* Chiefly extracted from a letter contributed to "*The Life and Letters of Sydney Dobell*," published in 1878.

of course, obvious in 'England in time of War,' and in his 'Sonnets on the War.' In both, while they present many phases of the experience of individuals, the love of country and the hatred of oppression may be recognised as pervading motives.

"In 'Balder,' the ethical purpose of the poet is less immediately apparent. Its influence, however, is not the less real. Primarily, the poem was designed to show the egotism of the intellect as contrasted with that of the heart. . . .

". . . I will not attempt to draw the line beyond which analysis of human disease ceases to be desirable in poetry. Of this poem of 'Balder' it may, at all events, be affirmed, that it enters into and reveals states of being and suffering which, however rare, are still real, and such as may, in large measure, consist with noble qualities in the persons delineated. Even those who protest most strongly against the analysis of diseased conditions of mind might surely find the highest claims to admiration in the number of separate poems which the plan of 'Balder' allows it to enclose as in a frame. Just, as in dealing with thoughts and emotions, it was, perhaps, the speciality of the writer to seize in them what is most subtle and latent, to catch their most delicate *nuances;* so, in his treatment of external nature, nothing seems to me so individual as his power to arrest and retain those aspects which are the most elusive and difficult of definition. Grandeur and breadth of utterance, as all his readers know, lay easily within his grasp when occasion called for them, but exquisite fineness of perception and expression was, probably, his most characteristic faculty.

" Purely imaginative, far beyond the correctness of mere literal painting, for instance, is his description of Winter.   Weird are the touches that give to the stern season an almost supernatural personality :—

> " ' More and more the observance
> Of the astonished year is turned and turned
> Upon the Solitary, and the leaves
> Grow wan with conscience, and a-sudden fall
> Liege at his feet, and all the naked trees
> Mourn audibly, lifting appealing arms.
> Which, when he knew, as a pale smoke that grows
> Keeping its shape, he rose into the air
> And froze it, and the broad land blanched with fear
> And every breathless stream and river stopped,
> And through him, walking white and like a ghost
> With grim unfurnished limbs, the cold light passed
> And cast no shade.'

" The exquisite description of the fairies is in the vein of Shakespeare's description of ' Queen Mab,' and it is hardly too much to say that it may mate well with that triumph of delicate imagination. The power of language to define the minute can hardly have a better illustration than the lines :—

> " 'The emerald wing
> Of summer beetle is a barge of state ;
> Her cock-boat, red and black, the painted scale
> Of lady-lly, aft in the fairy wake,
> Towed by a film, and tossed perchance in storm,
> When airy martlet, sipping of the pool,
> Touches it to a ripple that stirs not
> The lilies.   .   .   .

> .   .   .   Neither have fear
> To scare them drawing nigh, nor with thy voice
> To roll their thunder.   Thy wide utterance
> Is silence to the ears it enters not,
> Raising the attestation of a wind,
> No more.'

" Of a bolder but not less profound conception is the image that embodies the awfulness and the immemorial existence of the Alps, and informs the murmurs of Nature with a human burden :—

> " ' Round whose feet
> Are wrapped the shaggy forests, and whose beards
> Down from the great height unapproachable
> Descend upon their breasts.   There, being old,
> All days and years they maunder on their thrones
> Mountainous mutterings, or thro' the vale
> Roll the long roar from startled side to side,
> When whoso lifting up his sudden voice,
> A moment speaketh of his meditation
> And thinks again.'

" Fine is the whole passage—wonderfully fine the use of the word 'sudden,' so expressive of the abrupt ' roar ' which disturbs the subdued murmurs or the awful silence of Nature.

"Of Sydney Dobell's power of description and grandeur and subtle beauty of imagery the lines quoted furnish sufficient evidence. His power not only closely to observe nature, but, so to speak, to humanise, so that its objects stand, in many instances, as types of our states and feelings, may be seen almost continuously. Thus the Ash Tree, in ' Dead Maid's Pool,' while described with the most minute and graphic touches as a natural object, may also be recognised as a symbol of human desolation and remorse. Here is an extract from it :—

  " ' Thou art wizen and white, ash tree ;
   Other trees have gone on,
   Have gathered and grown,
   Have bourgeoned and borne,
   Thou hast wasted and worn.

   Thy knots are all eyes ;
   Every knot a dumb eye,
   That has seen a sight
   And heard a cry.

   Thy leaves are dry :
   The summer has not gone by
   But they're withered and dead,
   Like locks round a head
   That is bald with a secret sin,
   That is scorched by a hell within,

   Thy skin
   Is withered and wan
   Like a guilty man ;
   It was thin,
   Aye, silken and thin,
   It is houghed
   And ploughed
   Like a murderer's skin.

   Thou hast no shoots or wands,
   All thy arms turn to the deep,
   All thy twigs are crooked,
   Twined and twisted,
   Fingered and fisted,
   Like one who had looked
   On wringing hands
   Till his hands were wrung in his sleep.'

"Let the reader, again, carefully peruse the lyric,

"'In the Spring twilight, in the coloured twilight,'

and say if the exquisite description there of the youth of the year do not intimately correspond to the youth of man, with its opening receptivity to beauty and delicate tenderness of emotion. And here is a piece of grand description of the *Mer de Glace* which can scarcely be excelled :—

> "'Cold crested tides
> And cataracts more white than wintry foam
> Eternally in act of the great leap
> That never may be ta'en, these fill the gorge
> And rear upon the steep uplifted waves
> Immovable, that proudly feign to go,—
> And on the awful ramparts of the rock
> Bend forward, as in motion.'—

"For his power over the supernatural, let the reader turn not only to the ballad, 'Keith of Ravelston,' but, also, to a passage in 'Balder,' beginning :—

> "'One can be brave
> At noon, and with triumphant logic clear
> The demonstrable air, but ne'ertheless
> Sometimes at Hallow-e'en when, legends say,
> The things that stir among the rustling trees
> Are not all mortal, and the sick white moon
> Wanes o'er the season of the sheeted dead,
> We grow unreasonable and do quake
> With more than the cold wind.'

"And here is an instance of that delicate and suggestive perception which is a characterstic of the writer :—

> " ' Loveliness
> Is precious for its essence ; time and space
> Make it nor near, nor far, nor old, nor new,
> Celestial nor terrestrial. Seven snowdrops
> Sister the pleiads, the primrose is kin
> To Hesper, Hesper to the world to come.'

"Of the writer's tendency, at times, to avoid set and substantial description, and to furnish, in preference, hints to the imagination, many other proofs might be cited. No poet, perhaps, has ever shown more of that subtle instinct which teaches us that at certain intense points of feeling (whether they relate to external beauty or to human experience) to realise strictly is to limit, to define sharply is to degrade. Of work full of the highest suggestion, but in some degree purposely indefinite, the poem 'Dead Maid's Pool,' already referred to, is a special example. The story of terror is not actually told, but the germ from which it may be derived, with the climate and atmosphere—so to speak—under which it must inevitably, though gradually, shape itself, is so presented to the mind as to lead irresistibly to a ghastly inference far more powerful to the imagination than would have been circumstantial detail.

"With a mind that, on certain occasions, recoiled, even to a fault, from realistic precision of statement, it is not surprising that the poet should have relied unusually upon implication to indicate designs which he forbade himself to mark out with formal directness.

"That the author of 'Balder' could not only be realistic, but that in his realism he could make tune serve his purpose to the utmost, will hardly be doubted by those who have read his poems on familiar subjects. The song of 'The Betsey-Jane,' for instance, moves in a rhythm that has in it the whistle of the wind and the buoyancy of the wave ; while the 'Song of the *Chasseur*,' in its appropriate variety of metre, is a wonderful identification of sentiment with melody. The description of battle in 'An Evening Dream,' though in a yet higher strain, is equally successful as an example of emotion conveyed by rhythm. The poems included in the title, 'England in time of War,' express almost every legitimate feeling which war can arouse— patriotism, heroism, exultation, and suffering, while the expression of those feelings is dramatically modified by the individualities of the persons represented, and even by their positions in life. Dealing now with the emotions of a high-born woman, now with those of a Scottish peasant or a market-wife, or again with the vivacity of a French *chasseur*, or the tameless spirit of a British tar, or with the weird solemnity of a haunted life, as in 'Keith of Ravelston'—the width and impartiality of his sympathy, and the thorough identification of himself with his subject, are remarkably exhibited.

"Of the far greater number of these lays it may, I think, be affirmed, that they are not more remarkable for their dramatic character, their passion, and their felicity of expression, than for a rhythm happily conformed to their leading ideas and sentiments. . .

" . . . How many high qualities, rarely indeed combined, were united in his generous nature : the richest taste and judgment, with the widest appreciation of what is best in various forms of art ; earnestness of purpose, with spontaneous humour ; fine adherence to convictions, with the sweetest courtesy to opponents ; exquisite refinement, with a sympathy that was never checked by fastidious scruples. Prompt to recognise genius in his contemporaries, liberal to all men, it is not too much to say that he carried into letters the chivalry that is the glory of arms. With an almost religious reverence for the vocation of the Poet, the sentiment *noblesse oblige* seemed to influence his entire conduct and to make his life the illustration of his ideal."

SELECTIONS FROM

Sydney Dobell's Poems.

Poems.

A MUSING ON A VICTORY.

(1847.)

Down by the Sutlej shore,
Where sound the trumpet and the wild tum-tum,
At winter's eve did come
A gaunt old northern lion, at whose roar
The myriad howlers of thy wilds are dumb,
Blood-stained Ferozepore !

In the rich Indian night,
And dreaming of his mate beyond the sea,
Toil-worn but grand to sight,
He made his lair, in might,
Beneath thy dark palm-tree,
And thou didst rouse him to the unequal fight—
And woe for thee !
For some of that wild land
Had heard him in the desert where he lay;

And soon he snuffs upon their hurtling way,
The hunters—band by band ;
And up he gat him from the eastern sand
And leaped upon his prey.

.   .   .   .

Alas for man !   Alas for all thy dreams,
Thou great somnambulist, wherein, outlawed
From right and thought, thou workest out unawed
Thy grand fantastic fancies !   'Thro' the flood,
The pestilence, the whirlwind, the dread plain
Of thunders—thro' the earthquake and the storm,
The deluge and the snows, the whirling ice
Of the wild glacier, every ghastly form
Of earth's most vexed vicissitudes of pain,—
Thro' worlds of fire and seas of mingled bloods
Thou rushest, dreadful as a maniac god ;
And only finding that thou wert not sane
When some great sorrow thunders at thy brain
And wakes thee trembling by a precipice.

Alas for thee, thou grey-haired man that still
Art sleeping, and canst hold thy grandchild high
That he may see the gorgeous wrong go by
Which slew his father !   And for thee, thou bright
Inheritress of summer-time and light,
Alas for thee, that thy young cheek is flush'd
With dreaming of the lion and the foe,
Tho' it had been yet paler than the snow
Upon the battle-hill, if once had gush'd,
But once before thee, even the feeblest flow
Of that life's blood that swept in floods below.
Alas ! that even thy beauty cannot break
The vampyre spell of such a war-dream's woe,--

Alas ! tho' waking might have been to know
Things which had made it sweeter not to wake.

Alas for man !—poor hunchback—all so proud
And yet so conscious ; man that stalks divine
Because he feels so mortal, speaking loud
To drown the trembling whisper in his heart,
And wildly hurrying on from crowd to crowd,
In hope to shun the faithful shapes that start
Wherever lake doth sleep or streamlet shine
In silent solitudes.   When once in youth
Fresh from the spheres, and too severely wise,
Truth drew the face he longed yet feared to view,
Stung with the instinct that confessed it true
He dashed the tablets from her sacred hand ;
She drops her singing robes and leaves his land ;
And Fiction, decent in the garb of Truth,
While lurking mischief lights her lambent eyes,
Seizes the fallen pencil, and with grave
Historic features paints the lies we crave.

So war became a welcome woe.   The grass
Grows tear-bedewed upon a lonely grave,
And we plant sad flow'rs and sweet epitaphs,
And every grief of monumental stone,
Above a single woe ; but let men sleep
In thousands, and we choose their hideous heap
For Joy to hold his godless orgies on.
Is it that some strange law's unknown behest
Makes gladness of the greatest woes we have
And leaves us but to sorrow for the less ?
Even as in outward nature light's excess
Is blindness, and intensest motion rest ;
Or is it not—oh conscious heart declare—
That the vast pride of our o'erwrought despair

Seeing the infinite grief, and knowing yet
We have no tears to pay such deep distress,
Grown wild, repudiates the direful debt,
And in its very bankrupt madness laughs?—

Yet when this Victory's fame shall pass, as grand
And griefless as a rich man's funeral,
Thro' nations that look on with spell-bound eye,
While echoing plaudits ring from land to land,
Alas ! will there be none among the good
And great and brave and free, to speak of all
The pale piled pestilence of flesh and blood,
The common cold corruption that doth lie
Festering beneath the pall?

Alas ! when time has deified the thought
Of this day's desperate devilry, and men
(Who scorn to inherit virtue, but will ape   [shape
Their sires, and bless them, when they sin) shall
A graven image of the thought, and then
Fall down to worship it—will no one dare,
While nations kneel before the idol there,
To stand and tell them it is Juggernaut?
Alas for man ! if this new crime shall yield
To truth no harvest for the sighs it cost ;
If this crowned corpse, this pale ensceptred ghost
That stalks, Ferozepore, from thy red field
Robed as a king, shall all unchallenged pass
Down the proud scene of Time.   Alas, alas !
If there are some to weep and some to pray,
And none to bow their humbled heads and say,
Low sighing,—There hath been a mortal strife ;
And thirteen thousand murdered men lie there,
And day and night upon the tainted air
Blaspheme the Lord of Life.

ISABEL.

(1847.)

In the most early morn
I rise from a damp pillow, tempest-tost,
To seek the sun with silent gaze forlorn,
And mourn for thee, my lost
Isabel.

That early hour I meet
The daily vigil of my life to keep,
Because there are no other lights so sweet,
Or shades so long and deep,
Isabel.

And best I think of thee
Beside the duskest shade and brightest sun,
Whose mystic lot in life it was to be
Outshone, outwept by none,
Isabel.

Men said that thou wert fair :
There is no brightness in the heaven above,
There is no balm upon the summer air
Like thy warm love,
Isabel.

Men saw that thou wert bright :
There is no wildness in the winds that blow,
There is no darkness in the winter's night
Like thy dark woe,
Isabel.

And yet thy path did miss
Men's footsteps : in their haunts thou hadst no joy ;
The thoughts of other worlds were thine in this ;
In thy sweet piety, and in thy bliss
And grief, for life too coy,
Isabel.

And so my heart's despair
Looks for thee ere the firstling smoke hath curled ;
While the rapt earth is at her morning pray'r,
Ere yet she putteth on her workday air
And robes her for the world,
Isabel.

When the sun-burst is o'er,
My lonely way about the world I take,
Doing and saying much, and feeling more,
And all things for thy sake,
Isabel.

But never once I dare
To see thine image till the day be new,
And lip hath sullied not the unbreathed air,
And waking eyes are few,
Isabel.

Then that lost form appears
Which was a joy to few on earth but me :

In the young light I see thy guileless glee,
In the deep dews thy tears,
Isabel.

So with Promethean moan
In widowhood renewed I learn to grieve ;
Blest with one only thought—that I alone
Can fade : that thou thro' years shalt still shine on
In beauty, as in beauty art thou gone,
Thou morn that knew no eve,
Isabel.

In beauty art thou gone ;
As some bright meteor gleams across the night,
Gazed on by all, but understood by none,
And dying by its own excess of light,
Isabel.

From *THE ROMAN.*

Opening Song.

Sing lowly, foot slowly, oh why should we chase
The hour that gives heaven to this earthly embrace?
To-morrow, to-morrow, is dreary and lonely ;
Then love as they love who would live to love only!
Closer yet, eyes of jet,—breasts fair and sweet !
No eyes flash like those eyes that flash as they meet !
Weave brightly, wear lightly, the warm-woven chain,
Love on for to-night if we ne'er love again.
Fond youths ! happy maidens ! we are not alone !
Bright steps and sweet voices keep pace with our own.
Love-lorn Lusignuolo, the soft-sighing breeze,
The rose with the zephyr, the wind with the trees.
While Heaven, blushing pleasure, is full of love-notes,
Soft down the sweet measure the fairy world floats.

———

[Vittorio Santo *(the Roman, disguised as a Monk)
speaks to the people.*]

I pray you listen how I loved my mother,
And you will weep with me.   She loved me, nurst me,
And fed my soul with light.   Morning and Even
Praying, I sent that soul into her eyes,

And knew what Heaven was though I was a child.
I grew in stature, and she grew in goodness.
I was a grave child ; looking on her taught me
To love the beautiful : and I had thoughts
Of Paradise, when other men have hardly
Look'd out of doors on earth.   (Alas ! alas !
That I have also learn'd to look on earth
When other men see heaven.)   I toil'd, but ever
As I became more holy, she seem'd holier ;
Even as when climbing mountain-tops the sky
Grows ampler, higher, purer as ye rise.

    .   .   .   .   .   .

        Her name is ROME.   Look round,
And see those features which the sun himself
Can hardly leave for fondness.   Look upon
Her mountain bosom, where the very sky
Beholds with passion : and with the last proud
Imperial sorrow of dejected empire,
She wraps the purple round her outraged breast,
And even in fetters cannot be a slave.
Look on the world's best glory and worst shame.
You cannot count her beauties or her chains,
You cannot know her pangs or her endurance.
You, whom propitious skies may hardly coax
To threescore years and ten.   Your giant fathers
Call'd Atlas demigod.   But what is she,
Who, worn with eighteen centuries of bondage,
Stands manacled before the world, and bears
Two hemispheres—innumerable wrongs,
Illimitable glories.   Oh, thou heart
That art most tortured, look on her and say
If there be anything in earth or heaven,
In earth or heaven—now that Christ weeps no longer—
So most divinely sad.

VITTORIO SANTO *to Francesca.*

There was a song that in my wanderings
I heard in other years.   A wayward song
That caught the murmur of the waterfall,
By which I sang it.   But no matter.   'Twill
Find its way where the brawny words of manhood
Might be too rude.   I would, my poor disciple,
I had some foot more fit than an arm'd heel
To tread the dwelling of thy woman's soul.
And while we commune, daughter,—for alas,
A patriot militant has no to-morrows—
Hear this first lesson.   It may be remember'd
When I am not.   Stern duties need not speak
Sternly.   He who stood firm before the thunder,
Worshipp'd the still small voice.   Let the great world
That bears us—the all-preaching world—instruct thee
That teacheth every man, because her precepts
Are seen, not heard.   Oh, worship her.   Fear not
Whilst thou hast open eyes, and ears for all
The simplest words she saith.   Deaf, blind, to these,
Despair.   That worst incurable, perchance
Some voice may heal hereafter, but none here.
For before every man, the world of beauty,
Like a great artist, standeth day and night,
With patient hand retouching in the heart
God's defaced image.   Reverence sights and sounds,
Daughter; be sure the wind among the trees
Is whispering wisdom.
        . . . Now assist me, lute.

There went an incense through the land one night,
Through the hush'd holy land, when tired men slept
The haughty sun of June had walk'd, long days,
Through the tall pastures which, like mendicants,

Hung their sere heads and sued for rain : and he
Had thrown them none.   And now it was high haytime,
Through the sweet valley all her flowery wealth
At once lay low, at once ambrosial blood
Cried to the moonlight from a thousand fields.
And through the land the incense went that night,
Through the hush'd holy land when tired men slept.
It fell upon the sage ; who with his lamp
Put out the light of heaven.   He felt it come
Sweetening the musty tomes, like the fair shape
Of that one blighted love, which from the past
Steals oft among his mouldering thoughts of wisdom.
And SHE came with it, borne on airs of youth ;
Old days sang round her, old memorial days,
She crown'd with tears, they dress'd in flowers, all
    faded—
And the night-fragrance is a harmony
All through the old man's soul.   Voices of eld,
The home, the church upon the village green,
Old thoughts that circle like the birds of Even
Round the grey spire.   Soft sweet regrets, like sunset
Lighting old windows with gleams day had not.
Ghosts of dead years, whispering old silent names
Through grass-grown pathways, by halls mouldering now.
Childhood—the fragrance of forgotten fields ;
Manhood—the *un*forgotten fields whose fragrance
Pass'd like a breath ; the time of buttercups,
The fluttering time of sweet forget-me-nots ;
The time of passion and the rose—the hay-time
Of that last summer of hope !   The old man weeps,
The old man weeps.
His aimless hands the joyless books put by ;
As one that dreams and fears to wake, the sage
With vacant eye stifles the trembling taper,
Lets in the moonlight—and for once is wise.

There went an incense through the midnight land,
Through the hush'd holy land where tired men slept.
It fell upon a simple cottage child,
Laid where the lattice open'd on the sky,
And she look'd up and said, Those flowers the stars
Smelt sweet to-night.   God rest her ignorance !
There went an incense through the land one night,
Through the hush'd holy land when tired men slept ;
It pass'd above a lonely vale, and fell
Upon a poet looking out for signs
In heaven and earth, and went into his soul,
And like a fluttering bird among sweet strings,
Made strange Æolian music wild and dim.

A haggard man, silent beneath the stars,
Stood with bare head, a hasty step withdrawn
From a low tattered hut, wherefrom the faint
Low wail of famine, like a strange night-bird,
Cried on the air.   He had come forth to give
His dying child, his youngest one, repose.
" Father," it said, " you weep, I cannot die."
There went an incense through the land that night,
Through the hush'd holy land when tired men slept ;
It came upon his soul, and went down deep,
Deep to his heart, and threw the new-made hay
Upon the coals of fire that ember'd there.
And by the rising flame came pictures fair,
Of old ancestral fields that strangers till,
And patrimony that the spoiler reaps.
Then falls the flame upon the pallet near,
And forward on the canvas of the night,
To the wild father's eye, lights up that landscape
Of love and health and hope which yesterday
The poorest crumbs of the oppressor's feast
Might buy.   Oh God ! how coarse a crust may be

The bread of life.   He breathes the night-balm in,
And breathes it back the red-hot smoke of vengeance !

There was a lonely mother and one babe,
—A moon with one small star in all her heaven—
Too like the moon, the wan and weary moon,
In pallor, beauty, all, alas ! but change.
Through six long months of sighs that moon unwaning
Had risen and set beside the little star.
And now the little star, whom all the dews
Of heaven refresh not, westers to its setting,
Out of the moonlight to be dark for ever.
O'er the hush'd holy land where tired men sleep,
There went an incense through the night.   It fell
Upon the mother, and she slept—the babe,
It smil'd and dream'd of paradise.

Oh, prince's daughter, if
In some proud street, leaning 'twixt night and day
From out thy palace balcony to meet
The breeze—that tempted by the hush of eve,
Steals from the fields about a city's shows,
And like a lost child, scared with wondering, flies
From side to side in touching trust and terror,
Crying sweet country names and dropping flowers—
Leaning to meet that breeze, and looking down
To the so silent city, if below
With dress disorder'd and dishevell'd passions
Streaming from desperate eyes that flash and flicker
Like corpse-lights (eyes that once were known on high,
Morning and night, as welcome there as thine),
And brow of trodden snow, and form majestic

That might have walk'd unchallenged through the
    skies,
And reckless feet, fitful with wine and woe,
And songs of revel that fall dead about
Her ruin'd beauty—sadder than a wail—
(As if the sweet maternal eve for pity
Took out the joy, and, with a blush of twilight,
Uncrown'd the Bacchanal)—some outraged sister
Passeth, be patient, think upon yon heaven,
Where angels hail the Magdalen, look down
Upon that life in death and say—My country !

Song of Insurgents.

(Chanting as they march.)

Who would drone on in a dull world like this ?
    Heaven costs no more than a pang and a sigh ;
Dash off the fetters that bind us from bliss,
    Fair fall the freeman who foremost shall die !
Death's a siesta, lads, take it who can !
Wave the proud banners that wave for Milan !

Chanted in song, and remember'd in story,
    Sunk but to rest—like the sun in the wave—
Grandly the fallen shall sleep in his glory,
    Proudly his country shall weep at his grave,
And hallow like relics each clod where there ran
The blood of that hero who died for Milan !

Holy his name shall be, blest by the brave and free,
    Kept like a saint's day the hour when he died !

The mother that bore him, the maid that bends o'er
    him,
  Shall weep, but the tears shall be rich tears of pride.
Shout, brothers, shout for the first falling man,
Shout for the gallant that dies for Milan !

Long, long years hence, by the home of his truth,
  His fate, beaming eyes yet unborn shall bedew,
Beloved of the lovely, while beauty and youth
  Shall give their best sighs to the brave and the true !
On, spears ! spur, cavaliers ! Victory our van,
Fame sounds the trumpet that sounds for Milan !

FRANCESCA'S SOLILOQUY.

       I will but live in twilight,
I will seek out some lone Egerian grove,
Where sacred and o'er-greeting branches shed
Perpetual eve, and all the cheated hours
Sing vespers. And beside a sullen stream,
Ice-cold at noon, my shadowy self shall sit,
Crown'd with dull wreaths of middle-tinted flowers ;
With sympathetic roses, wan with weeping
For April sorrows ; frighten'd harebells, pale
With thunder ; last, half-scented honeysuckle,
That like an ill-starr'd child hides its brown head
Through the long summer banquet, but steals late
To wander through the fragments of the feast,
And glad us with remember'd words that fell
From guests of beauty ; sunburnt lilies, grey
Wind-whispering ilex, and whatever leaves
And changeling blossoms Flora, half-asleep,
Makes paler than the sun and warmer than the moon !
Was ever slave so dark and cold as I ?

Ah cruel, cruel night ! the very stars
Put me to shame !   I spur my soul all day
With thought of tyrants, woes and chains, and curse
As oft my pallid and ill-blooded nature,
That will not rage.   Oh for some separate slave
To pity every vassal by !   Some tyrant
By whom I might set down of all oppressors
That they are thus and thus !   Oh that some hand,
Oh that some one hand, faint and fetter-wrung,
Would thrust its clanking wrongs before my eyes,
And I could bleed to break them !

                         And thou ! country !
Thou stern and awful god, of which my reason
Preaches infallibly, but which no sense
Bears witness to—I would thou hadst a shape.
It might be dwarf, deform'd, maim'd,—anything,
So it was thine ; and it should stand to me
For beauty.   And my soul should wait on it,
And I would train my fancies all about it,
Till growing to its fashion, and most nurtured
With smiles and tears they strengthen'd into love.
But—Santo—this indefinite dim presence
I cannot worship.   O thou dear apostle,
Oh what a patriot could Francesca be
If *thou* wert Rome !   Oh what a fond disciple
Should his tongue have whose only eloquence
Was praise of thee !   To what a pile of vengeance
One look of retribution in thine eye
Were torch enough !   Be still, my heart, be still !
Ah wilful, wilful heart, dost thou refuse ?
Nay, be appeased—I bid thee silence, lest
Consenting cheeks attest how well thou sayest !
Too late, too late.   Nay, do you crave, you blushes,
Escort of spoken passion, to interpret

Your beauties to the moon, which, pale with love
And watching for the never-coming night,
Mistakes them for some rosy cloud of dawn,
And ends her vigil?   Heart, have all thy will!
Santo, I love thee!

———

OPENING OF SIXTH SCENE.

The Monk. This is the spot.   From hence my eye
　　　unseen
Commands their cottage.   Hither have I fared
Five times at this same hour, and five times learn'd
To love my nature better.   Here I stood,
And felt, when passing gales in snatches bore me
Their evening talk, as if some wayward child
Had pelted me with flowers.   She is a poet,
Or in or out of metre.   Rome must have her.
A mother too, 'tis well; then there is one thing
The poet will serve.   Ah! art thou forth to-day,
Thou little tyrant, that shalt rule for me?
My faith! a lovely boy! holy St. Mary!
Hark how he carols out his royalty,
And, born a sovereign, rules and knows it not.
The father must be mine too; he hath bone
And sinew, and—if the eye's gauge deceive not—
A soul as brawny.   Heavy deeds demand
Such carriers.   I will win or lose this night.
Let me draw near.

*Children sporting.   The girl hides among myrtles,
and sings.*

Girl.   Whither wingest thou, wingest thou, winny
　　　wind;

Where, winny wind, where, oh where?
   Boy (singing).   My sister, my sister, I flit forth to
    find,
My sister, my sister, the orange-flow'r fair!
   Girl.   Since thy songs thy soft sister seek,
What wouldst with her? say, oh say.
   Boy.   Oh, to pat her pearl-white cheek,
And court her with kisses all day!   [chord
   The Mother.   Husband! the music in my soul would
Most sweetly with thy voice.   Take down thy lute.
   The Father.   Nay, Lila: bid me not do violence
To this calm sunset.   List that golden laughter,
Hark to our children!   There is music like
The hour.   From each to each the heart can pass,
And know no change.
   The Mother.   Sing me a song about them,
Kind husband.   Sing that song I made for thee,
When once, on a sweet eve like this, we watch'd
As now our joyous babes—I blessing them,
Thou marvelling, with show of merry jest,
How they could be so fair.

SONG.

Oh, Lila! round our early love,
What voices went—in days of old!
Some sleep, and some are heard above,
And some are here—but changed and cold!

What lights they were that lit the eyes
That never may again be bright!
Some shine where stars are dim; and some
Have gone like meteors down the night.

I marvell'd not to see them beam,
Or hear their music round our way;
A part of life *they* used to seem,
But *these*—oh whence are they?

Ear hath not heard the tones they bring,
Lip hath not named their name,
Like primroses around the spring,
Each after each they came.

I should not wonder, love, to see
In dreams of elder day,
The forms of things that used to be,
But *these*—oh whence are they?

Dost thou remember when the days
Were all too short for love and me,
And we roam'd forth at eve in rays
Of mingled light from heaven and thee?

One gentle sign so often beam'd
Upon us with such favouring eyes,
That every vow we plighted seem'd
A secret holden with the skies.

Now sometimes, in strange phantasy,
I think, if stars could leave their sphere,
And won by the dear love of thee,
Renew the constellation here,

And shine here with the tender light
That glinted through the olden trees,
They would come silently and bright,
And one by one, like these.

How can a joy so pure and free
Have sprung from tears and cares?
I have no beauty—and for thee,
Thou hast no mirth like theirs.

Yet with strange right each takes his rest,
Even when he will, on thy fair breast,
    Nor doubts nor fears nor prays.
The daisy smiling on the lea
Comes not with kindlier trust to be
    Beloved of April days.

I look into their laughing eyes,
They cannot have more light than thine—
But treasured by ten thousand ties,
Mine own I know *thee*, Lila mine.

Wistful I gaze on *them* and say,—
Fond, checking with a doubtful sigh
The pride that swells, I know not why—
These, these, oh whence are they?

The Monk.   Thou little child,
Thy mother's joy, thy father's hope—thou bright,
Pure dwelling where two fond hearts keep their
    gladness—
Thou little potentate of love, who comest
With solemn sweet dominion to the old,
Who see thee in thy merry fancies charged
With the grave embassage of that dear past,
When they were young like thee—thou vindication

Of God—thou living witness against all men
Who have been babes—thou everlasting promise
Which no man keeps—thou portrait of our nature,
Which in despair and pride we scorn and worship—
Thou household-god, whom no iconoclast
Hath broken,—if I knew a parent's joys,
If I were proud and full of great ambitions,
Had haughty limbs that chafed at ill-borne chains,
If I had known a tyrant's scorn and felt
That vengeance though bequeathed is still revenge,
I would pray God to give me such a son !

.   .   .   .   .   'Tis the purblind
Dim sense of after years that makes our monsters.
The earth hath none to children and to angels.
Eyes weak with vigil, sear'd with scalding tears,
Betray us, and we start at death and phantoms
Because they are pale.   And the still-groping heart
Incredulous by over much believing—
Walking by sight dreads the unknown, and clings
Even to familiar sorrow, and loves more
The seen earth than the unseen God.

———

THE CAMPAGNA.

Here and there
Rude heaps, that had been cities, clad the ground
With history.   And far and near, where grass
Was greenest and the unconscious goat browsed free,
The teeming soil was sown with desolations,
As though Time—striding o'er the field he reap'd—
Warm'd with the spoil, rich droppings for the gleaners
Threw round his harvest way.   Frieze, pedestal,
Pillars that bore through years the weight of glory,

And take their rest.   Tombs, arches, monuments,
Vainly set up to save a name, as though
The eternal served the perishable ; urns,
Which winds had emptied of their dust, but left
Full of their immortality.   In shrouds
Of reverent leaves, rich works of wondrous beauty
Lay sleeping—like the children in the wood—
Fairer than they.   Columns like fallen giants,
The victor on the vanquish'd, stretch'd so stern
In death, that not a flower might dare to do
Their obsequies.   And some from sweet Ionia
With those Ionia bore to Roman skies
Lay mingled, like a goddess and her mother,
Who wear, with difference, the co-equal brightness
Of fadeless youth.   The plain thus strew'd with age
Flower'd in the sunshine of to-day, and bore me
The Present and the Past.   But there were some
Proud changeless stones that stood up in the sun,
And with their shadowy finger on the plain
Drew the same mystic circle day by day,
And these I worshipp'd.   Honouring them, because
It needs must be they knew the sense that sign
Bore in the language of Eternity ;
And fearing them for that dark hand which ever—
When I drew near their awful face at noon,
And, spent with wondering, sank down unconscious,
And slept upon the turf—came back at even
And cast me shuddering out.

                              So days wore on,
And childhood.   And the shade of all these ruins
Fell on my soul.   And *he*, my pride, grew up,
With, and without me.   And we were such brothers
As day and night.   We met at morn and eve.
Each sun uprose to find us hand in hand,

And see a tender parting.   Each first star
Led back the shades and us.   He flush'd with conquest,
Rich in the well slain antelope, and all
That feathery wage youth loves to take for labour ;
I laden with new thoughts.   Pale, travel-worn,
Spent with fierce exercise and faint with toil,
I, who—the shepherd of the plain would tell you—
Since sunbreak upon one same broken column
Sat like a Caryatid.   So youth was mine,
And seasons crown'd it manhood.

Music.

                          An art
Lightly esteem'd, but which to name divine
Is not the filial rapture of a son,
Since in the change of time it hath not changed ;
Indigenous to all the earth.   A spirit
Evoked by many, but a bound familiar
To no magician yet.   The equal tenant
Of loftiest palace and of lowliest cot,
Treading the rustic and the royal floor
To the same step and time.   In every age,
With all the reverence that man claims as man,
Preaching to clouted clown, and with no more
To throned kings.   The unrespective friend—
In such celestial wise as gods befriend—
By turns of haughtiest monarch, humblest swain ;
And, with impartial love and power, alike
Ennobling prince and peasant.   Giving all,
Receiving never.   What else makes a god ?
What human art looks so divine on earth ?
And, as you tell us, seraphs in high heaven
Find nothing worthier.

SONG.

The poet bends above his lyre and strikes—
No smile, no smile of rapture on his face ;
The poet bends above his lyre and strikes,
No fire, no fire of passion, in his eye ;—
The poet bends above his lyre and strikes,
No flush, no prophet's flush, upon his cheek ;—
Calm as the grand white cloud where thunders sleep,
Like a wrapt listener—not in vain to listen—
Feeling the winds with every sense to catch
Some far sound wandering in the depths of space,
The poet bends above his lyre and strikes.

The poet bends above his lyre and strikes.
Ah Heaven ! I hear ! Again. Ah Heaven, I hear !
Again :—the vacant eyes are moist with tears !
Again :—they gleam with vision. Bending lower,
Crowding his soul upon the strings.—Again.
Hark, hark, thou heart that leapest !   Ye thrill'd
      fibres !
See the triumphant minstrel in the dust,
To his own music. Hark ! Angels in heaven
Catch it on golden harps ! Down float their echoes
Richer than dews of Paradise. Inspired,
Tuning each chord to the enchanted key,
The poet sweeps the strings and wakes, awe-stricken,
The sounds that never die. From hill to hill
They vibrate round the world of time, as deep
Calleth to deep.

            But note like this stirs not
The wind of every day. And 'tis the ear
To know it, woo it, wait for it, and stand
Amid a Babel deaf to other speech,

That makes a poet.   And from ear like this,
That troubling of the air which common men
Call harmony, falls unrespected off,
As balls from a charm'd life.
                              Hear yet again
A better parable.   The good man hears
The voice in which God speaks to men.   The poet,
In some wrapt moment of intense attendance,
The skies being genial and the earthly air
Propitious, catches on the inward ear
The awful and unutterable meanings
Of a divine soliloquy.
                              Soul-trembling
With incommunicable things, he speaks
At infinite distance.   So a babe in smiles
Repeats the unknown and unknowable
Joys of a smiling mother.

THE WINTER'S NIGHT.

And she stood at its father's gate,
At its father's gate she stood,
With her baby at her breast ;
'Twas about the hour of rest—
There were lights within the place—
The old moon began to sink
(Long, like her, upon the wane),
It grew dark ; she drew her hood
Close about her pallid face ;
At the portal down she sate,
Where she will not sit again.
" Little one," she slowly said,
Bending low her lowly head,

" In all this wide world only thee,
And my shame, *he* gave to me.
When *thou* camest I did think
On that other gift of his—
Hating that I dreaded this.
Thou art fair—but so was he ;
'Tis a winning smile of thine,--
Ah ! what fatal praise it is !—
One such smile once won all mine.
Little one, I not repine,
It befits me well to wait
My lord's will, till I be dead--
Once it was a gentler will !"

With that, a night-breeze full chill
Shook some dead leaves from the lime ;
At the sad sound, loud and burly
Like a warder went the blast
Round about the lordly house ;
Hustled her with menial wrath,
Much compelling forth her cast,
Who was all too fain to go ;
She sank down upon the path—
She cower'd lower, murmuring low,
" What was I that I should earn,
For I loved him, more return
Than I look'd for of the sun,
When he smiled upon me early
In our merry milking-time ? "

Then was silence all ; the mouse
Rustled with the beechen mast,
The lank fox yelp'd round, the owl
Floating, shriek'd pale horror past ;
Strange and evil-omen'd fowl

Croak'd about her, and knew not.
Round her had the last bat fed.
" Little one," she said, " the cot
Where I bore thee was too low
For a haughty baron's bride.
Little one, I hope to go
Where the palace-halls are wide ;
When thou prattlest at his knee,
Wilt thou sometimes speak of me?
Tell him, in some eve," she said,
" Where thou knowest I shall be.
When he hears that I am grand,
In those mansions ever fair,
Will he look upon me there
As a lady of the land,
And think no more in scorn
Upon thee and on the dead ?"
All below the garden banks,
Where the blighted aspens grew,
Faded leaves faint breezes blew,
As in pity, round her.   Then
Low whispering in her plaintive plight,
Her shivering babe she nearer nurst.
" 'Tis a bitter night," said she,
" Little one, a dreary night.
Little shalt thou bless the first
Pass'd upon thy father's ground,
Aye ! cower closer in thy nest,
Birdie ! that didst never build.
There is warmth enough for thee,
Though the frost shall split the tree
Where it rocks."
" Little one," she said again,
" Babe," she said, " my little son,
Thou and I at last must part ;

There is in my freezing heart
Only life enough for one.
By the crowing of the cocks
Early steps will tread the way,
Could mine arms but wrap thee round
Till the dawning of the day!"
Silent then she seem'd to pray,
Then she spoke like one in pain,
"Little one, it shall be done,
I will keep thee back no more;
It were sweet to go together,
If thou couldst be mine alone;
As it is I must restore
Treasure not mine own.
All the gift and the sweet thanks
Will be over by to-morrow,
He must weep some tears to see
What at morn they will bring in
Where she dared not living come.
He will take thee to his home,
And bless the mother in the child.
Little one, 'tis sweet to me,
Who once gave him all I had—
Hoped it duty, found it sin—
Once more to give all, but now
Take no shame, and no more sorrow
Than a death-pang sets at rest."
Closer then her babe she prest,
Chiller sank the wintry weather.
Once again the owl cried near,
Once more croak'd the strange night-bird
From the stagnance of the fosse
Lorn pale mists, like winding gear,
Hung about her and look'd sad;
Then the blast, that all this while

Slumber'd by a freezing fountain,
Burst out rudely, like a prince
From a midnight revel rushing,
In his train a thousand airs,
Each ambitious of his guilt,
Each as cruel, cold, and wild,
Each as rugged, chill, and stark,
Hurtled round their leader crushing
All the fretwork of the dark ;
Frosty palace, turret, and tower,
Mosque and arabesque, mist-built
By winter-fairies. Then, grown gross
With the license of the hour,
They smote the mother and the child !
Dark night grew darker, not a smile
Came from one star. The moon long since
Had sunk behind the mountain.
At the mirkest somewhat stirred
The sere leaves, where the mother sate ;
For a moment the babe cried,
Something in the silence sigh'd,
And the night was still. Oh fate !
What hadst thou done? Oh that hard sight
Which morn must see ! When Winter went
About the earth at dawn, he rent
His locks in pain, and cast grey hairs
Upon it as he past. So when
Maids, poor mother, wail thy lot—
Mournful at the close of day—
By that legendary spot
Oft they tell us, weeping, how
Hoar frost lay on thy pale brow
When they found thee, and was not
Paler than the clay.

———

SONG.

Oh maiden ! touch gently the rose overblown,
And think of the mother thy childhood hath known ;
Smile not on the buds that exult from her stem,
Lest her pallor grow paler that thou lovest them.
From their beauties, oh maid, each bright butterfly
　　chase,
'Till his duties are paid to that dew-faded face,
And forbid the gay bee one deceitful sweet tone,
Till his vows are all said to the rose overblown.
Sorrow, oh maid, is more grateful than bliss,
Rosebuds were made for the light breeze to kiss.
And woo how thou wilt in the soft hope to see
Some bright bursting blossom that blooms but for thee,
Weep thy fond wish, thou shalt look up to find
Thy tears worn as gems to beguile the next wind.
Turn then thine eyes to the rose overblown,
Speak of its place in a tremulous tone,
Sigh to its leaves as they fall one by one,
And think how the young hopes the heart used to own
Are all shedding fast—like the rose overblown.
Yes, turn in thy gloom to the rose overblown,
Reverently gather each leaf that hath gone,
Watch every canker and wail every streak,
As thou countest the lines on thy mother's dim cheek ;
Twilight by twilight, and day after day,
Keep sweet attendance on sweeter decay.
When all is over weep tears—two or three—
And perchance long years hence, when the grass grows
　　o'er thee,
Fond fragrant tribute to days long by-gone,
Shall be shed on thy grave by some rose overblown.

SONG.

Brother, there is a vacant spot within our holy band,
And poorer is our earthly lot by one strong heart and
    hand ;
Yet, brother, it were ill to weep, when life hath been so
    drear,
That we are left alone to keep its painful vigil here.
'Twere ill if thou hast trod the way to count the
    labouring hours,
Or mourn that sorrow fill'd thy cup with hastier hand
    than ours.
Sleep softly by thy bending tree, till death's long sleep be
    o'er,
That thou canst not remember, we remember thee the
    more.
Sleep softly,—that thine heart hath pass'd through all
    death's deep distress,   [it less.
To such calm rest as now thou hast, shall make us dread
Sleep softly, brother, sleep. But oh, if there are hopes
    more blest
Than sleep, where seasons come and go about a dream-
    less rest ;
If we may deem this grave a shrine which summer rites
    observe,
Where autumn pours the votive wine, and white-robed
    winters serve ;
If we may think that those who now sit side by side with
    God,
Have sent for thee to ask thee how we tread the path
    they trod ;
Oh, brother, if it be not sin when God hath broke the
    chain
Of earthly thought, to bind thee in its fever'd links
    again,

This much of all that earth did know, and all that life
    hath given,
The sadness of our love below bequeathes thy bliss in
    heaven ;
Remember what the bounden bear, though thou for aye
    art free,
And speak of us as kindly there, as here we think of
    thee.

———

The Monk.   But, Roman,
Shall we obey the living or the dead ?
" The powers that be ! "   By what sign will ye know
The *powers* that be ?   My friends, we are the fools
Of eyesight and the earthly habitudes
Which cannot look aloft.   Walking the plank
Of life o'er the abyss, we fear to glance
Or upward to the stars, or downward to the grave.
Our souls, yoke-strain'd, in attitude of toil
Bend earthward.   Oft the *un*worshipp'd angel passeth
While we, with eyes fix'd on the ground from which
We came, adore his footsteps in the sand.
And God, this while, is in the heaven of heavens !

———

The Monk.   When the Baptist
Call'd to repentance, did he weigh the dust
And measure out the sackcloth ? Let a prophet
Wait upon silence.   Who can hold his peace
Hath said his message.   Things that once have dwelt
In heaven will make that prison, a man's heart,
Glad to release them.   Let the seer see
And he will cry.

The Silence of Desolation.

　　　　　　　　　　　　　　　Absolute calm,
A silence like the silence of the desert,
Silence beyond repose, lone, lifeless, stagnant,
Muter than any grave.　Silence too dead
For living tongue to name.　Silence more placid
Than peace or night or death (for these are strings
Unstruck but to be stricken) ; idiot silence,
Sterile, and blank, and blind.　A breathless pause
In heaven and earth ; held till the moving thought
Seems turbulence, this human nature grows
Unseemly on us, our life's common functions
Impertinent and gross, and conscious cheeks
Excuse the beating heart with blushes.　Silence
As of a listening world.　Such strange defect,
Such lean and hungry quiet, such keen sense
Of absence grown effectual, that the ear
Faints as for breath, and even the very substance
Of latent sound seems dead.　Alas ! for language,
We sing the healing darkness of sweet night,
But for Egyptian darkness that was felt
Have names no blacker.　When *you* speak of silence,
'Tis as the sweet content of voiceless woods
After the nightingale—as the home-genius
Sole watching by the sleep of happy babes
With finger at her lip, and shows of stillness,
Meanwhile the sleeper smileth and the air
Stirs with dream-music.　When *I* use the word
Think of some other silence.　In that other
I woke.

———

The Coliseum.

In my short rest
From imminent heights, the dust of slow decay –
Sands from the glass of time shaken of winds—
Crumbs from the feast of desolation—strew'd
My slumbering face upturn'd. The Gorgon Sleep
Made them a shower of stones. My wondering eyes
O'er-charged with sense, in shuddering unbelief
Unclose upon the lone inane expanse
Of summer turf, from which the mouldering walls
Shut not the sunshine ; like a green still lake
Girt by decaying hills. Urging my gaze
Round the tremendous circle, arch on arch,
And pile on pile, that tired the travell'd eye,
I saw the yawning jaws and sightless sockets
Gape to the heedless air. Like the death's-head
Of buried empire. And the sun shone through them
With calm avoidance that left them more dark,
And pleasured him with some small daisy's face
Grass-grown. As though even from the carrion of
    gods,
The instinct of the living universe
Held heaven and earth aloof. All through the lorn
Vacuity winds came and went, but stirr'd
Only the flowers of yesterday. Upstood
The hoar unconscious walls, bisson and bare,
Like an old man deaf, blind, and grey, in whom
The years of old stand in the sun and murmur
Of childhood and the dead. From parapets
Where the sky rests, from broken niches—each
More than Olympus,—for gods dwelt in them,—
Below from senatorial haunts and seats
Imperial, where the ever-passing fates
Wore out the stone, strange hermit birds croak'd forth

Sorrowful sounds, like watchers on the height
Crying the hours of ruin. When the clouds
Dress'd every myrtle on the walls in mourning
With calm prerogative the eternal pile
Impassive shone with the unearthly light
Of immortality.   When conquering suns
Triumph'd in jubilant earth, it stood out dark
With thoughts of ages : like some mighty captive
Upon his deathbed in a Christian land,
And lying, through the chant of Psalm and Creed
Unshriven and stern, with peace upon his brow,
And on his lips strange gods.
                              Rank weeds and grasses,
Careless and nodding, grew, and asked no leave,
Where Romans trembled.   Where the wreck was
        saddest
Sweet pensive herbs, that had been gay elsewhere,
With conscious mien of place rose tall and still,
And bent with duty.   Like some village children
Who found a dead king on a battle-field,
And with decorous care and reverent pity
Composed the lordly ruin, and sat down
Grave without tears.   At length the giant lay,
And everywhere he was begirt with years,
And everywhere the torn and mouldering Past
Hung with the ivy.   For Time, smit with honour
Of what he slew, cast his own mantle on him,
That none should mock the dead.

CRAZED.

(First printed in the "Athenæum" of November 23, 1850.)

" THE Spring again hath started on the course
Wherein she seeketh Summer thro' the Earth.
I will arise and go upon my way.
It may be that the leaves of Autumn hid
His footsteps from me ; it may be the snows.

" He is not dead.   There was no funeral ;
I wore no weeds.   He must be in the Earth.
Oh where is he, that I may come to him
And he may charm the fever of my brain.

" Oh Spring, I hope that thou wilt be my friend.
Thro' the long weary Summer I toiled sore ;
Having much sorrow of the envious woods
And groves that burgeoned round me where I came,
And, when I would have seen him, shut him in.

" Also the Honeysuckle and wild bine
Being in love did hide him from my sight ;
The Ash-tree bent above him ; vicious weeds
Withheld me ; Willows in the River-wind
Hissed at me, by the twilight, waving wands.

"Also, for I have told thee, oh dear Spring,
Thou knowest after I had sunk outworn
In the late summer gloom till Autumn came,
I looked up in the light of burning Woods
And entered on my wayfare when I saw
Gold on the ground and glory in the trees.

"And all my further journey thou dost know;
My toils and outcries as the lusty world
Grew thin to winter; and my ceaseless feet
In vales and on stark hills, till the first snow
Fell, and the large rain of the latter leaves.

"I hope that thou wilt be my friend, oh Spring,
And give me service of thy winds and streams.
It needs must be that he will hear thy voice,
For thou art much as I was when he woo'd
And won me long ago beside the Dee.

"If he should bend above you, oh ye streams,
And anywhere you look up into eyes
And think the star of love hath found her mate
And know, because of day, they are not stars;
Oh streams, they are the eyes of my beloved!
Oh murmur as I murmured once of old,
And he will stay beside you, oh ye streams,
And I shall clasp him when my day is come.

"Likewise I charge thee, west wind, zephyr wind,
If thou shalt hear a voice more sweet than thine
About a sunset rosetree deep in June,
Sweeter than thine, oh wind, when thou dost leap
Into the tree with passion, putting by
The maiden leaves that ruffle round their dame,

And singest and art silent,—having dropt
In pleasure on the bosom of the rose,—
Oh wind, it is the voice of my beloved ;
Wake, wake, and bear me to the voice, oh wind !

" Moreover, I do think that the spring birds
Will be my willing servants.   Wheresoe'er
There mourns a hen-bird that hath lost her mate
Her will I tell my sorrow—weeping hers.

" And if it be a Lark whereto I speak,
She shall be ware of how my Love went up
Sole singing to the cloud ; and evermore
I hear his song, but him I cannot see.

" And if it be a female Nightingale
That pineth in the depth of silent woods,
I also will complain to her that night
Is still.   And of the creeping of the winds
And of the sullen trees, and of the lone
Dumb Dark.   And of the listening of the stars.
What have we done, what have we done, oh Night ?

" Therefore, oh Love, the summer trees shall be
My watch-towers.   Wheresoe'er thou liest bound
I will be there.   For ere the spring be past
I will have preached my dolour through the land,
And not a bird but shall have all my woe.
—And whatsoever hath my woe hath me.

" I charge you, oh ye flowers fresh from the dead,
Declare if ye have seen him.   You pale flowers,
Why do you quake and hang the head like me ?

" You pallid flowers, why do ye watch the dust
And tremble ?   Ah, you met him in your caves,
And shrank out shuddering on the wintry air.

" Snowdrops, you need not gaze upon the ground,
Fear not.   He will not follow ye ; for then
I should be happy who am doomed to woe.

"Only I bid ye say that he is there,
That I may know my grief is to be borne,
And all my Fate is but the common lot."

She sat down on a bank of Primroses,
Swayed to and fro, as in a wind of Thought
That moaned about her, murmuring alow,
"'The common lot, oh for the common lot."

Thus spake she, and behold a gust of grief
Smote her.   As when at night the dreaming wind
Starts up enraged, and shakes the Trees and sleeps.

"Oh early Rain, oh passion of strong crying,
Say, dost thou weep, oh Rain, for him or me?
Alas, thou also goest to the Earth
And enterest as one brought home by fear.

" Rude with much woe, with expectation wild,
So dashest thou the doors and art not seen.
Whose burial did they speak of in the skies?

" I would that there were any grass-green grave
Where I might stand and say, ' Here lies my Love ; '
And sigh, and look down to him, thro' the Earth.
And look up, thro' the clearing skies, and smile."

Then the Day passed from bearing up the Heavens,
The sky descended on the Mountain tops
Unclouded ; and the stars embower'd the Night.

Darkness did flood the Valley; flooding her.
And when the face of her great grief was hid,
Her callow heart, that like a nestling bird
Clamoured, sank down with plaintive pipe and slow.
Her cry was like a strange fowl in the dark :
" Alas Night," said she ; then like a faint ghost,
As tho' the owl did hoot upon the hills,
" Alas Night."   On the murky silence came
Her voice like a white sea-mew on the waste
Of the dark deep ; a-sudden seen and lost
Upon the barren expanse of mid-seas
Black with the Thunder.   " Alas Night," said she,
" Alas Night."   Then the stagnant season lay
From hill to hill.   But when the waning Moon
Rose, she began with hasty step to run
The wintry mead ; a wounded bird that seeks
To hide its head when all the trees are bare.
Silent,—for all her strength did bear her dread —
Silent, save when with bursting heart she cried,
Like one who wrestles in the dark with fiends,
" Alas Night."   With a dim wild voice of fear
As though she saw her sorrow by the moon.

The morning dawns ; and earlier than the Lark
She murmureth, sadder than the Nightingale.

" I would I could believe me in that sleep
When on our bridal morn I thought him dead,
And dreamed and shrieked and woke upon his breast.

" Oh God, I cannot think that I am blind ;
I think I see the beauty of the world.
Perchance but I am blind, and he is near.

" Even as I felt his arm before I woke,
And clinging to his bosom called on him,
And wept, and knew and knew not it was he.

" I do thank God I think that I am blind.
There is a darkness thick about my heart
And all I seem to see is as a dream ;
My lids have closed, and have shut in the world.

" Oh Love, I pray thee take me by the hand ;
I stretch my hand, oh Love, and quake with dread ;
I thrust it, and I know not where,   Ah me,
What shall not seize the dark hand of the blind ?

" How know I, being blind, I am on Earth?
I am in Hell, in Hell, oh Love !   I feel
There is a burning gulph before my feet !
I dare not stir—and at my back the fiends !
I wind my arms, my arms that demons scorch,
Round this poor breast, and all that thou shouldst save
From rapine.   Husband, I cry out from Hell ;
There is a gulph. They seize my flesh." (She shrieked.)

" I will sink down here where I stand.   All round
How know I but the burning pit doth yawn ?
Here will I shrink and shrink to no more space
Than my feet cover."   (She wept.)   " So much up
My mortal touch makes honest.   Oh my Life,
My Lord, my Husband !   Fool that cryest in vain !
Ah Angel !   What hast thou to do with Hell?

" And yet I do not ask thee, oh my Love,
To lead me to thee where thou art in Heaven.
Only I would that thou shouldst be my star,
And whatsoever Fate thy beams dispense
I am content.   It shall be good to me.

" But tho' I may not see thee, oh my Love,
Yea, though mine eyes return and miss thee still,
And thou shouldst take another shape than thine,
Have pity on my lot, and lead me hence
Where I may think of thee.   To the old fields
And wonted valleys where we once were blest.
Oh Love, all day I hear them, out of sight,
The far Home where the Past abideth yet
Beside the stream that prates of other days.

" My Punishment is more than I can bear.
My sorrow groweth big unto my time.
Oh Love, I would that I were mad.   Oh Love,
I do not ask that thou shouldst change my Fate,
I will endure ; but oh my Life, my Lord,
Being as thou art a thronèd saint in Heaven,
If thou wouldst touch me and enchant my sense,
And daze the anguish of my heart with dreams,
And change the stop of grief ; and turn my soul
A little devious from the daily march
Of Reason, and the path of conscious woe
And all the truth of Life !   Better, oh Love,
In fond delusion to be twice betrayed,
Than know so well and bitterly as I.
Let me be mad."   (She wept upon her knees.)

" I will arise and seek thee.   This is Heaven·
I sat upon a cloud.   It bore me in.
It is not so, you Heavens !   I am not dead.
Alas ! there have been pangs as strong as Death.
It would be sweet to know that I am dead.

" Even now I feel I am not of this world,
Which sayeth, day and night, ' For all but thee,
And poureth its abundance night and day
And will not feed the hunger in my heart.

" I tread upon a dream, myself a dream,
I cannot write my Being on the world,
The moss grows unrespective where I tread.

" I cannot lift mine eyes to the sunshine,
Night is not for my slumber.   Not for me
Sink down the dark inexorable hours.

" I would not keep or change the weary day ;
I have no pleasure in the needless night,
And toss and wail that other lids may sleep.

" I am a very Leper in the Earth.
Her functions cast me out ; her golden wheels
That harmless roll about unconscious Babes
Do crush me.   My place knoweth me no more.

" I think that I have died, oh you sweet Heavens.
I did not see the closing of the eyes.
Perchance there is one death for all of us
Whereof we cannot see the eyelids close.

" Dear Love, I do beseech thee answer me.
Dear Love, I think men's eyes behold me not.
The air is heavy on these lips that strain
To cry ; I do not warm the thing I touch ;
The Lake gives back no image unto me.

" I see the Heavens as one who wakes at noon
From a deep sleep.   Now shall we meet again !
The Country of the blest is hid from me
Like Morn behind the Hills.   The Angel smiles.
I breathe thy name.   He hurleth me from Heaven.

" Now of a truth I know thou art on earth.
Break, break the chains that hold me back from thee.

I see the race of mortal men pass by;
The great wind of their going waves my hair;
I stretch my hands, I lay my cheek to them,
In love; they stir the down upon my cheek;
I cannot touch them, and they know not me.

" Oh God! I ask to live the saddest life!
I care not for it if I may but live!
I would not be among the dead, oh God!
I am not dead! oh God, I will not die!"

So throbbed the trouble of this crazèd heart.
So on the broken mirror of her mind
In bright disorder shone the shattered World
So, out of tune, in sympathetic chords,
Her soul is musical to brooks and birds,
Winds, seasons, sunshine, flowers, and maundering
    trees.

Hear gently all the tale of her distress.
The heart that loved her loves not now yet lives.
What the eye sees and the ear hears—the hand
That wooing led her thro' the rosy paths
Of girlhood, and the lenten lanes of Love,
The brow whereon she trembled her first kiss,
The lips that had sole privilege of hers,
The eyes wherein she saw the Universe,
The bosom where she slept the sleep of joy,
The voice that made it sacred to her sleep
With lustral vows; that which doth walk the World
Man among Men, is near her now.   But He
Who wandered with her thro' the ways of Youth,
Who won the tender freedom of the lip,
Who took her to the bosom dedicate
And chaste with vows, who in the perfect whole

Of gracious Manhood was the god that stood
In her young Heaven, round whom the subject stars
Circled : in whose dear train, where'er he passed
Thronged charmèd powers ; at whose advancing feet
Upspringing happy seasons and sweet times
Made fond court carolling ! who but moved to stir
All things submissive, which did magnify
And wane as ever with his changing will
She changed the centre of her infinite ; He
In whom she worshipped Truth, and did obey
Goodness ; in whose sufficient love she felt,
Fond Dreamer ! the eternal smile of all
Angels and men ; round whom, upon his neck,
Her thoughts did hang ; whom lacking they fell down
Distract to the earth ; He whom she *loved*, and who
Loved her of old,—in the long days before
Chaos, the empyrean days !—(Poor heart,
She phrased it so) is no more : and O God !
Thorough all Time, and that transfigured Time
We call Eternity, will be no more.

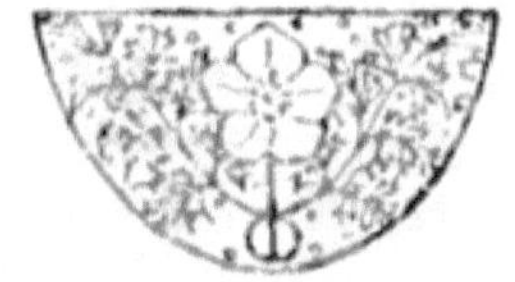

THE SNOWDROP IN THE SNOW.

*(First printed in the " Athenæum" of
1st March, 1851.)*

O FULL of Faith !   The Earth is rock,—the Heaven
The dome of a great palace all of ice,
Russ-built.   Dull light distils through frozen skies
Thickened and gross.   Cold Fancy droops her wing,
And cannot range.   In winding-sheets of snow
Lies every thought of any pleasant thing.
I have forgotten the green earth ; my soul
Deflowered, and lost to every summer hope,
Sad sitteth on an iceberg at the Pole ;
My heart assumes the landscape of mine eyes
Moveless and white, chill blanched with hoarest rime ;
The Sun himself is heavy and lacks cheer
Or on the eastern hill or western slope ;
The world without seems far and long ago ;
To silent woods stark famished winds have driven
The last lean robin—gibbering winds of fear !
Thou only darest to believe in spring,
Thou only smilest, Lady of the Time !
Even as the stars come up out of the sea
Thou risest from the Earth.   How is it down
In the dark depths?   Should I delve there, O Flower,
For beauty?   Shall I find the Summer there
Met manifold, as in an ark of peace ?

And Thou, a lone white Dove, art thou sent forth
Upon the winter deluge?   It shall cease,
But not for thee—pierced by the ruthless North
And spent with the Evangel.   In what hour
The flood abates thou wilt have closed thy wings
For ever.   When the happy living things
Of the old world come forth upon the new
I know my heart shall miss thee ; and the dew
Of summer twilights shall shed tears for me—
Tears liker thee, ah, purest ! than mine own—
Upon thy vestal grave, O vainly fair !

Thou should'st have noble destiny, who, like
A Prophet, art shut out from kind and kin :
Who on the winter silence comest in
A still small voice.   Pale Hermit of the Year,
Flower of the Wilderness ! oh, not for thee
The jocund playmates of the maiden spring.
For when she danceth forth with cymballed feet,
Waking a-sudden with great welcoming,
Each calling each, they burst from hill to dell
In answering music.   But thou art a bell,
A passing bell, snow-muffled, dim and sweet.
As is the Poet to his fellow-men,
So mid thy drifting snows, O Snowdrop, Thou.
Gifted, in sooth, beyond them, but no less
A snowdrop.   And thou shalt complete his lot
And bloom as fair as now when they are not..
Thou art the wonder of the seasons, O
First-born of Beauty.   As the Angel near
Gazed on that first of living things which, when
The blast that ruled since Chaos o'er the sere
Leaves of primeval Palms did sweep the plain,
Clung to the new-made sod and would not drive,

So gaze I upon thee amid the reign
Of Winter.   And because thou livest, I live.
And art thou happy in thy loneliness?
Oh couldst thou hear the shouting of the floods,
Oh couldst thou know the stir among the trees
When—as the herald-voice of breeze on breeze
Proclaims the marriage pageant of the Spring
Advancing from the South—each hurries on
His wedding-garment, and the love-chimes ring
Thro' nuptial valleys !   No, serene and lone,
I will not flush thy cheek with joys like these.
Songs for the rosy morning ; at grey prime
To hang the head and pray.   Thou doest well.
I will not tell thee of the bridal train.
No ; let thy Moonlight die before their day
A Nun among the Maidens, thou and they.
Each hath some fond sweet office that doth strike
One of our trembling heartstrings musical.
Is not the hawthorn for the Queen of May ?
And cuckoo-flowers for whom the cuckoo's voice
Hails, like an answering sister, to the woods ?
Is not the maiden blushing in the rose ?
Shall not the babe and buttercup rejoice,
Twins in one meadow !   Are not violets all
By name or nature for the breast of Dames ?
For them the primrose, pale as star of prime,
For them the wind-flower, trembling to a sigh,
For them the dew stands in the eyes of day
That blink in April on the daisied lea ?
Like them they flourish and like them they fade,
And live beloved and loving.   But for thee—
For such a bevy how art thou arrayed,
Flower of the Tempests ?   What hast thou with
    them ?
Thou shalt be pearl unto a diadem

Which the Heavens jewel.   *They* shall deck the brows
Of joy and wither there.   But *thou* shalt be
A Martyr's garland.   Thou who, undismayed,
To thy spring dreams art true amid the snows
As he to better dreams amid the flames.

THE HARPS OF HEAVEN.

ON a solemn day
I clomb the shining bulwark of the skies :
Not by the beaten way,
But climbing by a prayer,
That like a golden thread hung by the giddy stair
Fleck'd on the immemorial blue,
By the strong step-stroke of the brave and few,
Who, stirr'd by echoes of far harmonies,
Must either lay them down and die of love,
Or dare
Those empyrean walls that mock their starward eyes.
But midway in the dread emprize
The faint and fainter footsteps cease ;
And, all my footing gone,
Like one who gathers samphire, I hold on,
And in the swaying air look up and down :
And up and down through answering vasts descry
Nor Earth nor Heaven ;
Above,
The sheer eternal precipice ; below,
The sheer eternal precipice.
Then when I,
Gigantic with my desperate agony,
Felt even
The knotted grasp of bodily despair
Relaxing to let go,
A mighty music, like a wind of light,

Blew from the imminent height,
And caught me in its splendour ; and, as flame
That flickers and again aspires,
Rose in a moment thither whence it came ;
And I, that thought me lost,
Pass'd to the top of all my dear desires,
And stood among the everlasting host.
Then turn'd I to a seraph whose swift hands,
That lived angelic passion, struck his soul
Upon a harp—a seraph fair and strong,
And faultless for his harp and for his throne,
And yet, among
The Strength and Beauty of the heavenly bands,
No more to be remember'd than some one
Poor warrior, when a king of many kings
Stamps on the fields, and rears his glittering crop
Of standing steel, and the vex'd spirit wings
Above the human harvest, and in vain
Begins from morn till eve to sum the embattled plain ;
Or when,
After a day of peace, sudden and late
The beacon flashes and the war-drums roll,
And through the torches of the city gate,
All the long winter night a martial race
Streams to the nation's gathering-place,
And, like as water-drop to water-drop,
Pour on in changeless flood the innumerable men.
I turn'd, and as from footing in mid-seas
Looking o'er lessening waves thou may'st behold
The round horizon of unshadow'd gold,
I, standing on an amethyst, look'd round
The moving Heaven of Harpers throned and crown'd,
And said, " Was it from these
I heard the great sound ?"   And he said, " What
    sound ?"

Then I grown bolder, seeing I had thriven
To win reply—" This that I hear from thee,
This that everywhere I hear,
Rolling a sea of choristry
Up and down the jewel of Heaven ;
A sea which from thy seat of light,
That seems more loud and bright
Because more near,
To the white twinkle of yon furthest portal,
Swells up those circling shores of chrysolite,
And, like an odorous luminous mist, doth leap the
        eternal walls,
And falls
In wreaths of melody
Adown the azure mountain of the sky ;
And round its lower slopes bedew'd
Breathes lost beatitude ;
And far away,
Low, low, below the last of all its lucent scarps.
Sprinkles bewildering drops of immortality.
O angel fair, thou know'st what I would say—
This sound of harpers that I hear,
This sound of harpers harping on their harps."
Then he bent his head
And shed a tear
And said,
" I perceive thou art a mortal."
Then I to him—" Not only, O thou bright
Seraphic Pity ! to a mortal ear
These sacred sounds are dear,
Or why withholdest not thy ceaseless hand ?
And why,
Far as my dazzled eye
Can pierce the lustre of the radiant land,
See I the rapt celestial auditory,

Each, while he blessed hears, gives back his bliss
With never-tiring touch from golden harps, like this?"
Then he to me—"Oh, wherefore hast thou trod
Beyond the limit of thine earthly lot?
These that we bear
Within our hands are instruments of glory,
Wherewith, day without night,
We make the glory of immortal light
In the eyes of God,
As for the sound, we hear it not ;
Yet, speaking to thee, child of ignorance,
I do remember that I loved it once,
In the sweet lower air."
Yet he spake once more, —
"But thou, return to the remember'd shore :
Why shouldst thou leave thy nation,
Thy city, and the house of all most dear?
Do we not all dwell in eternity?
For we have been as thou, and thou
Shalt be as we."
And he lean'd and kissed me,
Saying, " But now
Rejoice, O child, in other joys than mine
Hear the dear music of thy mortal ear
While yet it is the time with thee,
Nor make haste to thine exaltation,
Though our state be better than thine."

SONNETS WRITTEN IN 1855.

(During the Crimean War.)

THE FUTURE.

I saw the human millions as the sand
Unruffled on the starlit wilderness.
The day was near, and every star grew less
In universal dawn.   Then woke a band
Of wheeling winds, and made a mighty stress
Of morning weather ; and still wilder went
O'er shifting plains, till, in their last excess,
A whirlwind whirled across the whirling land.
Heaven blackened over it ; a voice of woes
Foreran it ; the great noise of clanging foes
Hurtled behind ; beneath the earth was rent,
And howling Death, like an uncaverned beast,
Leaped from his lair.   Meanwhile morn oped the East,
And thro' the dusty tumult God arose.

THE ARMY SURGEON.

OVER that breathing waste of friends and foes,
The wounded and the dying, hour by hour,—
In will a thousand, yet but one in power,—
He labours thro' the red and groaning day.
The fearful moorland where the myriads lay
Moved as a moving field of mangled worms.
And as a raw brood, orphaned in the storms,
Thrust up their heads if the wind bend a spray
Above them, but when the bare branch performs
No sweet parental office, sink away
With hopeless chirp of woe, so as he goes
Around his feet in clamorous agony
They rise and fall; and all the seething plain
Bubbles a cauldron vast of many-coloured pain.

CZAR NICHOLAS.

WE could not turn from that colossal foe,
The morning shadow of whose hideous head
Darkened the furthest West, and who did throw
His evening shade on Ind.   The polar bow
Behind him flamed and paled, and through the red
Uncertain dark his vasty shape did grow
Upon the sleepless nations.   Lay him low !
Aye, low as for our priceless English dead
We lie and groan to-day in England !   Oh,
My God !   I think Thou hast not finished
This Thy fair world, where, triumph Ill or Good,
We still must weep ; where or to lose or gain
Is woe ; where Pain is medicined by Pain,
And Blood can only be washed out by Blood.

HOME, IN WAR-TIME.

SHE turned the fair page with her fairer hand—
More fair and frail than it was wont to be—
O'er each remembered thing he loved to see
She lingered, and as with a fairy's wand
Enchanted it to order.   Oft she fanned
New motes into the sun ; and as a bee
Sings thro' a brake of bells, so murmured she,
And so her patient love did understand
The reliquary room.   Upon the sill
She fed his favourite bird.   " Ah, Robin, sing !
He loves thee."   Then she touches a sweet string
Of soft recall, and towards the Eastern hill
Smiles all her soul—for him who cannot hear
The raven croaking at his carrion ear.

WARNING.

VIRTUE is Virtue, writ in ink or blood.
And Duty, Honour, Valour, are the same
Whether they cheer the thundering steps of Fame
Up echoing hills of Alma, or more blest,
Walk with her in that band where she is least,
Thro' smiling plains and cities doing good.
Yet, oh to sing them in their happier day !
Yon glebe is not the hind whose manhood mends
Its rudeness, yet it gains but while he spends,
And mulcts him rude.   Even that sinless Lord
Whose feet wan Mary washed, went not His way
Uncoloured by the Galilean field ;
And Honour, Duty, Valour, seldom wield
With stainless hand the immedicable sword.

AMERICA.

MEN say, Columbia, we shall hear thy guns.
But in what tongue shall be thy battle-cry?
Not that our sires did love in years gone by,
When all the Pilgrim Fathers were little sons
In merrie homes of Englaunde?   Back, and see
Thy satchelled ancestor !   Behold, he runs
To mine, and, clasped, they tread the equal lea
To the same village-school, where side by side
They spell " our Father."   Hard by, the twin-pride
Of that grey hall whose ancient oriel gleams
Thro' yon baronial pines, with looks of light
Our sister-mothers sit beneath one tree.
Meanwhile our Shakespeare wanders past and dreams
His Helena and Hermia.   Shall we fight?

AMERICA.

Nor force nor fraud shall sunder us !   Oh ye
Who north or south, on east or western land,
Native to noble sounds, say truth for truth,
Freedom for freedom, love for love, and God
For God ; Oh ye who in eternal youth
Speak with a living and creative flood
This universal English, and do stand
Its breathing book ; live worthy of that grand
Heroic utterance—parted, yet a whole,
Far, yet unsevered,—children brave and free
Of the great Mother-tongue, and ye shall be
Lords of an Empire wide as Shakespeare's soul,
Sublime as Milton's immemorial theme,
And rich as Chaucer's speech, and fair as Spenser's
      dream.

THE COMMON GRAVE

LAST night beneath the foreign stars I stood
And saw the thoughts of those at home go by
To the great grave upon the hill of blood.
Upon the darkness they went visibly,
Each in the vesture of its own distress.
Among them there came One, frail as a sigh,
And like a creature of the wilderness
Dug with her bleeding hands.   She neither cried
Nor wept: nor did she see the many stark
And dead that lay unburied at her side.
All night she toiled, and at that time of dawn,
When Day and Night do change their More or Less,
And Day is More, I saw the melting Dark
Stir to the last, and knew she laboured on.

ESSE ET POSSE.

The groan of fallen Hosts ; a torrid glare
Of cities ; battle-cries of Right and Wrong
Where armies shout to rocking fleets that roar
On thundering oceans to the thundering shore,
And high o'er all—long, long prolonged, along
The moaning caverns of the plaining air,—
The cry of conscious Fate.   The firmament
Waves from above me like a tattered flag ;
And as a soldier in his lowly tent
Looks up when a shot strikes the helpless rag
From o'er him, and beholds the canopy
Of Heaven, so, sudden to my startled eye
The Heavens that shall be !   The dream fades.
    I stand
Among the mourners of a mourning land.

:

GOOD-NIGHT IN WAR-TIME.

(To Alexander Smith.)

The stars we saw arise are high above,
And yet our Evensong seems sung too soon.
Good-Night!   I lay my hand—with such a love
As thou wert brother of my blood—upon
Thy shoulder, and methinks beneath the moon
Those sisters, Anglia and Caledon,
Lean towards each other.   Aye, for Man is one ;
We are a host ruled by one trumpet-call,
Where each, armed in his sort, makes as he may
The general motion.   The well-tuned array
We see ; yet to what victory in what wars
We see not ; but, like the revolving stars,
Move on ourselves.   The total march of all,
Or men or stars, God knows.   Lord, lead us on !

LYRICS FROM

ENGLAND IN TIME OF WAR.

(1856.)

DESOLATE.

FROM the sad eaves the drip-drop of the rain !
The water washing at the latchel door ;
A slow step plashing by upon the moor !
A single bleat far from the famished fold ;
The clicking of an embered hearth and cold ;
The rainy Robin tic-tac at the pane.

"So as it is with thee
Is it with me,
So as it is and it used not to be,
With thee used not to be,
Nor me."
So singeth Robin on the willow tree,
The rainy Robin tic-tac at the pane

Here in this breast all day
The fire is dim and low,
Within I care not to stay,
Without I care not to go.

A sadness ever sings
Of unforgotten things,
And the bird of love is patting at the pane ;
But the wintry water deepens at the door,
And a step is plashing by upon the moor
Into the dark upon the darkening moor,
And alas, alas, the drip-drop of the rain !

THE MARKET-WIFE'S SONG.

THE butter an' the cheese weel stowit they be,
I sit on the hen-coop the eggs on my knee,
The lang kail jigs as we jog owre the rigs,
The gray mare's tail it wags wi' the kail,
The warm simmer sky is blue aboon a',
An' whiddie, whuddie, whaddie, gang the auld wheels
    twa.

I sit on the coop, I look straight before,
But my heart it is awa' the braid ocean owre,
I see the bluidy fiel' where my ain bonny chiel',
My wee bairn o' a', gaed to fight or to fa',
An' whiddie, whuddie, whaddie, gang the auld wheels
    twa.

I see the gran' toun o' the big forrin' loun,
I hear the cannon soun', I see the reek aboon ;
It may be lang John lettin' aff his gun,
It may be the mist—your mither disna wist—
It may be the kirk, it may be the ha',
An' whiddie, whuddie, whaddie, gang the auld wheels
    twa.

 * In several of the Scottish songs of this volume, the author
wishes, notwithstanding whatever *couleur locale* they may
possess, to be understood as speaking rather for a class than a
locality. As most of the English provincial dialects are poeti-
cally objectionable, and are modifications of tongues which
exist more purely in the " Lallans " of Scotland, it seemed to
him that when expressing the general peasant life of the empire
he might employ the central truth of that noble Doric which is
at once rustic and dignified, heroic and vernacular.

An' I ken the Black Sea, ayont the rock o' dool,
Like a muckle blot o' ink in a buik fra' the schule,
An' Jock ! it gars me min' o' your buikies lang syne,
An' mindin' o' it a' the tears begin to fa',
An' whiddie, whuddie, whaddie, gang the auld wheels
    twa.

Then a bull roars fra' the scaur, ilka rock 's a bull agen,
An' I hear the trump o' war, an' the carse is fu' o' men,
Up an' doun the morn I ken the bugle horn,
Ilka birdie sma' is a fleein' cannon ba',
An' whiddie, whuddie, whaddie, gang the auld wheels
    twa.

Guid Heavens ! the Russian host ! We maun e'en gie
    up for lost !
Gin ye gain the battle hae ye countit a' the cost ?
Ye may win a gran' name, but wad wee Jock come hame ?
Dinna fecht, dinna fecht ! there's room for us a',
An' whiddie, whuddie, whaddie, gang the auld wheels
    twa.

In vain, in vain, in vain ! They are marchin' near and
    far !
Wi' swords an' wi' slings an' wi' instruments o' war !
Oh, day sae dark an' sair ! ilka man seven feet an' mair !
I bow my head an' say, " Gin the Lord wad smit them
    a' ! "
An' whiddie, whuddie, whaddie, gang the auld wheels
    twa.

Then forth fra' their ban' there steps an armed man,
His tairge at his breast an' his claymore in his han',

His gowd pow glitters fine an' his shadow fa's behin',
I think o' great Goliath as he stan's before them a',
An' whiddie, whuddie, whaddie, gang the auld wheels
    twa.

To meet the Philistine leaps a laddie fra' our line,
Oh, my heart ! oh, my heart ! 'tis that wee lad o' mine !
I start to my legs—an' doun fa' the eggs—
The cocks an' hens a' they cackle an' they ca',
An' whiddie, whuddie, whaddie, gang the auld wheels
    twa.

Oh, Jock, my Hielan' lad—oh, Jock, my Hielan' lad,
Never till I saw thee that moment was I glad !
Aye sooner sud thou dee before thy mither's e'e
Than a man o' the clan sud hae stept out but thee !
An' sae I cry to God—while the hens cackle a',
An' whiddie, whuddie, whaddie, gang the auld wheels
    twa.

THE LITTLE-GIRL'S SONG.

Do not mind my crying, Papa, I am not crying for
 pain.
Do not mind my shaking, Papa, I am not shaking
 with fear;
Tho' the wild wild wind is hideous to hear,
And I see the snow and the rain.
When will you come back again,
Papa, Papa?

Somebody else that you love, Papa,
Somebody else that you dearly love
Is weary, like me, because you're away.
Sometimes I see her lips tremble and move,
And I seem to know what they're going to say;
And every day, and all the long day,
I long to cry, "Oh Mamma, Mamma,
When will Papa come back again?"
But before I can say it I see the pain
Creeping up on her white white cheek,
As the sweet sad sunshine creeps up the white wall,
And then I am sorry, and fear to speak;
And slowly the pain goes out of her cheek,
As the sad sweet sunshine goes from the wall.
Oh, I wish I were grown up wise and tall,
That I might throw my arms round her neck
And say, " Dear Mamma, oh, what is it all
That I see and see and do not see
In your white white face all the livelong day?"
But she hides her grief from a child like me.
When will you come back again,
Papa, Papa?

Where were you going, Papa, Papa?
All this long while have you been on the sea?
When she looks as if she saw far away,
Is she thinking of you, and what does she see?
Are the white sails blowing,
And the blue men rowing,
And are you standing on the high deck
Where we saw you stand till the ship grew grey,
And we watched and watched till the ship was a
    speck,
And the dark came first to you, far away?
I wish I could see what she can see,
But she hides her grief from a child like me.
When will you come back again,
Papa, Papa?

Don't you remember, Papa, Papa?
How we used to sit by the fire, all three,
And she told me tales while I sat on her knee,
And heard the winter winds roar down the street,
And knock like men at the window pane,
And the louder they roared, oh, it seemed more
    sweet
To be warm and warm as we used to be,
Sitting at night by the fire, all three ?
When will you come back again,
Papa, Papa?

Papa, I like to sit by the fire ;
Why does she sit far away in the cold
If I had but somebody wise and old,
That every day I might cry and say,
" Is she changed, do you think, or do I forget ?
Was she always as white as she is to-day ?
Did she never carry her head up higher ? "

Papa, Papa, if I could but know !
Do you think her voice was always so low?
Did I always see what I seem to see
When I wake up at night and her pillow is wet ?
You used to say her hair it was gold—
It looks like silver to me.
But still she tells the same tale that she told,
She sings the same songs when I sit on her knee,
And the house goes on as it went long ago,
When we lived together, all three.
Sometimes my heart seems to sink, Papa,
And I feel as if I could be happy no more.
Is she changed, do you think, Papa,
Or did I dream she was brighter before ?
She makes me remember my snowdrop, Papa,
That I forgot in thinking of you,
    The sweetest snowdrop that ever I knew !
But I put it out of the sun and the rain :
It was green and white when I put it away,
It had one sweet bell and green leaves four ;
It was green and white when I found it that day,
It had one pale bell and green leaves four,
But I was not glad of it any more.
Was it changed, do you think, Papa,
Or did I dream it was brighter before ?

Do not mind my crying, Papa,
I am not crying for pain.
Do not mind my shaking, Papa,
I am not shaking for fear ;
Tho' the wild wild wind is hideous to hear,
And I see the snow and the rain.
When will you come back again,
Papa, Papa?

"*HE IS SAFE.*"

"AND it shall come to pass at eventide
There shall be light." Lord, it hath come to pass.
As one day to the world so now to me
Thine advent. My dark eve is white as noon ;
My year so sour and green is gold and red ;
Mine eyes have seen Thy Goodness. All is done.

All things bespeak an end. I am come near
The crown o' this steep earth. My feet still stand
Cold in the western shadow, but my brow
Lives in the living light. The toil is o'er,
Surely "He giveth His beloved Rest."

I feel two worlds : one ends and one begins.
Methinks I dwell in both ; being much here,
But more hereafter : even as when the nurse
Doth give the babe into the mother's arms,
And she who hath not quite resigned, and she
Who hath not all received, support in twain
The single burden ; ne'ertheless the babe
Already tastes its mother. Lord, I come.
Thy signs are in me. "He shall wipe away
All tears : " Thou see'st my tears are wiped away.
"There shall be no more pain : " Lord, it is done,
Here there is no more pain. "The sun no more
Shall be their light by day ; " even so, Lord,
I need no light of sun or moon ! My heart

Is as a lamp of jasper, crystal-clear,
Dark when Thy light is out, but lit with Thee
The sun may be a suckling at this breast,
And milk a nobler glory.   Lord, I know
Mine hour.   This painful world, that was of thorns,
Is roses.   Like a fragrance thro' my soul
I breathe a balm of slumber.   Let me sleep.
Bring me my easy pillows, Margery.
I am asleep; this oak is soft: all things
Are rest: I sink as into bliss.   O Lord,
Now lettest Thou Thy servant depart in peace

LADY CONSTANCE.

My Love, my Lord,
I think the toil of glorious day is done.
I see thee leaning on thy jewelled sword,
And a light-hearted child of France
Is dancing to thee in the sun,
And thus he carols in his dance.

> "Oh, a gallant sans peur
> Is the merry chasseur,
> With his fanfaron horn and his rifle ping-pang !
> And his grand haversack
> Of gold on his back,
> His pistol cric-crac !
> And his sword cling-clang !

> "Oh, to see him blithe and gay
> From some hot and bloody day,
Come to dance the night away till the bugle blows
> 'au rang,'
> With a wheel and a whirl
> And a wheeling waltzing girl,
And his bow, 'place aux dames !' and his oath,
> 'feu et sang !'
> And his hop and his fling
> Till his gold and silver ring
To the clatter and the clash of his sword cling-clang !

> "But hark,
> 'Thro' the dark,
> Up goes the well-known shout !
> The drums beat the turn out !

    Cut short your courting, Monsieur l'Amant !
    Saddle ! mount ! march ! trot !
    Down comes the storm of shot,
    The foe is at the charge !   En avant !

  " His jolly haversack
    Of gold is on his back,
    Hear his pistol cric-crac ! hear his rifle ping-pang !

  " Vive l' Empereur !
    And where's the Chasseur ?

  " He's in
    Among the din
    Steel to steel cling-clang ! "

And thou within the doorway of thy tent
Leanest at ease with careless brow unbent,
Watching the dancer in as pleased a dream
As if he were a gnat i' the evening gleam,
And thou and I were sitting side by side
Within the happy bower
Where oft at the same hour
We watched them the sweet year I was a bride.

My Love, my Lord,
Leaning so grandly on thy jewelled sword,
Is there no thought of home to whisper thee,
None can relieve the weary guard I keep,
None wave the flag of breathing truce for me,
Nor sound the hours to slumber or to weep ?
Once in a moon the bugle breaks thy rest,
I count my days by trumpets and alarms :
Thou liest down in thy warcloak and art blest,
While I, who cannot sleep but in thine arms,
Wage night and day fresh fields unknown to fame,
Arm, marshal, march, charge, fight, fall, faint, and die,

Know all a soldier can endure but shame,
And every chance of warfare but to fly.
I do not murmur at my destiny :
It can but go with love, with whom it came,
And love is like the sun—his light is sweet,
And sweet his shadow—welcome both to me !
Better for ever to endure that hurt
Which thou canst taste but once than once to lie
At ease when thou hast anguish.   Better I
Be often sad when thou art gay than gay
One moment of thy sorrow.   Tho' I pray
Too oft I shall win nothing of the sky
But my unfilled desire and thy desert
Can take it and still lack.   Oh, might I stay
At the shut gates of heaven ! that so I meet
Each issuing fate, and cling about his feet
And melt the dreadful purpose of his eye,
And not one power pass unimpleaded by
Whose bolt might be for thee !   Aye, love is sweet
In shine or shade !   But love hath jealousy,
That knowing but so little thinks so much !
And I am jealous of thee even with such
A fatal knowledge.   For I wot too well
In the set season that I cannot tell
Death will be near thee.   This thought doth deflour
All innocence from time.   I dare not say
"Not now," but for the instant cull the hour,
And for the hour reap all the doubtful day,
And for the day the year : and so, forlorn,
From morn till night, from startled night till morn,
Like a blind slave I bear thine heavy ill
Till thy time comes to take it ; come when 't will
The broken slave will bend beneath it still.

THE MILKMAID'S SONG.

Turn, turn, for my cheeks they burn,
Turn by the dale, my Harry !
Fill pail, fill pail,
He has turned by the dale,
And there by the stile waits Harry.
Fill, fill,
Fill pail, fill,
For there by the stile waits Harry !
The world may go round, the world may stand still,
But I can milk and marry,
Fillpail,
I can milk and marry.

Wheugh, wheugh !
Oh, if we two
Stood down there now by the water,
I know who'd carry me over the ford
As brave as a soldier, as proud as a lord,
Tho' I don't live over the water.
Wheugh, wheugh ! he's whistling thro',
He's whistling "the farmer's daughter.'
Give down, give down,
My crumpled brown !
He shall not take the road to the town
For I'll meet him beyond the water.
Give down, give down,
My crumpled brown !
And send me to my Harry.

The folk o' towns
May have silken gowns,
But I can milk and marry,
Fillpail,
I can milk and marry.

Wheugh, wheugh ! he has whistled thro'
He has whistled thro' the water.
Fill, fill, with a will, a will,
For he's whistled thro' the water,
And he's whistling down
The way to the town,
And it's not " the farmer's daughter ! "
Churr, churr ! goes the cockchafer,
The sun sets over the water,
Churr, churr ! goes the cockchafer,
I'm too late for my Harry !
And, oh, if he goes a-soldiering,
The cows they may low, the bells they may ring,
But I'll neither milk nor marry,
Fillpail,
Neither milk nor marry.

My brow beats on thy flank, Fillpail,
Give down, good wench, give down !
I know the primrose bank, Fillpail,
Between him and the town.
Give down, good wench, give down, Fillpail,
And he shall not reach the town !
Strain, strain ! he's whistling again,
He's nearer by half a mile.
More, more !   Oh, never before
Were you such a weary while !
Fill, fill ! he's crossed the hill,
I can see him down by the stile,
He's passed the hay, he's coming this way,

He 's coming to me, my Harry !
Give silken gowns to the folk o' towns,
He 's coming to me, my Harry !
There's not so grand a dame in the land,
That she walks to-night with Harry !
Come late, come soon, come sun, come moon,
Oh, I can milk and marry,
Fillpail,
I can milk and marry.

Wheugh, wheugh ! he has whistled thro',
My Harry ! my lad ! my lover !
Set the sun and fall the dew,
Heigho, merry world, what's to do
That you 're smiling over and over ?
Up on the hill and down in the dale,
And along the tree-tops over the vale
Shining over and over,
Low in the grass and high on the bough,
Shining over and over,
Oh, world, have you ever a lover ?
You were so dull and cold just now,
Oh, world, have you ever a lover ?
I could not see a leaf on the tree,
And now I could count them, one, two, three,
Count them over and over,
Leaf from leaf like lips apart,
Like lips apart for a lover.
And the hill-side beats with my beating heart,
And the apple-tree blushes all over,
And the May bough touched me and made me start
And the wind breathes warm like a lover.

Pull, pull ! and the pail is full,
And milking's done and over.

Who would not sit here under the tree ?
What a fair fair thing 's a green field to see
Brim, brim, to the rim, ah me !
I have set my pail on the daisies !
It seems so light—can the sun be set ?
The dews must be heavy, my cheeks are wet,
I could cry to have hurt the daisies !
Harry is near, Harry is near,
My heart 's as sick as if he were here,
My lips are burning, my cheeks are wet,
He hasn't uttered a word as yet,
But the air's astir with his praises,
My Harry !
The air's astir with your praises.
He has scaled the rock by the pixy's stone,
He 's among the kingcups—he picks me one.
I love the grass that I tread upon
When I go to my Harry !
He has jumped the brook, he has climbed the knowe,
There's never a faster foot I know,
But still he seems to tarry.
Oh, Harry ! oh, Harry ! my love, my pride,
My heart is leaping, my arms are wide !
Roll up, roll up, you dull hill-side,
Roll up, and bring my Harry !
They may talk of glory over th. sea,
But Harry's alive, and Harry's for me
My love, my lad, my Harry !
Come spring, come winter, come sun, come snow,
What cares Dolly whether or no,
While I can milk and marry ?
Right or wrong, and wrong or right,
Quarrel who quarrel, and fight who fight,
But I'll bring my pail home every night
To love, and home, and Harry !

We'll drink our can, we'll eat our cake,
There's beer in the barrel, there's bread in the bake,
The world may sleep, the world may wake,
But I shall milk and marry,
And marry,
I shall milk and marry.

THE GERMAN LEGION.

In the cot beside the water,
In the white cot by the water,
The white cot by the white water,
There they laid the German maid.

There they wound her, singing round her,
Deftly wound her, singing round her,
Softly wound her, singing round her,
In a shroud like a cloud.

And they decked her as they wound her,
With a wreath of leaves they bound her,
Lornest leaves they scattered round her,
Singing grief with every leaf.

Singing grief with every leaf,
Sadder grief with sadder leaf,
Sweeter leaf with sweeter grief,
So 't was sung in a dark tongue.

Like a latter lily lying,
O'er whom falling leaves are sighing,
And Autumn vapours crying,
Pale and cold on misty mould,

So I saw her sweet and lowly,
Shining shining pale and holy,
Thro' the dim woe slowly, slowly,
Said and sung in that dark tongue.

Such an awe her beauty lent her,
While they sang I dared not enter
That charmed ring where she was centre,
But I stood with stirring blood

Till the song fell like a billow,
And I saw them leave her pillow,
And go forth to the far willow,
For the wreath of virgin death.

And I stood beside her pillow,
While they plucked the distant willow
And my heart rose like a billow
As I said to the pale dead—

" Oh, thou most fair and sweet virginity,
Of whom this heart that beats for thee doth know
Nor name nor story, that these limbs can be
For no man evermore, that thou must go
Cold to the cold, and that no eye shall see
That which thine unsolved womanhood doth owe
Of the incommunicable mystery
Shakes me with tears. I could kneel down by thee,
And o'er thy chill unmarriageable rest
Cry, ' Thou who shalt no more at all be prest
To any heart, one moment come to this !
And feel me weeping with thy want of bliss,
And all the unpraisèd beauties of thy breast—
Thy breast which never shall a lover kiss !' "

Then I slowly left her pillow,
For they came back with the willow,
And my heart sinks as a billow
Doth implore towards the shore,

As I see the crown they weave her,
And I know that I must leave her,
And I feel that I could grieve her
Sad and sore for evermore.

And again they sang around her,
In a richer robe they wound her,
With the willow wreath they bound her
And the loud song like a cloud

Of golden obscuration,
With the strange tongue of her nation,
Filled the house of lamentation,
Till she lay in melody,

Like a latter lily lying,
O'er whom falling leaves are sighing,
And the Autumn vapours crying,
In a dream of evening gleam.

And I saw her sweet and lowly,
Shining shining pale and holy,
Thro' the dim woe slowly slowly
Said and sung in a dark tongue.

In the cot beside the water,
The white cot by the white water,
English cot by English water
That shall see the German sea.

WOE IS ME.

Far in the cradling sky,
Dawn opes his baby eye,
Then I awake and cry,
Woe is me !

Morn, the young hunter gay,
Chases the shadows gray,
Then I go forth and say,
Woe is me !

Noon ! drunk with oil and wine,
Tho' not a grief is thine,
Yet shalt thou shake with mine !
Woe is me !

Eve kneeleth sad and calm,
Bearing the martyr's palm ;
I shriek above her psalm,
Woe is me !

Night, hid in her black hair
From eyes she cannot dare,
Lies loud with fierce despair ;
Then I sit silent where
She cries from her dark lair
Woe is me !

THE YOUNG MAN'S SONG

At last the curse has run its date !
  The heavens grow clear above,
And on the purple plains of Hate
  We'll build the throne of Love !

One great heroic reign divine
  Shall mock the Elysian isles,
And love in arms shall only shine
  Less fair than Love in smiles !

Old Clio, burn thine ancient scroll,
  The scroll of Rome and Greece !
Our war shall be a parable
  On all the texts of peace.

And saints look down, with eyes of praise,
  Where on our modern field
The new Samaritan forelays
  The wrongs that other healed !

What virtue is beyond our prize ?
  What deed beneath yon sun
More Godlike than the prodigies
  We mortal men have done ?

We wearied of the lagging steed,
  The dove had not a quill

To fledge the imaginable speed
  Of our wild shaft of will ;

What Force can meet our matchless might ?
  What Power is not our slave ?
We bound the angel of the light,
  We scourged him in a cave.

And when we saw the prisoner pine
  For his immortal land,
We wrung a ransom, half divine,
  From that celestial hand

Whose skill the heavy chain subdued,
  And all a captive's woe
Did tame to such a tempered good
  As mortal eyes can know.

Who comes, who comes, o'er mountains laid,
  Vales lifted, straightened ways ?
'Tis he ! the mightier horse we made
  To serve our nobler days !

But now, unheard, I saw afar
  His cloud of windy mane,
Now, level as a blazing star,
  He thunders thro' the plain !

The life he needs, the food he loves,
  This cold earth bears no more ;
He fodders on the eternal groves
  That heard the dragons roar.

Strong with the feast he roars and runs,
  And, in his maw unfurled,

Evolves the folded fires of suns
  That lit a grander world !

You bird, the swiftest in the sky,
  Before him sprang, but he
Has passed her as a wind goes by
  A struggler in the sea.

With forward beak and forward blows
  She slides back from his side ;
While ever as the monster goes,
  With needless power and pride,

Disdainful from his fiery jaws
  He snorts his vital heat,
And, easy as his shadow, draws,
  Long-drawn, the living street.

He's gone !   Methinks that over him,
  Like Curtius in the abyss,
I see great gulphs close rim to rim,
  And Past and Future kiss !

Oh, Man ! as from the flood sublime
  Some alp rose calm and slow,
So from the exhaling floods of time
  I see thy stature grow.

Long since thy royal brow, uncrowned,
  Allegiant nature saw,
Long since thine eye of empire frowned
  The heavenly thrones to awe ;

.   .   .   .   .

So sang a youth of glorious blood.
  Below, the wind-hawk shook her wings,
And lower, in its kingdom, stood
  A tower of ancient kings.

Above, the autumn sky was blue,
  Far round the golden world was fair,
And, gun by gun, the ramparts blew
  A battle on the air.

DEAD-MAID'S-POOL.

Oh water, water—water deep and still,
In this hollow of the hill,
Thou belenge well o'er which the long reeds lean.
Here a stream and there a stream,
And thou so still, between,
Thro' thy coloured dream,
Thro' the drownèd face
Of this lone leafy place,
Down, down, so deep and chill,
I see the pebbles gleam !

Ash-tree, ash-tree,
Bending o'er the well,
Why there thou bendest,
Kind hearts can tell.
'Tis that the pool is deep,
'Tis that—a single leap,
And the pool closes :
And in the solitude
Of this wild mountain wood,
None, none, would hear her cry,
From this bank where she stood
To that peak in the sky
Where the cloud dozes.

Ash-tree, ash-tree,
Thou art so sweet and good,

If any creeping thing
Among the summer games in the wild roses
Fall from its airy swing, ·
(While all its pigmy kind
Watch from some imminent rose-leaf half uncurled)—
I know thou hast it full in mind
(While yet the drowning minim lives,
And blots the shining water where it strives),
To touch it with a finger soft and kind,
As when the gentle sun, ere day is hot,
Feels for a little shadow in a grot,
And gives it to the shades behind the world.

And oh ! if some poor fool
Should seek the fatal pool,
Thine arms—ah, yes ! I know
For this thou watchest days, and months, and years,
For this dost bend beside
The lone and lorn well-side,
The guardian angel of the doom below,
Content if, once an age, thy helping hand
May lift repentant madness to the land :
Content to hear the cry
Of living love from lips that would have died :
To seem awhile endowed
With all thy limbs did save,
And in that voice they drew out of the grave,
To feel thy dumb desire for once released aloud,
And all thy muffled century
Repaid in one wild hour of sobs, and smiles, and tears.

Aye, aye, I envy thee,
Pitiful ash-tree !

Water, water—water deep and still,
In the hollow of the hill,

Water, water, well I wot,
Thro' the weary hours,
Well I wot thee lying there,
As fair as false, as false as fair.
The crows they fly o'er,
The small birds flit about,
The stream it ripples in, the stream it ripples out,
But what eye ever knew
A rinkle wimple thee?
And what eye shall see
A rinkle wimple thee
Evermore?
'Thro' thy gauds and mocks,
All thy thin enchantment thro'—
The green delusion of thy bowers,
The cold flush of thy feignèd flowers,
All the treacherous state
Of fair things small and great,
That are and are not,
Well I wot thee shining there,
As fair as false, as false as fair.
Thro' the liquid rocks,
Thro' the watery trees,
Thro' the grass that never grew,
Thro' a face God never made,
Thro' the frequent gain and loss
Of the cold cold shine and shade,
Thro' the subtle fern and moss,
Thro' the humless, hiveless bees,
Round the ghosts of buds asleep,
Thro' the disembodied rose,
Waving, waving in the deep,
Where never wind blows,
I look down, and see far down,
In clear depths that do nothing hide,

Green in green, and brown in brown,
The long fish turn and glide !

Ash-tree, ash-tree,
Bending o'er the water—
Ash-tree, ash-tree,
Hadst thou a daughter ?
Ash-tree, ash-tree, let me draw near,
Ash-tree, ash-tree, a word in thine ear !

Thou art wizen and white, ash-tree ;
Other trees have gone on,
Have gathered and grown,
Have bourgeoned and borne :
Thou hast wasted and worn.

Thy knots are all eyes ;
Every knot a dumb eye,
That has seen a sight
And heard a cry.

Thy leaves are dry :
The summer has not gone by,
But they're withered and dead,
Like locks round a head
That is bald with a secret sin,
That is scorched by a hell within.

Thy skin
Is withered and wan,
Like a guilty man :
It was thin,
Aye, silken and thin,
It is houghed
And ploughed,
Like a murderer's skin.

Thou hast no shoots nor wands,
All thy arms turn to the deep,
All thy twigs are crooked,
Twined and twisted,
Fingered and fisted,
Like one who had looked
On wringing hands
'Till his hands were wrung in his sleep

Pardon my doubt of thee,
What is this
In the very groove
Of thy right arm ?
There is not a snake
So yellow and red,
There is not a toad
So sappy and dread !
It doth not move,
It doth not hiss—
Ash-tree—for God's sake—
Hast thou known
What hath not been said
And the summer sun
Cannot keep it warm,
And the living wood
Cannot shut it down !
And it grows out of thee
And will be told,
Bloody as blood,
And yellow as gold !

Ash-tree, ash-tree,
That once wert so green !
Ash-tree, ash-tree !
What hast thou seen ?

Was I a mother—nay or aye ?
Am I childless—aye or nay ?
Ash-tree, ash-tree;
Bending o'er the water !
Ash-tree, ash-tree,
Give me my daughter !
Curse the water,
Curse thee,
Ash-tree,
Bending o'er the water !
Leaf on the tree,
Flower on the stem,
Curse thee,
And curse them !
Trunk and shoot,
Herb and weed,
Bud and fruit,
Blossom and seed,
Above and below,
About and about,
Inside and out,
Grown and to grow,
Curse you all,
Great and small,
'That cannot give back my daughter !

But if there were any,
Among so many,
Any small thing that did lie sweet for her,
Any newt or marish-worm that, shrinking
Under the pillow of the water weed,
Left her a cleaner bed,
Any least leaves that fell with little plashes,
And sinking, sinking,
Sank soft and slow, and settled on her lashes,

And did what was so meet for her,
Them I do not curse.

See, see up the glen,
The evening sun agen ?
It falls upon the water,
It falls upon the grass,
Thro' the birches, thro' the firs,
Thro' the alders, catching gold,
Thro' the bracken and the brier,
Goes the evening fire
To the bush-linnet's nest.

There between us and the west,
Dost thou see the angels pass ?
Thro' the air, with streaming hair,
The golden angels pass ?
Hold, hold ! for mercy, hold !
I know thee ! ah, I know thee !
I know thou wilt not pass me so—
The grey old woman is ready to go.
Call me to thee, call me to thee,
My daughter ! oh, my daughter !

THE SAILOR'S RETURN.

THIS morn I lay a-dreaming,
This morn, this merry morn,
When the cock crew shrill from over the hill,
I heard a bugle horn.

And thro' the dream I was dreaming,
There sighed the sigh of the sea,
And thro' the dream I was dreaming,
This voice came singing to me.

" High over the breakers,
    Low under the lee,
    Sing ho
    The billow,
    And the lash of the rolling sea !

" Boat, boat, to the billow,
    Boat, boat, to the lee !
    Love, on thy pillow,
    Art thou dreaming of me ?

" Billow, billow, breaking,
    Land us low on the lee !
    For, sleeping or waking,
    Sweet love, I am coming to thee !

" High, high, o'er the breakers,
    Low, low, on the lee,
    Sing ho !
    The billow
    That brings me back to thee ! "

AN EVENING DREAM.

I'm leaning where you loved to lean in eventides of
  old,
The sun has sunk an hour ago behind the treeless wold,
In this old oriel that we loved how oft I sit forlorn,
Gazing, gazing, up the vale of green and waving corn.
The summer corn is in the ear, thou knowest what I see
Up the long wide valley, and from seldom tree to tree,
The serried corn, the serried corn, the green and serried
  corn,
From the golden morn till night, from the moony night
  till morn.
I love it, morning, noon, and night, in sunshine and in
  rain,
For being here it seems to say, "The lost come back
  again."
And being here as green and fair as those old fields we
  knew,
It says, "The lost when they come back, come back
  unchanged and true."
But more than at the shout of morn, or in the sleep of
  noon,
Smiling with a smiling star, or wan beneath a wasted
  moon,
I love it, soldier brother! at this weird dim hour, for
  then
The serried ears are swords and spears, and the fields are
  fields of men.
Rank on rank in faultless phalanx stern and still I can
  discern,

Phalanx after faultless phalanx in dumb armies still
    and stern ;
Army on army, host on host, till the bannered nations
    stand,
As the dead may stand for judgment silent on the o'er-
    peopled land.
Not a bayonet stirs : down sinks the awful twilight,
    dern and dun,
On an age that waits its leader, on a world that waits the
    sun.
Then your dog—I know his voice—cries from out the
    courtyard nigh,
And my love too well interprets all that long and
    mournful cry !
In my passion that thou art not, lo ! I see thee as thou art,
And the pitying fancy brings thee to assuage the
    anguished heart.
"Oh my brother !" and my bosom's throb of welcome
    at the word,
Claps a hundred thousand hands, and all my legions
    hail thee lord.
And the vast unmotioned myriads, front to front, as at
    a breath,
Live and move to martial music, down the devious
    dance of death,
Ah, thou smilest, scornful brother, at a maiden's dream
    of war !
And thou shakest back thy locks as if—a glow-worm for
    thy star—
I dubbed thee with a blade of grass, by earthlight, in a
    fairy ring,
Knight o' the garter o' Queen Mab, or lord in-waiting-to
    her king.
Brother, in thy plumèd pride of tented field and turreted
    tower,

Smiling brother, scornful brother, darest thou watch
    with me one hour ?
Even now some fate is near, for I shake and know not
    why,
And a wider sight is orbing, orbing, on my moistened
    eye,
And I feel a thousand flutterings round my soul's still
    vacant field,
Like the ravens and the vultures o'er a carnage yet
    unkilled.
Hist ! I see the stir of glamour far upon the twilight wold,
Hist ! I see the vision rising ! List ! and as I speak
    behold !
These dull mists are mists of morning, and behind yon
    eastern hill,
The hot sun abides my bidding : he shall melt them
    when I will.
All the night that now is past, the foe hath laboured for
    the day,
Creeping thro' the stealthy dark, like a tiger to his prey.
Throw this window wider ! Strain thine eyes along the
    dusky vale !
Art thou cold with horror ? Has thy bearded cheek
    grown pale ?
'Tis the total Russian host, flooding up the solemn plain,
Secret as a silent sea, mighty as a moving main !
Oh, my country ! is there none to rouse thee to the
    rolling sight ?
Oh thou gallant sentinel who has watched so oft so well,
    must thou sleep this only night ?
So hath the shepherd lain on a rock above a plain,
Nor beheld the flood that swelled from some embowelled
    mount of woe,
  Waveless, foamless, sure and slow,
  Silent o'er the vale below,

Till nigher still and nigher comes the seethe of fields on
    fire,
And the thrash of falling trees, and the steam of rivers
    dry,
And before the burning flood the wild things of the wood
  Skulk and scream, and fight, and fall, and flee, and fly.

A gun ! and then a gun ! I' the far and early sun
  Dost thou see by yonder tree a fleeting redness rise,
As if, one after one, ten poppies red had blown,
  And shed in a blinking of the eyes ?
They have started from their rest with a bayonet at each
    breast,
  Those watchers of the west who shall never watch
    again !
'Tis nought to die, but oh, God's pity on the woe
  Of dying hearts that know they die in vain !
Beyond yon backward height that meets their dying
    sight,
  A thousand tents are white, and a slumbering army
    lies.
" Brown Bess," the sergeant cries, as he loads her while
    he dies,
"Let this devil's deluge reach them, and the good old
    cause is lost."
He dies upon the word, but his signal gun is heard,
  Yon ambush green is stirred, yon labouring leaves are
    tost,
And a sudden sabre waves, and like dead from opened
    graves,
  A hundred men stand up to meet a host.
Dumb as death, with bated breath,
Calm upstand that fearless band,
  And the dear old native land, like a dream of sudden
    sleep,

Passes by each manly eye that is fixed so stern and dry
  On the tide of battle rolling up the steep.
They hold their silent ground, I can hear each fatal
    sound
  Upon that summer mound which the morning sun-
    shine warms,
The word so brief and shrill that rules them like a will,
  The sough of moving limbs, and the clank and ring of
    arms.
"Fire!" and round that green knoll the sudden war-
    clouds roll,
  And from the tyrant's ranks so fierce an answ'ring
    blast
Of whirling death came back that the green trees turned
    to black,
  And dropped their leaves in winter as it passed.
A moment on each side the surging smoke is wide,
  Between the fields are green, and around the hills are
    loud,
But a shout breaks out, and lo! they have rushed upon
    the foe,
  As the living lightning leaps from cloud to cloud.
Fire and flash, smoke and crash,
The fogs of battle close o'er friends and foes, and they
    are gone!
Alas, thou bright-eyed boy! alas, thou mother's joy!
  With thy long hair so fair, thou didst so bravely lead
    them on!
I faint with pain and fear.   Ah, heaven! what do I
    hear?
  A trumpet-note so near?
What are these that race like hunters at a chase?
  Who are these that run a thousand men as one!
What are these that crash the trees far in the waving
    rear?

Fight on, thou young hero ! there's help upon the way !
The light horse are coming, the great guns are coming,
  The Highlanders are coming ;—good God, give us the
    day !
Hurrah for the brave and the leal ! Hurrah for the strong
    and the true !
Hurrah for the helmets of steel ! Hurrah for the bonnets
    o' blue !
A run and a cheer, the Highlanders are here ! a gallop
    and a cheer, the light horse are here !
A rattle and a cheer, the great guns are here !
  With a cheer they wheel round and face the foe !
As the troopers wheel about, their long swords are out,
  With a trumpet and a shout, in they go !
Like a yawning ocean green, the huge host gulphs them
    in,
  But high o'er the rolling of the flood,
Their sabres you may see like lights upon the sea
  When the red sun is going down in blood.
Again, again, again ! And the lights are on the wane !
  Ah, Christ ! I see them sink, light by light,
As the gleams go one by one when the great sun is down,
  And the sea rocks in foam beneath the night.
Aye, the great sun is low, and the waves of battle flow
  O'er his honoured head ; but, oh, we mourn not he is
    down,
For to-morrow he shall rise to fill his country's eyes,
  As he sails up the skies of renown !
Ye may yell, but ye shall groan !
Ye shall buy them bone for bone !
Now, tyrant, hold thine own ! blare the trumpet, peal
    the drum !
From yonder hill-side dark, the storm is on you !
    Hark !
  Swift as lightning, loud as thunder, down they come !

As on some Scottish shore, with mountains frowning
    o'er,
  The sudden tempests roar from the glen,
And roll the tumbling sea in billows to the lee,
  Came the charge of the gallant Highlandmen!
And as one beholds the sea tho' the wind he cannot see,
  But by the waves that flee knows its might,
So I tracked the Highland blast by the sudden tide that
    past
  O'er the wild and rolling vast of the fight.
Yes, glory be to God! they have stemmed the foremost
    flood!
  I lay me on the sod and breathe again!
In the precious moments won, the bugle call has gone
  To the tents where it never rang in vain,
And lo! the landscape wide is red from side to side,
  And all the might of England loads the plain!
Like a hot and bloody dawn, across the horizon drawn,
  While the host of darkness holds the misty vale,
As glowing and as grand our bannered legions stand,
  And England's flag unfolds upon the gale!
At that great sign unfurled, as morn moves o'er the world
  When God lifts His standard of light,
With a tumult and a voice, and a rushing mighty noise,
  Our long line moves forward to the fight.
Clarion and clarion defying,
Sounding, resounding, replying,
Trumpets braying, pipers playing, chargers neighing,
Near and far
The to and fro storm of the never-done hurrahing,
Thro' the bright weather banner and feather rising and
    falling, bugle and fife
Calling, recalling—for death or for life—
Our host moved on to the war,
While England, England, England, England, England!

Was blown from line to line near and far,
And like the morning sea, our bayonets you might see,
Come beaming, gleaming, streaming,
Streaming, gleaming, beaming,
Beaming, gleaming, streaming, to the war.
Clarion and clarion defying,
Sounding, resounding, replying,
Trumpets braying, pipers playing, chargers neighing,
Near and far
The to and fro storm of the never-done hurrahing,
Thro' the bright weather, banner and feather rising and
          falling, bugle and fife
Calling, recalling—for death or for life—
Our long line moved forward to the war.

From *A SHOWER IN WAR-TIME*.

RAIN, rain, sweet warm rain,
On the wood and on the plain !
Rain, rain, warm and sweet,
Summer wood lush leafy and loud,
With note of a throat that ripples and rings.
Sad sole sweet from her central seat,
Bubbling and trilling,
Filling, filling, filling
The shady space of the green dim place
With an odour of melody,
Till all the noon is thrilling,
And the great wood hangs in the balmy day
Like a cloud with an angel in the cloud,
And singing because she sings !

In the sheltering wood,
At that hour I stood ;
I saw that in that hour
Great round drops, clear round drops,
Grew on every leaf and flower,
And its hue so fairly took
And faintly, that each tinted elf
Trembled with a rarer self,
Even as if its beauty shook
With passion to a tenderer look.

Rain, rain, sweet warm rain.
On the wood and on the plain !

Rain, rain, warm and sweet,
Summer wood lush leafy and loud,
With note of a throat that ripples and rings,
Sad sole sweet from her central seat,
Bubbling and trilling,
Filling, filling, filling
The shady space of the green dim place
With an odour of melody,
Till all the noon is thrilling,
And the great wood hangs in the balmy day
Like a cloud with an angel in the cloud,
And singing because she sings !

Then out of the sweet warm weather
There came a little wind sighing, sighing :
Came to the wood sighing, and sighing went in,
Sighed thro' the green grass, and o'er the leaves
    brown,
Sighed to the dingle, and, sighing, lay down,
While all the flowers whispered together.
Then came swift winds after her who was flying,
Swift bright winds with a jocund din,
Sought her in vain, her boscage was so good,
And spread like baffled revellers thro' the wood.
Then, from bough, and leaf, and bell,
The great round drops, the clear round drops,
In fitful cadence drooped and fell—
Drooped and fell as if some wanton air
Were more apparent here and there,
Sphered on a favourite flower in dewy kiss,
Grew heavy with delight and dropped with bliss.

Rain, rain, sweet warm rain,
On the wood and on the plain ;
Rain, rain, still and sweet,

For the winds have hushed again,
And the nightingale is still,
Sleeping in her central seat.
Rain, rain, summer rain,
Silent as the summer heat.
Doth it fall, or doth it rise ?
Is it incense from the hill,
Or bounty from the skies ?
Or is the face of earth that lies
Languid, looking up on high,
To the face of Heaven so nigh
That their balmy breathings meet ?

Rain, rain, summer rain,
On the wood and on the plain :
Rain, rain, rain, until
The tall wet trees no more athirst,
As each chalice green doth fill,
See the pigmy nations nurst
Round their distant feet, and throw
The nectar to the herbs below.
The droughty herbs, without a sound,
Drink it ere it reach the ground.

Rain, rain, sweet warm rain,
On the wood and on the plain,
And round me like a dropping well,
The great round drops they fell and fell.

I say not War is good or ill ;
Perchance they may slay, if they will,
Who killing love, and loving kill.

   .   .   .

Whether our bloodsheds flow or cease,
I know that as the years increase,
The flower of all is human peace.

"The flower."   Vertumnus hath repute
O'er Flora ; yet methinks the fruit
But alter ego of the root ;

And that which serves our fleshly need,
Subserves the blossom that doth feed
The soul which is the life indeed.

Nor well he deems who deems the rose
Is for the roseberry, nor knows
The roseberry is for the rose.

And Autumn's garnered treasury,
But prudent Nature's guarantee
That Summer evermore shall be,

And yearly, once a-year, complete
That top and culmen exquisite
Whereto the slanting seasons meet.

Whether our bloodsheds flow or cease,
I know that, as the years increase,
The flower of all is human peace.

"The flower."   Yet whether shall we sow
A blossom or a seed ?   I know
The flower will rot, the seed will grow.

By this the rain had ceased, and I went forth
From that Dodona green of oak and beech.

But ere my steps could reach
The hamlet, I beheld along the verge
A flight of fleeing cloudlets that did urge
Unequal speed, as when a herd is driven
By the recurring pulse of shoutings loud.
I saw ; but held the omen of no worth.
For by the footway not a darnel stirred,
And still the noon slept on, nor even a bird
Moved the dull air ; but, at each silent hand,
Upon the steaming land
The hare lay basking, and the budded wheat
Hung slumberous heads of sleep.
Then I was 'ware that a great northern cloud
Moved slowly to the centre of the heaven.
His white head was so high
That the great blue fell round him like the wide
And ermined robe of kings.   He sat in pride
Lonely and cold ; but methought when he spied
From that severe inhospitable height
The distant dear delight,
The melting world with summer at her side,
His pale brow mellowed with a mournful light,
And like a marble god he wept his stony tears.
The loyal clouds that sit about his feet,
All in their courtier kinds,
Do weep to see him weep.
After the priceless drops the sycophant winds
Leap headlong down, and chase, and swirl, and sweep
Beneath the royal grief that scarce may reach the
    ground.
To see their whirling zeal,
Unlikely things that in the kennel lie
Begin to wheel and wheel ;
The wild tarantula-will spreads far and nigh,
And spinning straws go spiral to the sky,

And leaves long dead leap up and dance their ghastly
    round.
And so it happened in the street
'Neath a broad eave I stood and mused again,
And all the arrows of the driving rain
Were tipped with slanting sleet.
I mused beneath the straw pent of the bricked
And sodded cot, with damp moss mouldered o'er,
The bristled thatch gleamed with a carcanet,
And from the inner eaves the reeking wet
Dripped ; dropping more
And more, as more the sappy roof was sapped,
And wept a mirkier wash that splashed and clapped
The plain-stones, dribbling to the flooded door.
A plopping pool of droppings stood before,
Worn by a weeping age in rock of easy grain.
O'erhead, hard by, a pointed beam o'erlapped,
And from its jewelled tip
The slipping slipping drip
Did whip the lillipped pool whose hopping plashes
    ticked.

    Let one or thousands loose or bind,
    That land's enslaved whose sovran mind
    Collides the conscience of mankind.

    And free—whoever holds the rood—
    Where Might in Right, and Power in Good,
    Flow each in each, like life in blood.

    If England's head and heart were one,
    Where is that good beneath the sun
    Her noble hands should leave undone !

Small unit, hast thou hardiness
To bid mankind to battle ?   Yes.
The worm will rout them, and is less.

The world assaults ?   Nor fight nor fly.
Stand in some steadfast truth, and eye
The stubborn siege grow old and die.

My army is mankind.   My foe
The very meanest truth I know.
Shall I come back a conqueror ?   No.

Wouldst light ?   See Phosphor shines confest,
Turn thy broad back upon the west ;
Stand firm.   The world will do the rest.

Stand firm.   Unless thy strength can climb
Yon alp, and from that height sublime
See, ere we see, the advancing time.

Act for to-day ?   Friend, this " to-day "
Washed Adam's feet and streams away
Far into yon Eternity.

A HERO'S GRAVE.

O'ER our evening fire the smoke is like a pall,
And funeral banners hang about the arches of the hall,
In the gable end I see a catafalque aloof,
And night is drawn up like a curtain to the girders of
    the roof.

Thou knowest why we silent sit, and why our eyes are
    dim,
Sing us such proud sorrow as we may hear for him.

Reach me the old harp that hangs between the flags he
    won,
I will sing what once I heard beside the grave of such a
    son. .

My son, my son,
A father's eyes are looking on thy grave,
Dry eyes that look on this green mound and see
The low weed blossom and the long grass wave,
Without a single tear to them or thee,
My son, my son.

Why should I weep? The grass is grass, the weeds
Are weeds. The emmet hath done thus ere now.
I tear a leaf; the green blood that it bleeds
Is cold. What have I here? Where, where art thou,
My son, my son?

On which tall trembler shall the old man lean?
Which chill leaf shall lap o'er him when he lies
On that bed where in visions I have seen
Thy filial love? or, when thy father dies,
Tissue a fingered thorn to close his childless eyes?

Aye, where art thou?   Men tell me of a fame
Walking the wondering nations; and they say,
When thro' the shouting people thy great name
Goes like a chief upon a battle-day,
They shake the heavens with glory.   Well-away!

As some poor hound that thro' thronged street and square
Pursues his loved lost lord, and fond and fast
Seeks what he feels to be but feels not where,
Tracks the dear feet to some closed door at last,
And lies him down and lornest looks doth cast,

So I, thro' all the long tumultuous days,
Tracing thy footstep on the human sands,
O'er the signed deserts and the vocal ways
Pursue thee, faithful, thro' the echoing lands,
Wearing a wandering staff with trembling hands:

Thro' echoing lands that ring with victory,
And answer for the living with the dead,
And give me marble when I ask for bread,
And give me glory when I ask for thee—
It was not glory I nursed on my knee.

And now, one stride behind thee, and too late,
Yet true to all that reason cannot kill,
I stand before the inexorable gate
And see thy latest footstep on the sill,
And know thou canst not come, but watch and wait
    thee still.

"Old man !"—Ah, darest thou ? yet thy look is kind.
Didst thou, too, love him ?   "Thou grey-headed sire,
Seest thou this path which from that grave doth wind
Far thro' those western uplands higher and higher,
Till, like a thread, it burns in the great fire

"Of sunset ?   The wild sea and desert meet
Eastward by yon unnavigable strand,
Then wherefore hath the flow of human feet
Left this dry runnel of memorial sand
Meandering thro' the summer of the land ?

" See where the long immeasurable snake,
Between dim hall and hamlet, tower and shed,
Mountain and mountain, precipice and lake,
Lies forth unfinished to this final head,
This green dead mound of the unfading dead ! "

Do they then come to weep thee ?   Do they kiss
Thy relics ?   Art thou then as wholly gone
As some old buried saint ?   My son, my son,
Ah, could I mourn thee so !   Such tears were bliss !
" Old man, they do not mourn who weep at graves like
      this."

They do not mourn ?   What ! hath the insolent foe
Found out my child's last bed ?   Who, who, are they
That come and go about him ?   I cry, " Who ? "
I am his father—I ;—I cry " Who ? "   " Aye,
Gray trembler, I will tell thee who are they.

" The slave who, having grown up strong and stark
To the set season, feels at length he wears
Bonds that will break, and thro' the slavish dark
Shines with the light of liberated years,
And still in chains doth weep a freeman's tears.

"The patriot, while the unebbed force that hurled
His tyrant throbs within his bursting veins,
And, on the ruins of a hundred reigns,
That ancient heaven of brass, so long unfurled,
Falls with a crash of fame that fills the world,
And thro' the clangour lo the unwonted strains
Of peace, and, in the new sweet heavens upcurled,
The sudden incense of a thousand plains.

"Youth, whom some mighty flash from heaven hath
          turned
In his dark highway, and who runs forth, shod
With flame, into the wilderness untrod,
And as he runs his heart of flint is burned,
And in that glass he sees the face of God,
And falls upon his knees—and morn is all abroad.

"Age, who hath heard amid his cloistered ground
The cheer of youth, and steps from echoing aisles,
And at a sight the great blood with a bound
Melts his brow's winter, which the free sun smiles
To jewels, and he stands a young man crowned
With glittering years among a young world shouting
          round.

"Girls that do blush and tremble with delight
On the St. John's eve of their maidenhood ;
When the unsummered woman in her blood
Glows through the Parian maid, and at the sight
The flushing virgin weeps and feels herself too bright.

"He who first feels the world-old destiny,
The shaft of gold that strikes the poet still,
And slowly in its victim melts away,
Who knows his wounds will heal but when they kill,
And drop by vital drop doth bleed his golden ill.

" All whom the everpassing mysteries
Have rapt above the region of our race,
And, blinded by the glory and the grace,
Break from the ecstatic sphere—as he who dies
In darkness, and in heaven's own light doth rise,
Dazed with the untried glory of the place
Looks up and sees some well-remembered face,
And thro' the invulnerable angels flies
To that dear human breast and hides his dazzled eyes.

" All who, like the sun-ripened seed that springs
And bourgeons in the sun, do hold profound
An antenatal stature, which the round
Of the dull continent flesh hath cribbed and wound
Into this kernelled man ; but having found
Such soil as grew them, burst in blossomings
Not native here, or, from the hallowed ground,
Tower their slow height, and spread like sheltering wings,
Those boughs wherein the bird of omen sings
High as the palms of heaven, while to the sound
Lo kingdoms jocund in the sacred bound
Till the world's summer fills her moon, and brings
The final fruit which is the feast and fate of kings.

" And darest thou mourn ? Thy bones are left behind,
But where art thou, Anchises ? Dost thou see
Him who once bare the slow paternity,
Foot-burnt o'er stony Troy ? So, thou, reclined
Goest thro' the falling years. Here, here where we
Two stand, lies deep the flesh thou hast so pined
To clasp, and shalt clasp never. Verily,
Love and the worm are often of one mind !
God save them from election ! Pity thee ?
True he lifts not thy load, but he hath signed
And at his beck a nation rose up free ;

Thy wounds his living love may never bind,
But at the dead man's touch posterity
Is healed.   To thee, thou poor, and halt, and blind,
He is a staff no more : but times to be
Lean on his monumental memory
As the moon on a mountain.   Thou shalt find
A silent home, a cheerless hearth : but he
Shall be a fire which the enkindling wind,
Blowing for ever from eternity,
Fans till its universal blaze hath shined
The yule of thankful ages,   Pity thee?
A son is lost to thine infirmity ;
Poor fool, what then ?   A son thou hast resigned
To give a father to the virtues of mankind."

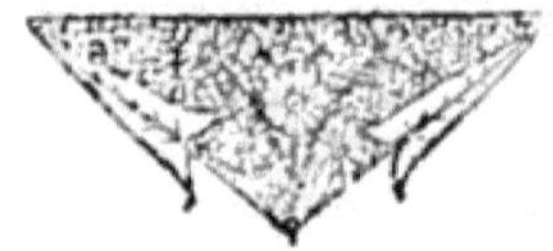

IN WAR-TIME.

An Aspiration of the Spirit.

Lord Jesus, as a little child,
  Upon some high ascension day
  When a great people goes to pay
Allegiance, and the tumult wild

Roars by its thousand streets, and fills
  The billowy nation on the plain,
  As roar into the heaving main
A thousand torrents from the hills,

Caught in the current of the throng
  Is drawn beneath the closing crowd,
  And, drowning in the human flood,
Is whirled in its dark depths along ;

And low under the ruthless feet,
  Or high as to the awful knees
  Of giants that he partly sees,
Blinded with fear and faint with heat,

Mindless of all but what doth seem,
  And shut out from the upper light,
  Maddens within a monstrous night
Of limbs that crush him like a dream ;

And when his strength no more can stand,
  And while he sinks in his last swound,
  Is lifted from the deadly ground,
And led by a resistless hand,

 And thro' the opening agony
  Goes on and knows not where, beside
  The mastery of his guardian guide,
Goes on, and knows not where nor why,

Till, when the sky no more is hid,
  Between the rocking heads he sees
  A mount that rises by degrees
Above them like a pyramid,

And on the summit of the mount
  A vacant throne, and round the throne
  Bright-vestured princes, zone by zone,
In circles that he cannot count,

And feels, at length, a slanting way,
  And labours by his guardian good
  Till forth, as from a lessening wood,
They step into the dazzling day,

And from the mount he sees below
  The marvel of the marshalled plain,
  And what was tumult is a reign,
And, as he climbs, the princes know

His guide, and fall about his feet,
  Before his face the courtiers fall,
  And lo ! it is the Lord of all,
And on his throne he takes his seat ;

And, while strong fears transfix the boy,
  The mighty people far and near
  Throw up upon the eye and ear
The flash and thunder of their joy,

And, round the royal flag unfurled,
  In sequent love and circling awe
  The legions lead their living law,
And what was Chaos is a World:

So, Lord, Thou seest this mortal me,
  Deep in Titanic days that press
  Incessant from unknown access
To issues that I cannot see.

Caught in the current stern and strong
  I sink beneath the closing crowd,
  And drowning in the awful flood
Am whirled in its dark depths along,

Struggling with shows so thronged and thrust
  On these wide eyes which bruise and burn,
  And flash with half-seen sights, or turn
To that worse darkness thick with dust,

That mindful of but what doth seem,
  And hopeless of the upper light,
  I madden in a monstrous night
Of shapes that crush me like a dream.

Then when my strength no more can stand,
  And while I sink in my last swound,
  Lo! I am lifted from the ground,
And led by a resistless hand;

And thro' the opening agony
 Go on and know not where, beside
 The mastery of my guardian guide,
Go on, and know not where or why ;

Nor, tho' I cannot see Thy brow,
 Distrust the hand I feel so dear,
 Nor question how Thou wert so near,
Nor ask Thee whither goest Thou,

Nor whence Thy footsteps first began.
 Whence, Lord, Thou knowest : whither, Lord,
 Thou knowest : how Thou knowest.   Oh Word
That can be touched, oh Spoken Man,

Enough, enough, if Thou wilt lead,
 To know Thou knowest ; enough to know
 That darkling at Thy side I go,
And this strong hand is Thine indeed.

Yet by that side, unspent, untrod,
 Oh let me, clinging still to Thee,
 Between the swaying wonders see
The throne upon the mount of God.

And—tho' they close before mine eye,
 And all my course is choked and shut—
 Feel Time grow steeper under foot,
And know the final height is nigh.

And as one sees, thro' cambered straits
 Of forests, on his forward way,
 Horizons green of coloured day,
Oh let me thro' the crowding Fates

Behold the light of skies unseen,
  Till on that sudden Capitol
  I step forth to the sight of all
That is, and shall be, and hath been,

And Thou, O King, shalt take Thine own
  Triumphant; and, Thy place fulfilled,
  The flaw of Nature shall be healed,
And joyous round Thy central throne

I see the vocal ages roll,
  And all the human universe
  Like some great symphony rehearse
The order of its perfect whole;

And seek in vain where once I fell,
  Nor know the anarchy I knew
  In those congenial motions due
Of this great work where all is well,

And smile, with dazzled wisdom dumb,
  —Remembering all I said and sung—
  That man asks more of mortal tongue
Than skill to say, "Thy kingdom come."

HOME, WOUNDED

WHEEL me into the sunshine,
Wheel me into the shadow,
There must be leaves on the woodbine,
Is the king-cup crowned in the meadow ¿

Wheel me down to the meadow,
Down to the little river,
In sun or in shadow
I shall not dazzle or shiver,
I shall be happy anywhere,
Every breath of the morning air
Makes me throb and quiver.

Stay wherever you will,
By the mount or under the hill,
Or down by the little river :
Stay as long as you please,
Give me only a bud from the trees,
Or a blade of grass in morning dew,
Or a cloudy violet clearing to blue,
I could look on it for ever

Wheel, wheel thro' the sunshine,
Wheel, wheel thro' the shadow ;
There must be odours round the pine,
There must be balm of breathing kine
Somewhere down in the meadow.

Must I chcose ? Then anchor me there
Beyond the beckoning poplars, where
The larch is snooding her flowery hair
With wreaths of morning shadow.

Among the thicket hazels of the brake
Perchance some nightingale doth shake
His feathers, and the air is full of song ;
In those old days when I was young and strong.
He used to sing on yonder garden tree,
Beside the nursery.
Ah, I remember how I loved to wake,
And find him singing on the self-same bough
(I know it even now)
Where, since the flit of bat,
In ceaseless voice he sat,
Trying the spring night over, like a tune,
Beneath the vernal moon ;
And while I listed long,
Day rose, and still he sang,
And all his stanchless song,
As something falling unaware,
Fell out of the tall trees he sang among,
Fell ringing down the ringing morn, and rang —
Rang like a golden jewel down a golden stair.

Is it too early ? I hope not.
But wheel me to the ancient oak,
On this side of the meadow ;
Let me hear the raven's croak
Loosened to an amorous note
In the hollow shadow.
Let me see the winter snake
Thawing all his frozen rings
On the bank where the wren sings.

Let me hear the little bell,
Where the red-wing, top-mast high,
Looks towards the northern sky,
And jangles his farewell.
Let us rest by the ancient oak,
And see his net of shadow,
His net of barren shadow,
Like those wrestlers' nets of old,
Hold the winter dead and cold,
Hoary winter, white and cold,
While all is green in the meadow.

And when you've rested, brother mine,
Take me over the meadow ;
Take me along the level crown
Of the bare and silent down,
And stop by the ruined tower.
On its green scarp, by and by,
I shall smell the flowering thyme,
On its wall the wall-flower.

In the tower there used to be
A solitary tree.
Take me there, for the dear sake
Of those old days wherein I loved to lie
And pull the melilote,
And look across the valley to the sky,
And hear the joy that filled the warm wide hour
Bubble from the thrush's throat,
As into a shining mere
Rills some rillet trebling clear,
And speaks the silent silver of the lake
There mid cloistering tree-roots, year by year,
The hen-thrush sat, and he, her lief and dear,
Among the boughs did make

A ceaseless music of her married time,
And all the ancient stones grew sweet to hear,
And answered him in the unspoken rhyme
Of gracious forms most musical
That tremble on the wall
And trim its age with airy fantasies
That flicker in the sun, and hardly seem
As if to be beheld were all,
And only to our eyes
They rise and fall,
And fall and rise,
Sink down like silence, or a-sudden stream
As wind-blown on the wind, as streams a wedding-chime

But you are wheeling me while I dream,
And we've almost reached the meadow !
You may wheel me fast thro' the sunshine,
You may wheel me fast thro' the shadow,
But wheel me slowly, brother mine,
Thro' the green of the sappy meadow ;
For the sun, these days have been so fine,
Must have touched it over with celandine,
And the southern hawthorn, I divine,
Sheds a muffled shadow.

There blows
The first primrose,
Under the bare bank roses :
There is but one,
And the bank is brown,
But soon the children will come down,
The ringing children come singing down.
To pick their Easter posies,
And they'll spy it out, my beautiful,
Among the bare brier-roses ;

And when I sit here again alone,
The bare brown bank will be blind and dull,
Alas for Easter posies !
But when the din is over and gone,
Like an eye that opens after pain,
I shall see my pale flower shining again :
Like a fair star after a gust of rain
I shall see my pale flower shining again ;
Like a glow-worm after the rolling wain
Hath shaken darkness down the lane
I shall see my pale flower shining again ;
And it will blow here for two months more,
And it will blow here again next year,
And the year past that, and the year beyond ;
And thro' all the years till my years are o'er
I shall always find it here.
Shining across from the bank above,
Shining up from the pond below,
Ere a water-fly wimple the silent pond,
Or the first green weed appear.
And I shall sit here under the tree,
And as each slow bud uncloses,
I shall see it brighten and brighten to me,
From among the leafing brier-roses,
The leaning leafing roses,
As at eve the leafing shadows grow,
And the star of light and love
Draweth near o'er her airy glades,
Draweth near thro' her heavenly shades,
As a maid thro' a myrtle grove.
And the flowers will multiply,
As the stars come blossoming over the sky,
The bank will blossom, the waters blow,
Till the singing children hitherward hie
To gather May-day posies ;

And the bank will be bare wherever they go,
As dawn, the primrose-girl, goes by,
And alas for heaven's primroses !

Blare the trumpet, and boom the gun,
But, oh, to sit here thus in the sun,
To sit here, feeling my work is done,
While the sands of life so golden run,
And I watch the children's posies,
And my idle heart is whispering
"Bring whatever the years may bring,
The flowers will blossom, the birds will sing,
And there'll always be primroses."

Looking before me here in the sun,
I see the Aprils one after one,
Primrosed Aprils one by one,
Primrosed Aprils on and on,
Till the floating prospect closes
In golden glimmers that rise and rise,
And perhaps are gleams of Paradise,
And perhaps—too far for mortal eyes—
New years of fresh primroses,
Years of earth's primroses,
Springs to be, and springs for me
Of distant dim primroses.

My soul lies out like a basking hound,
A hound that dreams and dozes ;
Along my life my length I lay,
I fill to-morrow and yesterday,
I am warm with the suns that have long since set
I am warm with the summers that are not yet,
And like one who dreams and dozes
Softly afloat on a sunny sea,
Two worlds are whispering over me.

And there blows a wind of roses
From the backward shore to the shore before,
From the shore before to the backward shore,
And like two clouds that meet and pour
Each thro' each, till core in core
A single self reposes,
The nevermore with the evermore
Above me mingles and closes ;
As my soul lies out like the basking hound,
And wherever it lies seems happy ground,
And when, awakened by some sweet sound,
A dreamy eye uncloses,
I see a blooming world around,
And I lie amid primroses—
Years of sweet primroses,
Springs of fresh primroses,
Springs to be, and springs for me
Of distant dim primroses.

Oh to lie a-dream, a-dream,
To feel I may dream and to know you deem
My work is done for ever,
And the palpitating fever
That gains and loses, loses and gains,
And beats the hurrying blood on the brunt of a thousand
　　　　pains
Cooled at once by that blood-let
Upon the parapet ;
And all the tedious taskèd toil of the difficult long
　　　　endeavour
Solved and quit by no more fine
Than these limbs of mine,
Spanned and measured once for all
By that right hand I lost,
Bought up at so light a cost

As one bloody fall
On the soldier's bed,
And three days on the ruined wall
Among the thirstless dead.
Oh to think my name is crost
From duty's muster-roll ;
That I may slumber tho' the clarion call,
And live the joy of an embodied soul
Free as a liberated ghost.

Oh to feel a life of deed
Was emptied out to feed
That fire of pain that burned so brief a while—
That fire from which I come, as the dead come
Forth from the irreparable tomb,
Or as a martyr on his funeral pile
Heaps up the burdens other men do bear
Thro' years of segregated care,
And takes the total load
Upon his shoulders broad,
And steps from earth to God.

Oh to think, thro' good or ill,
Whatever I am you'll love me still ;
Oh to think, tho' dull I be,
You that are so grand and free,
You that are so bright and gay,
Will pause to hear me when I will,
As tho' my head were grey ;
And tho' there's little I can say,
Each will look kind with honour while he hears.
And to your loving ears
My thoughts will halt with honourable scars,
And when my dark voice stumbles with the weight
Of what it doth relate

(Like that blind comrade—blinded in the wars—
Who bore the one-eyed brother that was lame),
You'll remember, tis the same
That cried " Follow me,"
Upon a summer's day ;
And I shall understand with unshed tears
This great reverence that I see,
And bless the day—and Thee,
Lord God of victory !

And she,
Perhaps oh even she
May look as she looked when I knew her
In those old days of childish sooth,
Ere my boyhood dared to woo her.
I will not seek nor sue her,
For I'm neither fonder nor truer
Than when she slighted my love-lorn youth,
My giftless, graceless, guinealess truth,
And I only lived to rue her.
But I'll never love another,
And, in spite of her lovers and lands,
She shall love me yet, my brother !
As a child that holds by his mother,
While his mother speaks his praises,
Holds with eager hands,
And ruddy and silent stands
In the ruddy and silent daisies,
And hears her bless her boy,
And lifts a wondering joy,
So I'll not seek nor sue her,
But I'll leave my glory to woo her,
And I'll stand like a child beside,
And from behind the purple pride
I'll lift my eyes unto her,

And I shall not be denied.
And you will love her, brother dear,
And perhaps next year you'll bring me here
All thro' the balmy April-tide,
And she will trip like spring by my side,
And be all the birds to my ear.
And here all three we'll sit in the sun,
And see the Aprils one by one,
Primrosed Aprils on and on,
Till the floating prospect closes
In golden glimmers that rise and rise,
And perhaps are gleams of Paradise,
And perhaps, too far for mortal eyes,
New springs of fresh primroses,
Springs of earth's primroses,
Springs to be and springs for me,
Of distant dim primroses.

A NUPTIAL EVE.

Oh, happy, happy maid,
In the year of war and death
She wears no sorrow !
By her face so young and fair,
By the happy wreath
That rules her happy hair,
She might be a bride to-morrow !
She sits and sings within her moonlit bower,
Her moonlit bower in rosy June,
Yet, ah, her bridal breath,
Like fragrance from some sweet night-blowing flower,
Moves from her moving lips in many a mournful tune !
She sings no song of love's despair,
She sings no lover lowly laid,
No fond peculiar grief
Has ever touched or bud or leaf
Of her unblighted spring.
She sings because she needs must sing :
She sings the sorrow of the air
Whereof her voice is made.
That night in Britain howsoe'er
On any chords the fingers strayed,
They gave the notes of care.
A dim sad legend old
Long since in some pale shade
Of some far twilight told,
She knows not when or where,
She sings, with trembling hand on trembling lute-
    strings laid :—

The murmur of the mourning ghost
  That keeps the shadowy kine,
" Oh, Keith of Ravelston,
  The sorrows of thy line ! "

Ravelston, Ravelston,
  The merry path that leads
Down the golden morning hill,
  And thro' the silver meads;

Ravelston, Ravelston,
  The stile beneath the tree,
The maid that kept her mother's kine,
  The song that sang she !

She sang her song, she kept her kine,
  She sat beneath the thorn
When Andrew Keith of Ravelston
  Rode thro' the Monday morn.

His henchmen sing, his hawk-bells ring,
  His belted jewels shine !
Oh, Keith of Ravelston,
  The sorrows of thy line !

Year after year, where Andrew came,
  Comes evening down the glade,
And still there sits a moonshine ghost
  Where sat the sunshine maid.

Her misty hair is faint and fair,
  She keeps the shadowy kine;
Oh, Keith of Ravelston,
  The sorrows of thy line !

I lay my hand upon the stile,
  The stile is lone and cold,
The burnie that goes babbling by
  Says nought that can be told.

Yet, stranger ! here, from year to year,
  She keeps her shadowy kine ;
Oh, Keith of Ravelston,
  The sorrows of thy line !

Step out three steps, where Andrew stood—
  Why blanch thy cheeks for fear ?
The ancient stile is not alone,
  'Tis not the burn I hear !

She makes her immemorial moan,
  She keeps her shadowy kine ;
Oh, Keith of Ravelston,
  The sorrows of thy line !

ALONE.

THERE came to me softly a small wind from the sea,
And it lifted a curl as it passed by me.
But I sang sorrow and ho the heavy day !
And I sang heigho and well-away !

Again there came softly a small wind from the sea,
And it lifted a curl as it passed by me.
And still I sang sorrow and ho the heavy day !
And I sang heigho and well-away !

Once more there came softly that small wind from
    the sea,
And it lifted a curl as it passed by me.
I hushed my song of sorrow and ho the heavy day,
And I hushed my heigho and well-away.

Then, when I was silent, that small wind from the
    sea,
It came the fourth time tenderly to me ;
To me, to me,
Sitting by the sea,
Sitting sad and solitary thinking of thee.
Like warm lips it touched me—that soft wind from
    the sea,
And I trembled and wept as it passed by me.

FAREWELL.

HEAR me, hear me, now !
By this heaven less pure than thou,
Fare thee well !
By this living light,
Less bright,
Fare thee well !

By the boundless sea
Of mine agony,
Fare thee well !
That unfathomed sea
Which must roll from me to thee,
Must roll from thee to me,
Fare thee well !

By the tears that I have bled for thee,
Farewell !
By the life's-blood I will shed for thee,
Farewell !
By that field of death and fear
Where I'll fight with sword and spear
The fight I'm fighting here,
Fare thee well !

By a form amid the storm,
Fare thee well !
By a sigh above the cry,
Fare thee well !

By the war-cloud and the shout
That shall wrap me round about,
But can never shut thee out,
Fare thee well !

By the wild and bloody close,
When I loose this hell of woes,
And these fires shall eat our foes,
Fare thee well !

By all thou'lt not forget,
Fare thee well !
By the joy when first we met,
Fare thee well !

By the mighty love and pain
Of the frantic arms that strain
What they ne'er shall clasp again,
Fare thee well !

By the bliss of our first kiss,
Fare thee well !
By the locked love of our last,
Till a passion like a blast
Tore the future from the past,
Fare thee well !

By the nights that I shall weep for thee,
Farewell !
By the vigils I shall keep for thee,
Farewell !
By the memories that will beam of thee,
Farewell !
By the dreams that I shall dream of thee,
Farewell !

By the passion when I wake
Of this heart that will not break,
That can bleed, but cannot break,
Fare thee well !

By that holier woe of thine,
Fare thee well !
By thy love more pure than mine,
Fare thee well !

By the days thou shalt hold dear for me,
The lone life thou shalt bear for me,
The grey hairs thou shalt wear for me,
Farewell !

By thy good deeds offered up for me,
Farewell !
When thou fillest the wanderer's cup for me,
Farewell !
When thou givest the hungry bread for me,
Farewell !
When thou watchest by the dead for me,
Farewell !

By the faith of thy pure eyes,
By the hopes that shall arise
Day and night to the deaf skies,
Fare thee well !

By that faith I cannot share,
Fare thee well !
By this hopeless heart's despair,
Fare thee well !

By the days I have been glad for thee,
The years I shall be sad for thee,
The hours I shall be mad for thee,
Farewell !

SLEEPING AND WAKING.

I HAD a dream—I lay upon thy breast,
In that sweet place where we lay long ago :
I thought the morning woodbine to and fro
With playful shadows whipped away my rest,
And in my sleep I cried to thee, too blest,

" Rise, oh my love, the morning sun is bright,
Let us arise, oh love, let us arise ;
The flowers awake, the lark is in the skies,
I will array myself in my delight,
And we will—" and I woke to death and night !

:

"HE LOVES AND HE RIDES AWAY."

'TWAS in that island summer where
They spin the morning gossamer,
And weave the evening mist,
That, underneath the hawthorn-tree,
I loved my love, and my love loved me,
And there we lay and kissed,
And saw the happy ships upon the yielding sea.

Soft my heart, and warm his wooing,
What we did seemed, while 'twas doing,
Beautiful and wise ;
Wiser, fairer, more in tune,
Than all else in that sweet June,
And sinless as the skies
That warmed the willing earth thro' all the languid
    noon.

Ah, that fatal spell !
Ere the evening fell
I fled away to hide my frightened face,
And cried that I was born,
And sobbed with love and scorn,
And in the darkness sought a darker place,
And blushed, and wept, and blushed, and dared not
    think of morn.

Day and night, day and night,
And I saw no light,
Night and day, night and day,
And in my woe I lay
And dreamed the dreams they dream who cannot sleep:
My speech was withered, and I could not pray;
My tears were frozen, and I could not weep.

I saw the hawthorn rise
Between me and the skies,
I felt the shadow was from pole to pole,
I felt the leaves were shed,
I felt the birds were dead,
And on the earth I snowed the winter of my soul.

Like to the hare wide eyed,
That with her throbbing side
Pressed to the rock, awaits the coming cry,
In my despair I sate
And waited for my fate;
And as the hunted hare returns to die,
And with her latest breath
Regains her native heath,
So, when I heard the feet of destiny
Near and more near, and caught the yelp of death,
Toward the sounding sea,
Toward my hawthorn-tree,
Under the ignorant stars I darkly crept:
"There," I said, "they'll find me dead,
Lying within my maidenhead."
And at my own unwonted voice, I wept;
And for my great heart-ache,
Within a little brake

I lay me weary down and weary slept,
Nor ever oped mine eyes till Morn had left the lake.

Her morning bath was o'er,
And on the golden shore
She stood like Flora with her floral train,
And all her track was seen
Among the watery sheen,
That blushed, and wished, and blushing wished again,
And parted still, and closed, with pleasure that had
    been.

Oh the happy isle,
The universal smile
That met, as love meets love, the smile of day,
And touched and lit delight
Within the common light,
Till all the joy of life was ecstasy,
And morn's wild maids ran each her flowery way,
And shook her dripping locks o'er hill, and dale, and
    lea !
"At least," I said, "my tree is sear and blight,
My tree, my hawthorn-tree ! "

With downcast eyes of fear
I drew me near and near,
Dazed with the dewy glory of the hour,
Till under-foot I see
A flower too dear to me :
I pause, and raise my full eyes from the flower,
And lo ! my hawthorn-tree !

As a white-limbed may,
In some illumined bay,

Flings round her shining charms in starry rain,
And with her body bright
Dazzles the waters white,
That fall from her fair form, and flee in vain,
Dyed with the dear unutterable sight,
And circle out her beauty thro' the circling main,

So my hawthorn-tree
Stood and seemed to me
The very face that smiled the summer smile:
All lesser light-bearers
Did light their lamps at hers—
She lit her own at heaven's, and looked the while
A purer, sweeter sun,
Whence beauty was begun,
And blossomed from her blossoms thro' the blossoming
    isle.
Then I took heart, and as I looked upon
Her unstained white, I said, "I am not wholly vile."

Thus my hawthorn-tree
Was my witness unto me,
And so I answered my impleading sin
Till blossom-time was o'er,
And with the autumn roar
Mine unrebuked accuser entered in,
And I fell down convinced, and strove with shame no
    more.

Some time after came to me,
An image of the hawthorn-tree,
And bore the old sweet witness; and I heard,
And from among the dead
I lifted up my head,

As one lifts up to hear a little bird,
And finds the night is past and all the east is red.

Small and fair, choice and rare,
Snowy pale with moonlight hair,
My little one blossoms and springs !
Like joy with woe singing to it,
Like love with sorrow to woo it,
So my witty one, so my pretty one, sings !
And I see the white hawthorn-tree and the bright
    .summer bird singing thro' it,
And my heart is prouder than kings !

While I look on her I seem
Once again in the sweet dream
Of that enchanted day,
When, underneath the hawthorn-tree,
I loved my love and my love loved me :
And lost in love we lay,
And saw the happy ships upon the yielding sea.

While I look on her I seem
Once again in that bright dream,
Beautiful and wise :
Wiser, fairer, more in tune,
Than all else in that sweet June,
And sinless as the skies
That warmed the willing earth thro' all the languid
    noon.

Like my hawthorn-tree,
She stands and seems to me
The very face that smiles the summer smile :
All lesser light-bearers
Do light their lamps at hers --

She lights her own at heaven's, and looks the while
A sweeter, purer sun,
Whence beauty is begun,
To blossom from that blossom thro' the blossoming
    isle.

Thou shalt not leave me, child !
Come weather fierce or mild,
My babe, my blossom ! thou shalt never leave me !
Life shall never wean us,
Nor death shall e'er have room to come between us,
And time may grieve me but shall ne'er bereave me,
Nor see us more apart than he hath seen us.

For I will fall with thee,
As a bird from the tree
Falls with a butterfly petal whitely shed,
And falling—thou and I—
I shall not dread to die,
But like a child I'll take my flower to bed.
And when the long cold death-night hath gone by,
In the great darkness of the sepulchre
I'll feel and find thee near,
My babe, my white, white blossom !
And when the trumpet cries,
I shall not fear to rise,
But wear thee o'er the spot upon my bosom,
And come out of my grave and bear the awful eyes.

———

THE CAPTAIN'S WIFE.

I no not say the day is long and weary,
  For while thou art content to be away,
  Living in thee, oh Love, I live thy day,
And reck not if mine own be sad and dreary.

I do not count its sorrows or its charms:
  It lies as cold, as empty, and as dead,
  As lay my wedding-dress beside my bed
When I was clothed in thy dear arms.

Yet there is something here within this breast
  Which, like a flower that never blossoms, lieth,
  And tho' in words and tears my sorrow crieth,
I know that it hath never been exprest.

Something that blindly yearneth to be known,
  And doth not burn, nor rage, nor leap, nor dart;
  But struggles in the sickness of my heart,
As a root struggles in a vault of stone.

Now, by my wedding ring,
I charge thee do not move
That heavy stone that on the vault doth lie;
I charge thee be of merry cheer, my love,

Nor ever let me know that thou dost sigh,
For, ah ! how light a thing
Would shake me with the sorrow I deny !

I am as one who hid a giant's child
In her deep prison, and, from year to year,
He grew to his own stature, fierce and wild,
And what she took for love she kept for fear.

Oh, thou enchanter, who dost hold the spells
Of all my sealèd cells,
Oh Love, that hast been silent all too long,
A little longer, Love, oh, silent be ;
My secret hath waxed strong,
My giant hath grown up to angry age ;
Do thou but say the word that sets him free,
And, lo ! he tears me in his rage !

I do not say the day is sad and dreary,
For while thou art content to be away,
Living in thee, oh Love, I live thy day,
And reck not if mine own be wan and weary.

I look down on it from my far love-dream,
As some drowned saint may see with musing eyes
Her lifeless body float adown the stream,
While she is smiling in her skies.

But do thou silence keep !
For I am one who walketh on the ledge
Of some great rock's sheer edge :
I walk in beauty and in light,
Self-balanced on the height :
A breath ! and I am breathless in the deep.

Oh, my own Love, I warn
Thy grief to be as still as they who tread
The snow of alpine peak,
And see the pendulous avalanche o'erhead
Hang like a dew-drop on a thorn !

I charge thee silence keep !
My life stands breathless by her agony,
Oh, do not bid her leap !
I am as calm as air
Before a summer storm ;
The ocean of my thoughts hath ceased to roll ;
This living heart that doth not beat is warm ;
I think the stillness of my face is fair ;
The cloud that fills my soul
Is not a cloud of pain.
Beware, beware ! one rash
Sweet glance may be the flash
That brings it raving down in thunder and in rain !

No, do not speak :
Nor, oh ! let any tell of thy pale cheek,
Nor paint the silent sorrow of thine eye,
Nor tell me thou art fond, or gay, or glad ;
For, ah ! so tuned and lightly strung am I,
That howsoe'er thou stir, I ring thereby.

Thy manly voice is deep,
But if thou touch from sleep
The woman's treble of my shrill reply,
Ah, who shall say thine echoes may not weep?
A jester's ghost is sad,
The shades of merriest flowers do mow and creep,
And oh, the vocal shadows that should fly

About the simplest word that thou canst say,
What after-spell shall ever lay?

Hast thou forgot when I sat down to sing
To my forsaken harp, long, long ago,
How thou, for sport, wouldst strike a single string,
And hark the hovering chorus come and go,
Low and high, high and low,
Till round the throbbing wire
Rose such a quivering quire,
As all King David's wives were echoing
The tenor of their king.

Like those dear strings, my silent soul is full
Of cries, as a ripe fruit is full of wine.
The fruit is hanging fair and beautiful,
And dry-eyed as a rose in the sunshine,
But try it with a single touch of thine,
And, lo ! the drops that start,
And all the golden vintage of its heart !

So, thinking of thy debt to Love and me,
In some dull hour beyond the sea,
Do thou but only say—
As carelessly as men do pay their debts—
" Oh, weary day ! "
And that one sigh o'ersets
The hive of my regrets,
" Ah, weary, weary day,
Oh, weary, weary day,
Oh, day so weary, oh, day so dreary,
Oh, weary, weary, weary, weary, weary,
Oh, weary, weary ! "

GRASS FROM THE BATTLE-FIELD

SMALL sheaf
Of withered grass, that hast not yet revealed
Thy story, lo! I see thee once more green
And growing on the battle-field,
On that last day that ever thou didst grow!

I look down thro' thy blades and see between
A little lifted clover leaf
Stand like a cresset : and I know
If this were morn there should be seen
In its chalice such a gem
As decks no mortal diadem
Poised with a lapidary skill
Which merely living doth fulfil
And pass the exquisite strain of subtlest human will.
But in the sun it lifteth up
A dry unjewelled cup,
Therefore I see that day doth not begin ;
And yet I know its beaming lord
Hath not yet passed the hill of noon,
Or thy lush blades
Would be more dry and thin,
And every blade a thirsty sword
Edged with the sharp desire that soon
Should draw the silver blood of all the shades.
I feel 't is summer.   This whereon I stand
Is not a hill, nor, as I think, a vale ;

The soil is soft upon the generous land,
Yet not as where the meeting streams take hand
Under the mossy mantle of the dale.
Such grass is for the meadow.   If I try
To lift my heavy eyelids, as in dreams
A power is on them, and I know not why.
Thou art but part ; the whole is unconfest :
Beholding thee I long to know the rest.
As one expands the bosom with a sigh,
I stretch my sight's horizon ; but it seems,
Ere it can widen round the mystery,
To close in swift contraction, like the breast.
The air is held, as by a charm,
In an enforcèd silence, as like sound
As the dead man the living.   'T is so still,
I listen for it loud.
And when I force my eyes from thy sole place
And see a wider space,
Above, around,
In ragged glory like a torn
And golden-natured cloud,
O'er the dim field a living smoke is warm ;
As in a city on a sabbath morn
The hot and summer sunshine goes abroad
Swathed in the murky air,
As if a god
Enrobed himself in common flesh and blood,
Our heavy flesh and blood,
And here and there
As unaware
Thro' the dull lagging limbs of mortal make,
That keep unequal time, the swifter essence brake.

But hark a bugle horn !
And, ere it ceases, such a shock

As if the plain were iron, and thereon
An iron hammer, heavy as a hill,
Swung by a monstrous force, in stroke came down
And deafened Heaven.   I feel a swound
Of every sense bestunned.
The rent ground seems to rock,
And all the definite vision, in such wise
As a dead giant borne on a swift river,
Seems sliding off for ever,
When my reviving eyes,
As one that holds a spirit by his eye
With set inexorable stare,
Fix thee : and so I catch, as by the hair,
The form of that great dream that else had drifted by.
I know not what that form may be ;
The lock I hold is all I see,
And thou, small sheaf ! art all the battle-field to me.

The wounded silence hath not time to heal
When see ! upon thy sod
The round stroke of a charger's heel
With echoing thunder shod !
As the night-lightning shows
A mole upon a momentary face,
So, as that gnarled hoof strikes the indented place,
I see it, and it goes !
And I hear the squadrons trot thro' the heavy shell
    and shot,
And wheugh ! but the grass is gory !
Forward ho ! blow to blow, at the foe in they go,
And 'tis hieover heigho for glory !

The rushing storm is past,
But hark ! upon its track the far drums beat,

And all the earth that at thy roots thou hast   [of feet
Stirs, shakes, shocks, sounds, with quick strong tramp
In time unlike the last.
Footing to tap of drum
The charging columns come ;
And as they come their mighty martial sound
Blows on before them as a flaming fire
Blows in the wind ; for, as old Mars in ire
Strode o'er the world encompassed in a cloud,
So the swift legion, o'er the quaking ground,
Strode in a noise of battle.   Nigh and nigher
I heard it, like the long swell gathering loud
What-time a land-wind blowing from the main
Blows to the burst of fury and is o'er,
As if an ocean on one fatal shore
Fell in a moment whole, and threw its roar
Whole to the further sea : and as the strain
Of my strong sense cracked in the deafened ear,
And all the rushing tumult of the plain
Topped its great arch above me, a swift foot
Was struck between thy blades to the struck root,
And lifted : as into a sheath
A sudden sword is thrust and drawn again
Ere one can gasp a breath.
I was so near,
I saw the wrinkles of the leather grain,
The very cobbler's stitches, and the wear
By which I knew the wearer trod not straight ;
An honest shoe it seemed that had been good
To mete the miles of any country lane,
Nor did one sign explain
'Twas made to wade thro' blood.
My shoe, soft footstooled on this hearth, so far
From strife, hath such a patch, and as he past
His broken shoelace whipt his eager haste.

An honest shoe, good faith ! that might have stood
Upon the threshold of a village inn
And welcomed all the world : or by the byre
And barn gone peaceful till the day closed in,
And, scraped at eve upon some homely gate,
Ah, Heaven ! might sit beside a cottage fire
And touch the lazy log to softer flames than war.

Long, long, thou wert alone,
I thought thy days were done,
Flat as ignoble grass that lies out mown
By peaceful hands in June, I saw thee lie.
A worm crawled o'er thee, and the gossamer
That telegraphs Queen Mab to Oberon,
Lengthening his living message, passed thee by.
But rain fell : and thy strawed blades one by one
Began to stir and stir.

And as some moorland bird
Whom the still hunter's stalking steps have stirred,
When he stands mute, and nothing more is heard,
With slow succession and reluctant art
Grows upward from her bed,
Each move a muffled start,
And thro' the silent autumn covert red
Uplifts a throbbing head
That times the ambushed hunter's thudding heart ;
Or as a snow-drop bending low
Beneath a flake of other snow
Thaws to its height when spring winds melt the skies,
And drip by drip doth mete a measured rise ;

Or as the eyelids of a child's fair eyes
Lift from her lower lashes slow and pale
To arch the wonder of a fairy tale ;

So thro' the western light
I saw thee slowly rearing to thy height.

Then when thou hadst regained thy state,
And while a meadow-spider with three lines
Enschemed thy three tall pillars green,
And made the enchanted air between
Mortal with shining signs
(For the loud carrion-flies were many and late),

Betwixt thy blades and stems
There fell a hand,
Soft, small, and white, and ringed with gold and gems;
And on those stones of price
I saw a proud device,
And words I could not understand.

Idly, one by one,
The knots of anguish came undone,
The fingers stretched as from a cramp of woe,
And sweet and slow
Moved to gracious shapes of rest,
Like a curl of soft pale hair
Drying in the sun.
And then they spread,
And sought a wonted greeting in the air,
And strayed
Between thy blades, and with each blade
As with meeting fingers played
And tresses long and fair.
Then again at placid length it lay,
Stretched as to kisses of accustomed lips ;
And again in sudden strain
Sprang, falling clenched with pain,

Till the knuckles white,
Thro' the evening grey, ⸫
Whitened and whitened as the snowy tips
Of far hills glimmer thro' the night.
But who shall tell that agony
That beat thee, beat thee into bloody clay
Red as the sards and rubies of the rings ;
As when a bird, fast by the fowler's net,
A moment doth forget
His fetters, and with desperate wings
A-sudden springs and falls,
And (while from happy clouds the skylark calls)
Still feebler springs
And fainter falls,
And still untamed upon the gory ground
With failing strength renews his deadly wound ?
At length the struggle ceased ; and my fixed eye
Perceived that every finger wan
Did quiver like the quivering fan
Of a dying butterfly,
Nor long I watched until
Even the humming in the air was still.
Then I gazed and gazed,
Nor once my aching eyeballs raised
Till a poor bird that had a meadow nest
Came down, and like a shadow ran
Among the shadowy grass.
I followed with mine eyes ; and with a strain
Pursued her, till six cubits' length beyond
Thy central sheaf I found
A sight I could not pass.
The hacked and haggard head
Of a huge war-horse dead.
The evening haze hung o'er him like a breath,
And still in death

He stretched drawn lips of rage that grinned in vain;
A sparrow chirped upon
His wound, and in his dying slaver fed,
Or picked those teeth of stone
That bit with lifeless jaws the purple tongue of pain.

But I remembered that dead hand
I left to trace the childless lark,
And back o'er those six cubits of grass-land,
Blade by blade, and stalk by stalk,
As one doth walk
Who, mindful, counts by dark
Along the garden palings to the gate,
I felt along the vision to where late
There lay that dead hand white;
But now methought that there was something more
Than when I looked before,
And what was more was sweeter than the rest;
As when upon the moony half of night
Aurora lays a living light,
Softer than moonshine, yet more bright.
And as I looked I was aware
Another hand was on the hand,
A smaller hand, more fair
But not more white, as is the warm delight
That curves and curls and coyly glows
About the blushing heart of the white rose,
More fair but not more white
Than those broad beauties that expand
And fall, and falling blanch the morning air.

Both hands lay motionless,
The living on the dead.   But by-and-by
The living hand began to move and press
The cold dead flesh, and took its silent way

So often o'er the unrespective clay,
In such long-drawn caress
Of pleading passion, such an ecstasy
Of supplicating touch, that as they lay
So like, so unlike, twined with the fond art
And all the dear delay
And dreadful patience of a desperate heart,
Methought that to the tenement
From which it lately went,
The naked life had come back, and did try
By every gate to enter.   While I thought,
With sudden clutch of new intent
The living grasp had caught
The dead compliance.   Slowly thro'
The dusky air she raised it, and aloft,
While all her fingers soft
And every starting vein
Tightened as in a rack of pain,
Held it one straining moment fixed and mute,
And let it go.
And with a thud upon the sod,
It fell like falling fruit.

Then there came a cry,
Tearless, bloodless, dry
Of every sap of sorrow but its own—
It had no likeness among living cries ;
And to my heart my streaming blood was blown
As if before my eyes
A dead man sprang up dead, and dead fell down.
The carrion-hunting winds that prowl the wold,
Frenzied for prey, sweep in and bear it on,
Far, far and further thro' the shrieking cold,
And still the yelling pack devour it as they run.
And silence, like a want of air,

Was round me, and my sense burned low,
And darkness darkened ; and the glow
Of the living hand being gone,
The dead hand showed like a pale stone
Full fathom five
Under a quiet bay.
But still my sight did dive
To reach it where it lay,
And still the night grew dark, and by degrees
The dead thing glimmered with a drownèd light,
As faces seem and sink in depths of darkening seas.
Then, while yet
My set eyes saw it, as the sage doth set
His glass to some dim glimpse afar
That palpitates from mote to star,
It was touched and hid ;
Touched and hid, as when a deep sea-weed
Hides some white sea-sorrow.   All
My sight uprose, and all my soul
(As one who presses at the pane
When a city show goes by),
Crowded into the fixed eye,
And filled the starting ball.
Nor filled in vain.
I began to feel
The air had something to reveal.
Beyond the blank indifference
Was underlined another sense,
Was rained a gracious influence ;
And tho' the darkness was so deep,
I knew it was not wholly dead,
Nor empty, as we feel in sleep
That some one standeth by the bed.
I beheld, as who should look
In trance upon a sealèd book.

I perceived that in a place
The night was lighter, as the face
Of an Indian Queen when love
Draws back the dark blood from her sick
Pale cheek
Behind the sable curtain that doth not move.

No outer light was shed,
But as the mystery
Before my stronger will did slowly yield,
I saw, as in that dark hour before morn
When the shocks of harvest corn
Exhale about the midnight field
The wealth of yellow suns, and breathe a gentle day.
I saw the shape of a fair bended head,
And hair pale streaming long and low
Veiling the face I might not know,
And dabbling all the ground with sweet uncertain woe,
Much I questioned in my mind
Of her form and kind,
But my stern compelling eye
Brought no other answer from the air,
Nor did my rude hand dare
Profane that agony.
I watched apart
With such a sweet awe in my heart
As looks up dumb into the sky
When that goddess, lorn and lone,
Who slew grim winter like a polar bear,
And threw his immemorial white
Upon her granite throne,
Sits all unseen as Death,
Save for the loss of many a hidden star
And for the wintry mystery of her breath,
And at a far-sight that she sees,

Bowed by her great despair,
Bendeth her awful head upon her knees,
And all her wondrous hair
Dishevels golden down the northern night.

At length my weary gaze
Relents : and, haze in haze
Pervolving as in glad release,
I saw each separate shade
Slide from his place and fade,
And all the flowering dark did winter back
Into its undistinguished black.
So the sculptor doth in fancy make
His formèd image in the formless stone,
And while his spells compel,
Can see it there full well,
The ivory kernel in the ivory shell,
But shakes himself and all the god is gone.
Alas !
And have I seen thee but an hour ?
And shalt thou never tell
Thy story, oh thou broken flower,
Thou midnight asphodel
Among the battle grass ?

Too soon ! too soon !
But while I bid thee stay,
Night, like a cloud, dissolves into the day,
And from the city clock I hear the stroke of noon.

THE GHOSTS' RETURN.

SKIRLIN' an' birlin', tunin' an' croonin',
Reelin' an' skreelin', they piped doun the glen,
Lang Hugh an' black Sandie, Ian Dhu an' wee Dandie,
Wha wad na gang w i' the braw Hielan'men?

Skirlin' an' birlin', tunin' an' croonin',
Reelin' an' skreelin', they piped doun the glen,
Wi' a rout an' a shout, an' a' the lasses out,
Wha wad na gang wi' the braw Hielan'men?

Skirlin' an' birlin', tunin' an' croonin',
Reelin' an' skreelin', they piped doun the glen !
Wi' the hot light o' noon an' the blue sky aboon,
Ilka man sword in han' gaed the braw Hielan'men !

Ken ye why we weep ?   Think ye that they sleep,
Ilka man on his ain bluidy brae,
Ilk ane whar he died wi' a faeman by his side,
An' the pibroch can wauk him na mae ?

Or the news cam' fra the fiel' we ken'd it a' too weel,
Our bonnie, bonnie braw Hielan'men !
Not a foot ony stirred to meet the bluidy word,
As the death-roll cam' slow up the glen.

Had ye seen any sight of terror and affright ?
Did their ghosts walk in white up the glen ?
We saw na ony sight o' terror an' affright,
An' white 's no for braw tartaned men !

Fra the hour they gaed that day, oh the glen was fu' o'
    wae,
Our bonnie, bonnie braw Hielan'men !
Sair, sair, an' mair an' mair, our hearts were fu' o' care,
And our een speerit aye doun the glen ;

Till ae morn it did befa' that we waukit up a',
An' the light it was sweet, but an' ben,
An' a' that lang day we had na ony wae,
An' no ee cared to speer doun the glen.

Not a lassie but apart hid her wonder in her heart,
An' lay close till the day began to dee,
Lest her canty een confest the secret o' her breast,
For she said, " They will a' weep but me."

But when we met at een by the thorn upon the green,
An' the tale we a' tellt was the same,
Not a word mair we said, but ilk ane hid her head,
An' ken'd that her man was at hame.

AFLOAT AND ASHORE.

"TUMBLE and rumble, and grumble and snort,
Like a whale to starboard, a whale to port ;
Tumble and rumble, and grumble and snort,
And the steamer steams thro' the sea, love !"

" I see the ship on the sea, love,
I stand alone
On this rock,
The sea does not shock
The stone ;
The waters around it are swirled,
But under my feet
I feel it go down
To where the hemispheres meet
At the adamant heart of the world.
Oh, that the rock would move !
Oh, that the rock would roll
To meet thee over the sea, love !
Surely my mighty love
Should fill it like a soul,
And it should bear me to thee, love ;
Like a ship on the sea, love,
Bear me, bear me, to thee, love !"

"Guns are thundering, seas are sundering, crowds are
    wondering,
Low on our lee, love.
Over and over the cannon-clouds cover brother and
    lover, but over and over
The whirl-wheels trundle the sea, love,
And on thro' the loud pealing pomp of her cloud
The great ship is going to thee, love,
Blind to her mark, like a world thro' the dark,
Thundering, sundering, to the crowds wondering,
Thundering ever to thee, love."

"I have come down to thee coming to me, love,
I stand, I stand
On the solid sand,
I see thee coming to me, love ;
The sea runs up to me on the sand,
I start—'t is as if thou hadst stretched thine hand
And touched me thro' the sea, love.
I feel as if I must die
For there's something longs to fly,
Fly and fly, to thee, love.
As the blood of the flower ere she blows
Is beating up to the sun,
And her roots do hold her down,
And it blushes and breaks undone
In a rose,
So my blood is beating in me, love !
I see thee nigh and nigher,

And my soul leaps up like sudden fire,
My life's in the air
To meet thee there,
To meet thee coming to me, love !
Over the sea,
Coming to me,
Coming, and coming to me, love ! "

" The boats are lowered : I leap in first,
Pull, boys, pull ! or my heart will burst !
More ! more !—lend me an oar !—
I'm thro' the breakers ! I'm on the shore !
I see thee waiting for me, love ! "

" A sudden storm
Of sighs and tears,
A clenching arm,
A look of years.
In my bosom a thousand cries,
A flash like light before my eyes,
And I am lost in thee, love ! '

DAFT JEAN.

DAFT Jean,
The waesome wean,
She cam' by the cottage, she cam' by the ha',
The laird's ha' o' Wutherstanelaw,
The cottar's cot by the birken shaw ;
An' aye she gret,
To ilk ane she met,
For the trumpet had blawn an' her lad was awa'.

" Black, black," sang she,
" Black, black my weeds shall be,
My love has widowed me !
Black, black I" sang she.

Daft Jean,
The waesome wean,
She cam' by the cottage, she cam' by the ha',
The laird's ha' o' Wutherstanelaw,
The cottar's cot by the birken shaw ;
Nae mair she creepit,
Nae mair she weepit,
She stept 'mang the lasses the queen o' them a',
The queen o' them a',
The queen o' them a',
She stept 'mang the lasses the queen o' them a'.
For the fight it was fought i' the fiel' far awa',
An' claymore in han' for his love an' his lan',
The lad she lo'ed best he was foremost to fa'.

" White, white," sang she,
" White, white, my weeds shall be,
I am no widow," sang she,
" White, white, my wedding shall be,
White, white !" sang she.

Daft Jean,
The waesome wean,
She gaed na' to cottage, she gaed na' to ha',
But forth she creepit,
While a' the house weepit,
Into the snaw i' the eerie night-fa'.

At morn we found her,
The lammies stood round her,
The snaw was her pillow, her sheet was the snaw ;
Pale she was lying,
Singing and dying,
A' for the laddie wha fell far awa'.

" White, white," sang she,
" My love has married me,
White, white, my weeds shall be,
White, white, my wedding shall be,
White, white," sang she !

"WHEN THE RAIN IS ON THE ROOF."

LORD, I am poor, and know not how to speak,
But since Thou are so great,
Thou needest not that I should speak to Thee well.
All angels speak unto Thee well.

Lord, Thou hast all things: what Thou wilt is Thine,
More gold and silver than the sun and moon ;
All flocks and herds, all fish in every sea ;
Mountains and valleys, cities and all farms ;
Cots and all men, harvests and years of fruit.
Is any king arrayed like Thee, who wearest
A new robe every morning ?   Who is crowned
As Thou, who settest heaven upon thy head ?
But as for me—
For me, if he be dead, I have but Thee !
Therefore, because Thou art my sole possession,
I will not fear to speak to Thee, who art mine,
For who doth dread his own ?

Lord, I am very sorrowful.   I know
That Thou delightest to do well ; to wipe
Tears from all eyes ; to bind the broken-hearted ;
To comfort them that mourn ; to give to them
Beauty for ashes, and to garb with joy

The naked soul of grief.   And what so good
But Thou that wilt canst do it?   Which of all
Thy works is less in wonder and in praise
Than this poor heart's desire?   Give me, oh Lord,
My heart's desire !   Wilt Thou refuse my prayer
Who givest when no man asketh?   How great things,
How unbesought, how difficult, how strange,
Thou dost in daily pleasure !   Who is like Thee
Oh Lord of Life and Death?   The year is dead ;
It smouldered in its smoke to the white ash
Of winter : but Thou breathest and the fire
Is kindled, and Thy summer bounty burns.
This is a marvel to me.   Day is buried ;
And where they laid him in the west I see
The mounded mountains.   Yet shall he come back ;
Not like a ghost that rises from his grave.
But in the east the palace gates will ope,
And he comes forth out of the feast, and I
Behold him and the glory after him,
Like to a messaged angel with wide arms
Of rapture, all the honour in his eyes,
And blushing with the King.   In the dark hours
Thou hast been busy with him : for he went
Down westward, and he cometh from the east,
Not as toil-stained from travel, tho' his course
And journey in the secrets of the night
Be far as earth and heaven.   This is a sum
Too hard for me, oh Lord ; I cannot do it.
But Thou hast set it, and I know with Thee
There is an answer.   Man also, oh Lord,
Is clear and whole before Thee.   Well I know
That the strong skein and tangle of our life
Thou holdest by the end.   The mother dieth—
The mother dieth ere her time, and like
A jewel in the cinders of a fire,

The child endures.   Also, the son is slain,
And she who bore him shrieks not while the steel
Doth hack her sometime vitals, and transfix
The heart she throbbed with.   How shall these
    things be?
Likewise, oh Lord, man that is born of woman,
Who built him of her tenderness, and gave
Her sighs to breathe him, and for all his bones—
Poor trembler!—hath no wherewithal more stern
Than bowels of her pity, cometh forth
Like a young lion from his den.   Ere yet
His teeth be fangled he hath greed of blood,
And gambols for the slaughter: and being grown,
Sudden, with terrible mane and mouthing thunder,
Like a thing native to the wilderness
He stretches toward the desert ; while his dam,
As a poor dog that nursed the king of beasts,
Strains at her sordid chain, and, with set ear,
Hath yet a little longer, in the roar
And backward echo of his windy flight,
Him, seen no more.   This also is too hard—
Too hard for me, oh Lord ! I cannot judge it.
Also the armies of him are as dust.
A little while the storm and the great rain
Beat him, and he abideth in his place,
But the suns scorch on him, and all his sap
And strength, whereby he held against the ground,
Is spent ; as in the unwatched pot on the fire,
When that which should have been the children's
    blood
Scarce paints the hollow iron.   Then Thou callest
Thy wind.   He passeth like the stowre and dust
Of roads in summer.   A brief while it casts
A shadow, and beneath the passing cloud
Things not to pass do follow to the hedge,

Swift heaviness runs under with a show,
And draws a train, and what was white is dark ;
But at the hedge it falleth on the fields—
It falleth on the greenness of the grass ;
The grass between its verdure takes it in,
And no man heedeth. Surely, oh Lord God,
If he has gone down from me, if my child
Nowhere in any lands that see the sun
Maketh the sunshine pleasant, if the earth
Hath smoothed o'er him as waters o'er a stone,
Yet is he further from Thee than the day
After its setting? Shalt Thou not, oh Lord,
Be busy with him in the under dark,
And give him journey thro' the secret night,
As far as earth and heaven? Aye, tho' Thou slay
   me
Yet will I trust in Thee, and in his flesh
Shall he see God ! But, Lord, tho' I am sure
That thou canst raise the dead, oh what has he
To do with death ? Our days of pilgrimage
Are three-score years and ten ; why should he die ?
Lord, this is grievous, that the heathen rage,
And because they imagined a vain thing,
That Thou shouldst send the just man that feared
   Thee,
To smite it from their hands. Lord, who are they,
That this my suckling lamb is their burnt-offering ?
That with my staff, oh Lord, their fire is kindled,
My ploughshare Thou dost beat into Thy sword,
The blood Thou givest them to drink is mine ?
Let it be far from Thee to do to mine
What if I did it to mine own, Thy curse
Avengeth. Do I take the children's bread
And give it to the dogs ? Do I rebuke
So widely that the aimless lash comes down

On innocent and guilty?   Do I lift
The hand of goodness by the elbowed arm
And break it on the evil?   Not so.   Not so.
Lord what advantageth it to be God
If Thou do less than I ?

                        Have mercy on me !
Deal not with me according to mine anger !
Thou knowest if I lift my voice against Thee,
'T is but as he who in his fierce despair
Dasheth his head against the dungeon-stone,
Sure that but one can suffer.   Yet, oh Lord,
If Thou hast heard—if my loud passion reached
Thine awful ear—and yet, I think, oh Father,
I did not rage, but my most little anger
Borne in the strong arms of my mighty love
Seemed of the other's stature—oh, good Lord,
Bear witness now against me.   Let me see
And taste that Thou art good.   Thou who art slow
To wrath, oh pause upon my quick offence,
And show me mortal !   Thou whose strength is made
Perfect in weakness, ah, be strong in me,
For I am weak indeed !   How weak, oh Lord,
Thou knowest who hast seen the unlifted sin
Lie on the guilty tongue that strove in vain
To speak it.   Call my madness from the tombs !
Let the dumb fiend confess Thee !   If I sinned
In silence, if I looked the fool i' the face
And answered to his heart, " There is no God,"
Now in mine hour stretch forth Thy hand, oh Lord,
And let me be ashamed.   As when in sleep
I dream, and in the horror of my dream
Fall to the empty place below the world
Where no man is : no light, no life, no help,
No hope !   And all the marrow in my bones
Leaps in me, and I rend the night with fear !

And he who lieth near me thro' the dark
Stretcheth an unseen hand, and all is well.
Tho' Thou shouldst give me all my heart's desire,
What is it in Thine eyes? Give me, oh God,
My heart's desire ! my heart's desire, oh God !
As a young bird doth bend before its mother,
Bendeth and crieth to its feeding mother,
So bend I for that good thing before Thee.
It trembleth on the rock with many cries,
It bendeth with its breast upon the rock,
And worships in the hunger of its heart.
I tremble on the rock with many cries,
I bend my beating breast against the rock,
And worship in the hunger of my heart.
Give me that good thing ere I die, my God !
Give me that very good thing ! Thou standest, Lord,
By all things, as one standeth after harvest
By the threshed corn, and, when the crowding fowl
Beseech him, being a man and seeing as men,
Hath pity on their cry, respecting not
The great and little barley, but at will
Dipping one hand into the golden store
Straweth alike ; nevertheless to them
Whose eyes are near their meat and do esteem
By conscience of their bellies, grain and grain
Is stint or riches.   Let it, oh my God,
Be far from Thee to measure out Thy gifts
Smaller and larger, or to say to me
Who am so poor and lean with the long fast
Of such a dreary dearth—to me whose joy
Is not as Thine—whose human heart is nearer
To its own good than Thou who art in heaven—
" Not this but this : " to me who if I took
All that these arms could compass, all pressed down
And running over that this heart could hold,

All that in dreams I covet when the soul
Sees not the further bound of what it craves,
Might filch my mortal infinite from Thine
And leave Thee nothing less.   Give me, oh Lord,
My heart's desire !   It profiteth Thee nought
Being withheld ; being given, where is that aught
It doth not profit me ?   Wilt Thou deny
That which to Thee is nothing, but to me
All things ?   Not so.   Not so.   If I were God
And Thou—Have mercy on me ! oh Lord ! Lord !

    .   .   .   .   .   .

Lord, I am weeping.   As Thou wilt, oh Lord,
Do with him as Thou wilt ; but oh, my God,
Let him come back to die !   Let not the fowls
O' the air defile the body of my child,
My own fair child that when he was a babe
I lift up in my arms and gave to Thee !
Let not his garment, Lord, be vilely parted,
Nor the fine linen which these hands have spun
Fall to the stranger's lot !   Shall the wild bird
—That would have pilfered of the ox—this year
Disdain the pens and stalls ?   Shall her blind young,
That on the fleck and moult of brutish beasts
Had been too happy, sleep in cloth of gold
Whereof each thread is to this beating heart
As a peculiar darling ?   Lo, the flies
Hum o'er him !   Lo, a feather from the crow
Falls in his parted lips !   Lo, his dead eyes
See not the raven !   Lo, the worm, the worm
Creeps from his festering horse !   My God ! my God !

    .   .   .   .   .   .

Oh Lord, Thou doest well.   I am content.
If Thou have need of him he shall not stay.
But as one calleth to a servant, saying,

" At such a time be with me," so, oh Lord,
Call him to Thee ! ·Oh bid him not in haste
Straight whence he standeth.   Let him lay aside
The soilèd tools of labour.   Let him wash
His hands of blood.   Let him array himself
Meet for his Lord, pure from the sweat and fume
Of corporal travail !   Lord, if he must die,
Let him die here. Oh take him where Thou gavest !

And even as once I held him in my womb
Till all things were fulfilled, and he came forth,
So, oh Lord, let me hold him in my grave
Till the time come, and Thou, who settest when
The hinds shall calve, ordain a better birth ;
And as I looked and saw my son, and wept
For joy, I look again and see my son,
And weep again for joy of him and Thee !

THE ORPHAN'S SONG.

I HAD a little bird,
I took it from the nest ;
I prest it, and blest it,
And nursed it in my breast.

I set it on the ground,
I danced round and round,
And sang about it so cheerly,
With " Hey my little bird, and ho my little bird,
And oh but I love thee dearly ! "

I make a little feast
Of food soft and sweet,
I hold it in my breast,
And coax it to eat ;

I pit, and I pat,
I call it this and that,
And sing about it so cheerly,
With " Hey my little bird, and ho my little bird,
And ho but I love thee dearly ! "

I may kiss, I may sing,
But I can't make it feed,
It taketh no heed
Of any pleasant thing.

I scolded, and I socked,
But it minded not a whit,
Its little mouth was locked,
And I could not open it.

Tho' with pit, and with pat,
And with this, and with that,
I sang about it so cheerly,
And "Hey my little bird, and ho my little bird,
And ho but I love thee dearly."

But when the day was done,
And the room was at rest,
And I sat all alone
With my birdie in my breast,

And the light had fled,
And not a sound was heard,
Then my little bird
Lifted up its head,

And the little mouth
Loosed its sullen pride,
And it opened, it opened,
With a yearning strong and wide.

Swifter than I speak
I brought it food once more,
But the poor little beak
Was locked as before.

I sat down again,
And not a creature stirred,
I laid the little bird
Again where it had lain ;

And again when nothing stirred,
And not a word I said,
Then my little bird
Lifted up its head,
And the little beak
Loosed its stubborn pride,
And it opened, it opened,
With a yearning strong and wide.

It lay in my breast,
It uttered no cry,
'Twas famished, 'twas famished,
And I couldn't tell why.

I couldn't tell why,
But I saw that it would die,
For all that I kept dancing round and round,
And singing above it so cheerly,
With "Hey my little bird, and ho my little bird,
And ho but I love thee dearly!"

I never look sad,
I hear what people say,
I laugh when they are gay
And they think I am glad.

My tears never start,
I never say a word,
But I think that my heart
Is like that little bird.

Every day I read,
And I sing, and I play,
But thro' the long day
It taketh no heed.

It taketh no heed
Of any pleasant thing,
I know it doth not read,
I know it doth not sing.

With my mouth I read,
With my hands I play,
My shut heart is shut,
Coax it how you may.

You may coax it how you may
While the day is broad and bright,
But in the dead night
When the guests are gone away,

And no more the music sweet
Up the house doth pass,
Nor the dancing feet
Shake the nursery glass;

And I've heard my aunt
Along the corridor,
And my uncle gaunt
Lock his chamber door;

And upon the stair
All is hushed and still,
And the last wheel
Is silent in the square;

And the nurses snore,
And the dim sheets rise and fall,
And the lamplight's on the wall,
And the mouse is on the floor;

And the curtains of my bed
Are like a heavy cloud,
And the clock ticks loud,
And sounds are in my head ;

And little Lizzie sleeps
Softly at my side,
It opens, it opens,
With a yearning strong and wide !

It yearns in my breast,
It utters no cry,
'Tis famished, 'tis famished,
And I feel that I shall die.
I feel that I shall die,
And none will know why,
Tho' the pleasant life is dancing round and round
And singing about me so cheerly,
With " Hey my little bird, and ho my little bird,
And ho but I love thee dearly ! "

TOMMY'S DEAD.

You may give over plough, boys,
You may take the gear to the stead,
All the sweat o' your brow, boys,
Will never get beer and bread.
The seed's waste, I know, boys,
There's not a blade will grow, boys,
'Tis cropped out, I trow, boys,
And Tommy's dead.

Send the colt to fair, boys,
He's going blind, as I said,
My old eyes can't bear, boys,
To see him in the shed :
The cow's dry and spare, boys,
She's neither here nor there, boys,
I doubt she's badly bred ;
Stop the mill to-morn, boys,
There'll be no more corn, boys,
Neither white nor red ;
There's no sign of grass, boys,
You may sell the goat and the ass, boys,
The land's not what it was, boys,
And the beasts must be fed :
You may turn Peg away, boys,
You may pay off old Ned,
We've had a dull day, boys,
And Tommy's dead.

Move my chair on the floor, boys,
Let me turn my head :
She's standing there in the door, boys,
Your sister Winifred !
Take her away from me, boys,
Your sister Winifred !
Move me round in my place, boys,
Let me turn my head,
Take her away from me, boys,
As she lay on her death-bed,
The bones of her thin face, boys,
As she lay on her death-bed !
I don't know how it be, boys,
When all's done and said,
But I see her looking at me, boys,
Wherever I turn my head ;
Out of the big oak-tree, boys,
Out of the garden-bed,
And the lily as pale as she, boys,
And the rose that used to be red.

There's something not right, boys,
But I think it's not in my head,
I've kept my precious sight, boys—
The Lord be hallowed !
Outside and in
The ground is cold to my tread,
The hills are wizen and thin,
The sky is shrivelled and shred,
The hedges down by the loan
I can count them bone by bone,
The leaves are open and spread,
But I see the teeth of the land,
And hands like a dead man's hand,
And the eyes of a dead man's head.

There's nothing but cinders and sand,
The rat and the mouse have fed,
And the summer's empty and cold ;
Over valley and wold
Wherever I turn my head
There's a mildew and a mould,
The sun's going out overhead,
And I'm very old,
And Tommy's dead.

What am I staying for, boys,
You're all born and bred,
'Tis fifty years and more, boys,
Since wife and I were wed,
And she's gone before, boys,
And Tommy's dead.

She was always sweet, boys,
Upon his curly head,
She knew she'd never see't, boys,
And she stole off to bed ;
I've been sitting up alone, boys,
For he'd come home, he said,
But it's time I was gone, boys,
For Tommy's dead.

Put the shutters up, boys,
Bring out the beer and bread,
Make haste and sup, boys,
For my eyes are heavy as lead ;
There's something wrong in the cup, boys,
There's something ill wi' the bread,
I don't care to sup, boys,
And Tommy's dead.

I'm not right, I doubt, boys,
I've such a sleepy head,
I shall never more be stout, boys,
You may carry me to bed.
What are you about, boys,
The prayers are all said,
The fire's raked out, boys,
And Tommy's dead.

The stairs are too steep, boys,
You may carry me to the head,
The night's dark and deep, boys,
Your mother's long in bed,
'Tis time to go to sleep, boys,
And Tommy's dead.

I'm not used to kiss, boys,
You may shake my hand instead.
All things go amiss, boys,
You may lay me where she is, boys,
And I'll rest my old head :
'Tis a poor world, this, boys,
And Tommy's dead.

"*SHE TOUCHES A SAD STRING OF SOFT RECALL.*"

RETURN, return! all night my lamp is burning,
  All night, like it, my wide eyes watch and burn;
Like it, I fade and pale, when day returning
  Bears witness that the absent can return,
  Return, return.

Like it, I lessen with a lengthening sadness,
  Like it, I burn to waste and waste to burn,
Like it, I spend the golden oil of gladness
  To feed the sorrowy signal for return,
  Return, return.

Like it, like it, whene'er the east wind sings,
  I bend and shake; like it, I quake and yearn,
When Hope's late butterflies, with whispering wings,
  Fly in out of the dark, to fall and burn—
  Burn in the watchfire of return,
  Return, return.

Like it, the very flame whereby I pine
Consumes me to its nature.   While I mourn
My soul becomes a better soul than mine,
And from its brightening beacon I discern
My starry love go forth from me, and shine
Across the seas a path for thy return,
Return, return.

Return, return ! all night I see it burn,
All night it prays like me, and lifts a twin
Of palmèd praying hands that meet and yearn—
Yearn to the impleaded skies for thy return.
Day, like a golden fetter, locks them in,
And wans the light that withers, tho' it burn
As warmly still for thy return ;
Still thro' the splendid load uplifts the thin
Pale, paler, palest patience that can learn
Nought but that votive sign for thy return—
That single suppliant sign for thy return,
Return, return.

Return, return ! lest haply, love, or e'er
Thou touch the lamp the light have ceased to burn,
And thou, who thro' the window didst discern
The wonted flame, shalt reach the topmost stair
To find no wide eyes watching there,
No withered welcome waiting thy return !
A passing ghost, a smoke-wreath in the air,
The flameless ashes, and the soulless urn,
Warm with the famished fire that lived to burn—
Burn out its lingering life for thy return,
Its last of lingering life for thy return,
Its last of lingering life to light thy late return,
Return, return.

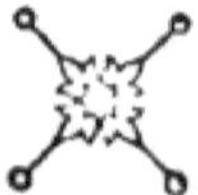

From "BALDER."

Amy's Song of the Willow.

THE years they come, and the years they go,
Like winds that blow from sea to sea ;
From dark to dark they come and go,
All in the dew-fall and the rain.
Down by the stream there be two sweet willows,
—Hush thee, babe, while the wild winds blow,—
One hale, one blighted, two wedded willows
All in the dew-fall and the rain.

She is blighted, the fair young willow,
—Hush thee, babe, while the wild winds blow,—
She hears the spring-blood beat in the bark ;
She hears the spring-leaf bud on the bough ;
But she bends blighted, the wan weeping willow,
All in the dew-fall and the rain.

The stream runs sparkling under the willow,
—Hush thee, babe, while the wild winds blow,—
The summer rose-leaves drop in the stream ;
The winter oak-leaves drop in the stream ;
But she bends blighted, the wan weeping willow,
All in the dew-fall and the rain.

Sometimes the wind lifts the bright stream to her,
—Hush thee, babe, while the wild winds blow,—

The false stream sinks, and her tears fall faster ;
Because she touched it her tears fall faster ;
Over the stream her tears fall faster,
All in the sunshine or the rain.

The years they come, and the years they go ;
Sing well-away, sing well-away !
And under mine eyes shines the bright life-river ;
Sing well-away, sing well-away !
Sweet sounds the spring in the hale green willow,
The goodly green willow, the green waving willow ;
Sweet in the willow, the wind-whispering willow ;
Sing well-away, sing well-away !
But I bend blighted, the wan weeping willow,
All in the sun, and the dew, and the rain.

———

Balder speaks.—I have lingered by the Past
As by a death-bed, with unwonted love
And such forgiveness as we bring to those
Who can offend no more.   The very stones
Of old memorial have been dear to me,
Sitting long days on ancient stiles worm-worn,
And gazing thro' green trees o'er grassy graves
Upon the living village and the dead,
The early and the latter tryst that all
Have kept so long and well ; or to the pile
Reared by those English whose ancestral feet
Trod the same path their children's children keep
Still hallowed, where the beauty of the vale,
The blushing girl of yonder bridal train,
Walks in her love and joy, and passing slow
Salutes unconscious with her wedding skirt
The gable end, no greyer than of yore,

When by the same dark yew for ever old,
The same grey Time did hold his scythe above
Her grandame's head, whose silk of long ago
So rustled on the wall when she went by
A happy bride, and heard perchance that day
Tales from wan lips of the far morning when
Her mother's mother passed as fair as she.
Or on the leafy and live-long repose
Of country labour, and the unhasted life
That plods with equal step the wonted way,
A-field at morn and homeward slow at eve,
And slow with eve and morn through drowsy day
Doth toil and feed and sleep and feed and toil.
Or on lone homesteads and the untrespassed rest
Of immemorial pastures, and the tread
Of dreamful herds in verdant peace unvexed
And taskless thro' the round of sauntering day,
And all the dewy leisure of the meads.

THE CUCKOO-LAMB.

Amy sings.—The cuckoo-lamb is merry on the lea,
The daisied lea ; I would I were the lamb !
While that the lark will pipe, the lamb will dance,
And when the lark is mute he danceth still ;
Up springs the lark, and pipes again for joy !
He, more by birth, than we by toil and skill,
Is happy with no labour but to live ;
He leapeth early, and he leapeth late ;
He leapeth in the sunshine and the rain,
Nor fears the hour that will not find him blest,
And milky plenty sauntering by his side.
Also the lamb that doth not toil nor spin,
Lies where he will, and where he lieth sleeps.

Sleeps on the hill-top like a cloud o' the hill,
Sleeps where the trembling Lily of the Vale,
Albeit she is so spotlesss, sleepeth not,
But like a naked fairy fears all night
The wind that for her beauty cannot sleep.
Sleeps on the nettle or the violet ;
Or where the sun doth warm his trance with light,
Or where the runnel murmureth cool dreams,
Or where the eglantine not yet in bloom,
Like a sweet girl full of her sweeter thought,
Reveals unheard the sweetness still to be.
Or where the darnel nods, and, as they tell
Of beauty nursed upon a savage dug,
Sucks grace from the harsh bosom of the waste.
Sleeps in the meadow butter-cups at noon,
—A babe a-slumber in a golden crib—
Or like a daisy by the way-side white,
And like a daisy quieteth the way.
The lamb, the lamb, I would I were the lamb !

BALDER TO AMY.

                         Thou most pure
And guileless voice, I never breathed thee ! No,
Thou meek misfortune, thou art not my past.
My Amy, my own Amy, whom of old
I found, as a wild sailor of the sea
Comes on some happy isle of Love and Peace,
Some isle where joys that in all other climes,
Sweet flying thro' the night of his dark way,
A moment rest upon his sail, pass on,
And are beheld no more, in equal haunts
And bright assured communion ever dwell,

Day without night, and native, brood and sing !
Thou who thro' the stern ordeal of this life
Didst cling beside me,
 . . . . .

My first Love and my last ; so far, so near,
So strong, so weak, so comprehensible
In these encircling arms, so undescribed
In any thought that shapes thee ; so divine,
So softly human, that to either stretch,
Extreme and farthest tether of desire
It finds thee still ; my ministering saint,
Attendant sprite, enshrined Egeria !
My ornament, my crown, my Indian gem
And incommunicable amulet
Upon my breast, not me but warm with me !

———

Amy. My lord, that walkest thro' the universe,
Did I not go beside thee, as a child,
With humble step and looking to thy face ?

My king, who reignest wheresoe'er thou art !
All do thy hest, my King, but who as I ?
Hast thou not all thy subjects here in me ?

My husband, who hast loved me like a god,
And blessed me, surely I did well to love
Thee as a god ?—but can a god forget ?

Wherein have I offended ? Nay, thy brow
Is sweet and cloudless—I have done no ill.

My husband, have I not been still thy bird,
Thy dove, thy snow-white dove, upon thy wrist,
Or in thy breast, or feeding from thy lips,
Or round thine head, or fluttering with fond feint
Before thy footsteps—with mine eyes on thee?

Was I not as a lamb around thy feet,
That loved thee?   For my neck thou didst entwine
Sweet garlands and I followed thee, nor knew
The inexorable sadness, till a door
Opened, and thou art among men, and I
Am but a lamb, and bleat about the gate.

My husband, I have been an orphan fawn
That ran beside the cubless lioness ;
Who spared her, and did make with her what sport
Befits the offspring of the forest king.
And the poor fawn still gambolled in her blood.

Have I not been a moth about thy light
Scorched, scorched ; but, husband ! when the wound
          was worst,
Winging with madder passion still to thee !

Wert thou nor always as a crescent moon,
And I thy star within thee, till the time
Came, and the lengthening distance, and I knew
My rising and my setting were not thine.

Oh was I not a floweret in thine hand
When thou didst stand upon the peak of thought
Gazing to heaven, which with a thunder-shock
Rolled back, and angels came to thee, and thou
Didst stretch to them thine open hands uplift
In welcome, and I fell to where I am.

I think they touched thine eyes, and that
    thenceforth
Thou seest all things clearly, and me here,
Nor knowest it is very far from thee.
Oh husband ! it is night here in the vale,
And I lie on the rugged earth who had
Thy bosom ; moreover I cannot hear
Thy voice, nor tho' thou seest me can I see
Thy face.   It is not with me as with thee ;
The shadows here are always long and deep,
Also the night comes sooner than to thee.

HAPPY EVE.

Happy eve, happy eve !
But the mavis singing in the eve,
Singeth for the silence of the eve.

Happy flower, happy flower,
But the golden secret of the flower,
Hidden honey sweeter than the flower.

Happy moon, happy moon,
But the loving moonlight of the moon,
Tender wonder fairer than the moon.

Little child, little child,
As the evening mavis unto me,
As the twilight mavis unto me.

Little child, little child,
As the hidden honey unto me,
As the golden honey unto me.

Little child, little child.
As the wondrous moonlight unto me,
As the better moonlight unto me.

Amy.   Is there no hostel by the way of life?
My wayfare was from far as I can see ;
As far my toil is hot and white before ;
I stagger with my load, and halt midway,
And trembling turn beseeching eyes and vain
Backward and forward from my pitiless place.
The weary miles lie infinite beyond,
And each might be the future and the past.
I would lay down my burden lest I die.
Is there no hostel by the way of life ?

Balder.   Tnis very morn
Thro' her green island home the laughing spring
Drove, flinging joy, her blossom-laden car.
Forth from the polar cavern of the snows,
Dripping with winter, leaped a northern storm,
And shook himself ; and she lay buried white
Beneath an avalanche.   At that dread sight
Up rose the West, and such a wind went by
As stunned the isle with voices, like a chief,
Rushing to battle with a sounding host
In shouting ranks wide on the echoing hills.
At first a roar of warning, " To the north ! "
Then like the shriek of all a ravished land,
" O Europe, Europe, Europe, Europe, Europe ! "
And then like the world's trumpet blown to war,
" The North, the North, the North, the North, the
      North ! "

SAILORS' SONG.

" How many? " said our good Captain.
" Twenty sail and more."
We were homeward bound,
Scudding in a gale with our jib towards the Nore.
Right athwart our tack,
The foe came thick and black,
Like Hell-birds and foul weather—you might count them
　　by the score.

The Betsy Jane did slack
To see the game in view.
They knew the Union Jack,
And the tyrant's flag we knew!
Our Captain shouted " Clear the decks!" and the
　　Bo'sun's whistle blew.

Then our gallant Captain,
With his hand he seized the wheel,
And pointed with his stump to the middle of the foe.
" Hurrah, lads, in we go ! "
(You should hear the British cheer,
Fore and aft.)

" There are twenty sail," sang he,
" But little Betsy Jane bobs to nothing on the sea !"
(You should hear the British cheer,
Fore and aft.)

" See yon ugly craft
With the pennon at her main !
Hurrah, my merry boys,
There goes the Betsy Jane !"
(You should hear the British cheer,
Fore and aft.)

The foe, he beats to quarters, and the Russian bugles
          sound ;
      And the little Betsy Jane she leaps upon the sea.
      " Port and starboard ! " cried our Captain ;
      " Pay it in, my hearts ! " sang he,
      " We're old England's sons,
      And we'll fight for her to-day ! "
      (You should hear the British cheer,
      Fore and aft.)
              " Fire away ! "
      In she runs,
      And her guns
      Thunder round.

AMY'S SONG.

Neither gold nor silver, oh ye heavens !
Only a little sunshine and sweet air,
The sunshine and the air of the old days !
Only to be a feather on the stream,
A thistle-plume upon the changing wind
Hither and thither ; to go to and fro
And up and down the joyance of the world,
The happy world, and be a part of all.

Ye are now unto me, oh ye bright heavens,
As one who should misuse the deaf and blind
In secret, but full loud when men are by
Speaketh rich words of love into the ears
That hear not, and before the sightless eyes
Makes vain ado of all they cannot see.

I pray ye ope the lattice of my soul
And let the wind blow on me ere I die,
And let me hold my forehead to the light,
And let me feel the falling of the dews,
And know the holy blessing of the rain !

Balder.   Had it been my portion here
With these obedient limbs and iron aid
Of some unconscious instrument to dig
The unquestionable soil, so that this hand
Thus armed should with no further cost than throes
Of definite volition—as to grasp,
To sink, to raise,—complete the stated dues
Of daily labour !

              Were I born to plough,
While the lark drops upon his meal, the long
Material black and measurable furrow,
Whereof the brute sense of returning steer,
Treading the line, observant, testifies
That it is made indeed, and grossest clown
Who holds two eyes in use is a critic
Superfluously endowed !

              Happier to drive
The patient ass along the beaten way,
Laden with humble fruits to the set mart
Of fixed reward, and back to certain rest,
And sweet assured possession, than like me
Bound helpless on the fury of the winds,
To scour the plains I seek not, scale the height
Where my brain swims, and leap, as in a dream,
Down into the unfathomable void. . . .

Amy.   If thou wouldst sleep, my babe, if thou
          wouldst sleep
And weary of the never-ending day !
Thou hast not milked me of my sorrow, babe,
Why must thou moan and watch and wake like me ?

My babe, my babe, is it not well with thee ?
And if not well, the end is come indeed.

My place was dark, and o'er a darker place
A great hand held me that I could not see.

Below us the dark gulph, for ever deep,
Above us, thro' the dark, a light of day,
And thou wert as a jewel on my breast,
Sweet shining in the light that lit not me.
The hand is weary with upholding me !
If ill hath touched thee, babe, we are given o'er,
Given o'er and dropt, a pillage and a prey !
Ah ! in the dark gulph what shall not seize thee !

If thou wouldst sleep, my baby, if thou wouldst
     sleep,
Nor scare me with the mystery of thine eyes.

Alas, thy parted lips, my babe, my babe !
Alas, the hot breath from the cankered rose !
Alas, the little limbs ! Alas, the heart
That beateth like a wounded butterfly !
My babe, my babe, what hath befallen thee ?

I see it all ; I see, I see it all !
How couldst thou lie upon my breast and live ?
The doom has run its date, the hour is here !
Not enough, babe, oh ! not enough, my babe.

That I who was the favourite and the flower,
Bruised and beaten by a thousand ills,
As to the utter shelter and mere shed
Of this great gilded palace-world did creep
With thee, not wholly lost since thou wert not,
Nor in my desolation desolate,
Because the glory could not give thee more
Than me, or the bare walls of sorrow less.
My babe, it was too good for thee and me.
God hath abandoned us, and from His home
Is driving forth the mother and her child.

My child, my child, the wolf is in the way,
And what if he doth choose the suckling lamb?

———

Balder.—One can be brave
At noon, and with triumphant logic clear
The demonstrable air, but ne'ertheless,
Sometimes at Hallowe'en when, legends say,
The things that stir among the rustling trees
Are not all mortal, and the sick white moon
Wanes o'er the season of the sheeted dead,
We grow unreasonable and do quake
With more than the cold wind.   The very soul,
Sick as the moon, suspects her sentinels,
And thro' her fortress of the body peers
Shivering abroad ; our heart-strings over-strung,
Scare us with strange involuntary notes
Quivering and quaking, and the creeping flesh
Knows all the starting horrors of surprise
But that which makes them, and for that, half-wild,
Quickens the winking lids, and glances out
From side to side, as if some sudden chance

Of vision, some unused slant of the eye,
Some accidental focus of the sight
O' th' instant might reveal a peopled world
Crowding about us, and the empty light
Alive with phantoms.　　Doubtless there are no
　　　ghosts ;
Yet somehow it is better not to move
Lest cold hands seize upon us from behind
Or forward thro' the dim uncertain time
Face close with paly face.　　My ominous dream
Leaves me in shuddering incredulity
As logically white.

———

If to the long mysterious trance of death
There be immortal waking, he who lifts
His head from the clay pillow, and doth stretch
Eternal life thro' all his quickening limbs,
And conscious on his opening orbs receives
Remembered light, and rises to be sure
He hath revived indeed, tastes in that first
Best moment what the infinite beyond
Can never give again.

———

Amy.　　My heart is shivered as a fallen cup,
And all the golden wine is in the earth.

My heart is stricken, and it cannot heal.
Tho' thou art but a little grave I know,
O little grave, it will bleed into thee
For evermore, and thou wilt not be filled.

The fountains of my fate are dry ; my soul
Is dying in the famine of my lot.
I am a dead leaf in a wintry wind ;
My stem is broken from the tree of life,
I wither in the sun and in the air,
I wither in the rain and in the dews.

And though the wind doth throw me on the tree,
Oh wind ! thou canst not bind what thou didst break ;
I wither in the verdure of the leaves.—
Beneath my window built the nightingale ;
Ah cruel, who despoiled her happy nest !
And in his wanton gripe he crushed her egg,
Her one lone egg ;—so doth Fate crush my heart.

The spring returns unto the nightingale,
The nightingale shall find a happier tree ;
The ravished nest must drift upon the day,
The wind shall toss it as an idle straw,
The rain shall tread its ruins to the earth,
And I am all despoiled for evermore.

Amy. Oh wounded dove, oh dove with broken
          wing,
Oh dying dove, wert thou not beautiful ?
Why didst thou hide thee, trembler, from the day,
And strain into the crevice of the cliff,
And press thy beating breast against the hill,
As if the rock should ope and let thee in ?

I took thee to my heart, oh snow-white dove,
I would have kissed and kissed thee o'er and o'er,
But thou wert fierce with fear, and with wild eyes
Didst turn upon me like a frantic maid
That struggles with a lover in the dark,
Bruising the hands that would have cherished her,

And gnashing on the lips that seek her own.
Oh dove, I also fall with broken wing,
I also strive and turn upon my fate,
And strike the inevitable hands in vain.
I also strain my bosom to the earth,
The earth that will not ope and let me in.

THE SWALLOW.

Swallow, that yearly art blown round the world,
What seekest thou that never may be found ?
Whither for ever sailing and to sail !
I think the gulphs have sucked thine haven down,
And thou still steerest for the vanished strand.
What cheer, what cheer, oh fairy marinere
Of windy billows, sea-mew of the air ?
The viewless oceans wash thee to and fro,
Spout thee to Heaven, and dive thee to the deep.
Swallow ! I also seek and do not find.

MILTON.

I ne'er see Milton, but I see the Alps,
As once sole standing on a peak supreme,
To the extremest verge summit and gulph
I saw, height after depth, Alp beyond Alp,
O'er which the rising and the sinking soul
Sails into distance, heaving as a ship
O'er a great sea that sets to strands unseen.
And as the mounting and descending bark
Borne on exulting by the under deep,
Gains of the wild wave something not the wave,
Catches a joy of going, and a will

Resistless, and upon the last lee foam
Leaps into air beyond it, so the soul
Upon the Alpine ocean mountain-tost,
Incessant carried up to heaven, and plunged
To darkness, and still wet with drops of death
Held into light eternal, and again
Cast down, to be again uplift in vast
And infinite succession, cannot stay
The mad momentum, but in frenzied sight
Of horizontal clouds and mists and skies
And the untried Inane, springs on the surge
Of things, and passing matter by a force
Material, thro' vacuity careers,
Rising and falling.

ENGLAND.

          This dear English land !
This happy England, loud with brooks and birds,
Shining with harvests, cool with dewy trees,
And bloomed from hill to dell ; but whose best
    flowers
Are daughters, and Ophelia still more fair
Than any rose she weaves ; whose noblest floods
The pulsing torrent of a nation's heart ;
Whose forests stronger than her native oaks
Are living men ; and whose unfathomed lakes,
For ever calm, the unforgotten dead
In quiet graveyards willowed seemly round,
O'er which To-day bends sad, and sees his face.
Whose rocks are rights, consolidate of old
Thro' unremembered years, around whose base
The ever-surging peoples roll and roar
Perpetual, as around her cliffs the seas
That only wash them whiter ; and whose mountains,

Souls that from this mere footing of the earth
Lift their great virtues thro’ all clouds of Fate
Up to the very heavens, and make them rise
To keep the gods above us !

CHARITY.

Learn this, my friend,
The secret that doth make a flower a flower,
So frames it that to bloom is to be sweet,
And to receive to give.   The flower can die,
But cannot change its nature; though the earth
Starve it, and the reluctant air defraud,
No soil so sterile and no living lot
So poor but it hath somewhat still to spare
In bounteous odours.   Charitable they
Who, be their having more or less, *so* have
That less is more than need, and more is less
Than the great heart’s goodwill.

SPRING.

Spring, who did scatter all her wealth last year,
Had gone to heaven for more ; and coming back
Flower-laden after three full seasons, found
The Earth, her mother, dead.

Far off, appalled
With the unwonted pallor of her face,
She flung her garlands down, and caught, distract,
The skirts of passing tempests, and thro’ wilds
Of frozen air fled to her, all uncrowned
With haste,—a bunch of snowdrops in her breast,
Her charms dishevelled, and her cheeks as white
As winter with her woe.   She fell upon

The corse, and warmed it.   The maternal earth,
Which was not dead, but slept, unclosed her eyes.
Then Spring, o'crawed at her own miracle,
Fell on her knees ; and then she smiled and wept.
Meanwhile the attendant birds her haste outstripped,
Chasing her voice, crowd round and fill the air
With jocund loyalty ; and eager winds,
Her suitors, at full speed with Love and wild,
Hie by her in the lusty cheer of March,
Crying her name.   Laughed Spring to see them pass,
—Laughing in tears.   Then it repented her
To see the old parental limbs of Earth
Lie stark as death ; and fared she forth alone
To where she left her burden in the void
Beyond the south horizon ; her fair hair
Streaming spring clouds among the vernal stars.
Returning slow, with flowers, she dressed the Earth
Which had sat up, and, being naked, blushed
And stretched her conscious arms to meet the Spring,
Who breathed upon her face, and made her young.
Then did her mother Earth rejoice in her ;
And she with filial love and joy admired,
Weeping and trembling in the wont of maids.
Meantime her pious fame had filled the skies ;
He that begat her, the almighty Sun,
Passing in regal state, did call her "child,"
And blessed her and her mother where they sat—
Her by the imposition of bright hands,
The Earth with kisses.   Then the Spring would go,
Abashed with bliss, decorous in the face
Of love parental.   But the Earth stood up,
And held her there ; and, them encircling, came
All kind of happy shapes that wander space,
Brightening the air.   And they two sang like gods
Under the answering heavens.

SUMMER.

                              Summer,
Mother of gods and men, with equal face
Unchangeable, and such wide eyes divine
As on the Athenian hill-top Phidian Jove
Inherited ; whose universal sense
Seems made with ampler vision to behold
A larger world than ours.   She leans in light
On rose-leaves, as a long and lazy cloud
Leans on the broad bed of the blushing west.
In her right hand a horn of plenty, red
With fragrant fruits exuberant ; in her left
The early harvest ; crowned with oak and ash,
Her hot feet slippered in the calid seas.
Her voice is like the murmur of the floods
Sluggard with noon, or the thick-leaved response
Of sultry forests to the languid winds
Dull with the dog-days.

AUTUMN.

He stands beside a throne of golden hills,
And up the steep steps of the royal throne
The burdened forests climb like countless slaves
Laden with gold.   He stands and heeds them not ;
Meanwhile his hand, with air abstract and wan,
From the abounding tribute of the earth
Scatters imperial largesse.   All her fields
Are his ; they own their lord ; his barns are full,
His rivers run with wine, and his red plains
Shout with the vintage.   Yet he stands beside
His golden throne, and looketh up to heaven,
And sigheth in the melancholy winds,

And smileth sweeter sadness.   He hath learned
The lesson of power ; therefore his locks are sere,
Therefore there is no light in the sunk eyes
Which day and night reproach the sun and stars
With the unsated hunger of a soul
That is no richer tho' the world be won.

The Death of Autumn.

Sometimes an aged king upon his bed,
He dieth 'mid the conscious hush of all
His reverent realm, and silent snows him wind.
Or, haply, at midnight a choir of winds
Chanting great anthems, bear him to his rest.
And sometimes doing battle with his fate,
A wreathèd wrestler from a gorge of wine,
He falls in pride ; a giant in his blood,
Dashed with the purple feast as to his robes
Of azure triumph and his golden crown
Olympic, while his dying eye on fire
Brings a red glow into the cheeks of Death,
His ghastly foe, and his felled stature shakes
The sounding halls.
           And sometimes as a maid
Dead and undone, the pale and drowned year
Lies still and silent on the mortal shore,
With dank unmeaning lips and sightless eyes
Ooze-filled, and blanch limbs stark and stiff beyond
The draggled robes soaked with a colder death.
And sometimes as a trusting maid who waits
Her far false lover, and thro' long lone hours
Expects in vain, but as the sun goes down,
Chilled with the bitter day where love is not,

Blighted and mute, astonied beyond speech,
Stands utterless ; while all within is changed
From life to death, and under that pale breast
Unheaving and those glittering eyes transacts
The alchemy of ruin.   Nor she weeps,
Nor starts, nor shrieks, nor throws her arms to heaven,
But motionless and crimson with her wrong
Dies in her silence, and falls still as leaves
Thro' stiller air.

WINTER.

Who is he
That o'er green pastures of the latter year,
And on the mountain-tops, and through the woods
Passeth amid the pageant of the world
Silent and ceaseless, laying hand on nought?
Not as content, for greed is in his eye,
But patient in the confidence of fate.
Downward in face, and as to his bent head
Covered ; by night and day, in sun or rain,
Unlooked for, unforeseen, but ever found,
And keeping ever on an aimless way
With the firm foot of purpose, as in dreams
We walk to airy biddings, and as on
A king's death-day, while all the court stand round
Power unresigned, the inevitable heir
Doth eye the crown and pace the palace floors
Expectant.   But none know him for a king
Nor do him homage.   The too-lusty green
Of the o'er-confident time unawed stands out
Into his path, and the insulting growth
Below retards his unrespected feet.

He sees, and a cold smile comes on his face
As moonlight upon ice ; the shivering wind
Starts from his side, and fleeing ominous,
Spreads such a sign as in the latter day
Shall blow from chill Damascus ; but no roll
Of answering thunder nor dread bolt of wrath
Smites the roused world that listens and forgets.
Yet some are wise.   With him on hill-tops hoar
The o'erruling spirits and attentive hours
Confer, and seek and take his high behest
In secret, and make peace with things to come.
And failing Autumn, like an aged king,
Talked with him on the field of cloth of gold,
And as he spake fell dead ; and the lush powers,
And pleasures full, which ruled the summer reign
(Like ships on a calm sea, that, sinking slow,
Of all their gallant bulk above the wave
Leave but a naked mast) sank one by one
Into the earth, and in the wonted place
Were found in lesser fashion, daily less.
And now the fields are empty, but He walks
Hale and unminished to and fro and up
And down, and more and more the observance
Of the astonished year is turned and turned
Upon the Solitary, and the leaves
Grow wan with conscience, and a-sudden fall
Liege at his feet, and all the naked trees
Mourn audibly, lifting appealing arms.
Which when he knew, as a pale smoke that grows
Keeping its shape, he rose into the air
And froze it, and the broad land blanched with fear,
And every breathless stream and river stopped,
And thro' him, walking white and like a ghost
With grim unfurnished limbs, the cold light passed
And cast no shade.   Then was he king indeed,

And all the undefended World he saw
Bare at his will.   His brow grew black on her;
And with a sound that killed her shuddering heart,
He whistled for the North.

DAWN.

See her in naked beauty, calm as snow,
And cradled in a cloud upon the east.
Unblushed, unconscious, with unopened lids,
Fair as the first of women where she lay
Among the asphodels of Paradise
Before God breathed for her the breath of life.

MORN.

                    Lo, Morn,
When she stood forth at universal prime,
The angels shouted, and the dews of joy
Stood in the eyes of earth.   While here she reigned
Adam and Eve were full of orisons,
And could not sin.   And so she won of God
That ever when she walketh in the world
It shall be Eden.   And around her come
The happy wonts of early Paradise.
Again the mist ascendeth from the earth
And watereth the ground, and at the sign
Nature, that silent saw our woe, breaks forth
Into her olden singing, near and far
The full and voluntary chorus tune
Spontaneous throats, and the ten thousand strings

That by meridian day, being struck, give out
A muffled answer, peal their notes, and ring
Reverberating music.   Once again
The heavens forget their limits, pinions bright
O'er-passing mix the ethereal bounds with ours,
And winds of morning lead between their wings
Ambrosial odours and celestial airs
Warm with the voices of a better world.
Dews to the early grass, Light to the eyes,
Brooks to the murmuring hills, Spring to the earth,
Sweet winds to opening flowers, MORN to the heart !
But more than dew to grass or light to eyes
Or brooks to murmuring hills or spring to earth
Or winds to opening flowers, MORN to the heart !
Once more to live is to be happy ; Life
With backward-streaming hair and eyes of haste
That look beyond the hills, doth urge no more
Her palpitating feet ; her wild hair falls
Soft thro' the happy light upon her limbs,
She turns her wondering gaze upon herself,
Sweet saying—" It is good."   Once more the soul
Rises in Eden to immortal gifts,
And by the side of morning,—new from heaven,
Fresh from the stores of all things, and within
Her limpid face still wearing reflex bright
Of joys that shall be,—dances glad with strange
Unutterable Knowledge.   We are healed ;
The curse falls from our eyelids ; all the thorns
And thistles that do plague us, clad in gems
Stand round ; and we behold them as they are,
And call them jewelled friends.   All fetters break ;
From the tremendous girdle that doth round
The globe and keep her, to these heavy bonds
That bind us to her, and whose last stronghold
Is clenched in central fires.   We are not dogs

Nailed to a needful den, but wingèd lions,
And walk the earth from choice,—the fair free earth
That willeth to be here, and cares not yet
To mount up like a coloured cloud to God.
The pulse of Being flows, the ill that ran
Along her veins, the hand of Incubus
Upon her throat, are gone like night !   All things
Do well, and still his function is to each
Consummate welfare.   As the unheeded garb
Upon the rising and the falling breast
Of beauty, that still moveth as she moves,
Breathes with her breath and quivers with her sighs,
So Nature's varied robe lies light on her,
The beautiful broad surface of the world
And all its kingdoms.   Memory that stirred
And murmured thro' the helpless dreamy dark,
Snuffing the eternal air, sinks silent down
To utter sleep, for whereas day that is
Bendeth beneath the golden multitude
Of all the days that have been, each to-morrow
Heavier for yesterday, Morn hath no past.
Primeval, perfect, she, not born to toil,
Steppeth from under the great weight of life,
And stands as at the first.

                    The feast is spread,
And none know wherefore.   Wherefore ? who shall
      ask ?
Who cannot feast ?   As a rich bride in smiles
And blushes for her much bliss eateth not,
And seeth that they serve a sacrament
And something more than wine, the poet sits.
While Who stood glorious at the shining head
Of jubilee, where men a light beheld
And he a presence, clad in sounding joy

Moves down the festal aisles.   As a true queen,
In whose ennobling eyes her lowliest guests
Are princes, so she slow descends to far
Forgotten places, and with her mere smile
Rights the unequal board.   Light shines to light
Down to the earth and upward to the heaven,
And whatsoe'er unknown it is whereof
Our lives default, whatever of divine
Whose all irreparable absence makes
The nameless dolour of a mortal day,
Returns in full.   As love, that hath his cell
In the deep secret heart, doth with his breath
Enrich the precincts of his sanctuary
And glorify the brow and tint the cheek ;
As in a summer garden one beloved
Whom roses hide, unseen fills all the place
With happy presence ; as to the void soul
Beggared with famine and with drought, lo God !
And there is great abundance ; so comes MORN,
Plenishes all things and completes the world.

FAIRIES.

                I knew a family
Of fairies.   Thou wouldst hear their history ?
But how ?   I cannot speak of them apart ;
Nay, hardly of the matter of this breath
May frame their common story.   Our least word
Too palpable is grosser than the strength
Of all, as one bright water-drop contains
An animalcular people.   Oberon,
Step forth, and let me fit thee with a sound
Wherein from top to toe thou wouldst not stand

Hid as an urchin in his grandsire's coat !
Their dwelling-place was by the water's edge
Under a stone.   The mosses of the brink
Spread ample shade with branching arms at noon,
And there each day they lay at ease, all three
Singing a drowsy chorus like the hum
Of hovering gnat above a bed at night,
Heard when the house is still.   Such needful rest
Concludes the daily feast ;—a grain of grass
In no more honey-dew than loads an ant
Driven like an ass before them.   Once a day
They fed at home, but morn and eve I saw
Where in green ambush under milking kine,
Looking up, all, as to a precipice,
They watched the pail, and when the white plash fell
Cupped in some patent floweret, gathering round,
Climbed the laborious stem, and bending o'er,
Drank deep ; which done, they seek the lucid lake,
And sailing forth in pride, the emerald wing
Of summer beetle is a barge of state ;
Her cock-boat, red and black, the painted scale
Of lady-fly aft in the fairy wake
Towed by a film, and tossed perchance in storm,
When airy martlet, sipping of the pool,
Touches it to a ripple that stirs not
The lilies.   Thus I knew the tiny band,
Nor only so, but singly, and of each
The several favour ; yet I can but speak
With organs made to tell of gods and men.
Thou who wouldst know them better *think* the rest,
And with some fine suggestion which has taste
Of a remembered odour, silent sweet,
Or what rare power divides the last result
Of mortal touch, and to the atomy
Gives an unnamed interior, or what sense

Responds the tremors of the soul and takes
The sound of wings that, unbeheld by eyes,
Mystic and seldom thro' its upper air
Pass as in wandering flight ; therewith behold
My vision, and therewith accept the parts
Of the so delicate whole which my strained care
Brought not unminished, nor could bring, but found
As 'twere an elfin draught in faëry cup,
And to be spilled by the mere pulse of hands
Like mine.   Therewith attach each separate grace
Of those thus fair together ; know what made
Each brother beauteous, what more subtle charm
The lovelier sister, and what golden hair
Hung over her as sometimes shimmereth light
From smallest dew-drop, else unseen, that crowns
The slimmest grass of all the shaven green
At morning.   Love them by their names, for names
They had, and speech that any word of ours
Would drop between its letters uncontained ;
Love them, but hope not for impossible knowledge.
In their small language they are not as we ;
Nor could, methinks, deliver with the tongue
Our gravid notions ; nor of this our world
They speak, tho' earth-born, but have heritage
From our confines, and property in all
That thro' the net of our humanity
Floats down the stream of things.   Inheriting
Below us even as we below some great
Intelligence, in whose more general eyes
Perchance Mankind is one.   Neither have fear
To scare them, drawing nigh, nor with thy voice
To roll their thunder.   Thy wide utterance
Is silence to the ears it enters not,
Raising the attestation of a wind,
No more.   As we, being men, nor hear but see

The clamour and the nniversal tramp
Of stars, and the continual Voice of God
Calling above onr heads to all the world.

CHAMOUNI.

If
Thou hast known anywhere amid a storm
Of thunder, when the Heavens and Earth were moved,
A gleam of quiet sunshine that hath saved
Thine heart; Or where the earthquake hath made
    wreck,
Knowest a stream, that wandereth fair and sweet
As brooks go singing thro' the fields of home ;
Or on a sudden when the sea distent
With windy pride, upriseth thro' the clouds
To set his great head equal with the stars
Hast sunk Hell-deep, thy noble ship a straw
Betwixt two billows ; Or in any wild
Barbaric, hast, with half-drawn breath, passed by
The sleeping savage, dreadful still in sleep,
Scarred by a thousand combats, by his side
His rugged spouse—in aught but sex a chief—
Their babe between ; Or where the stark roof-tree
Of a burnt home blackened and scar lies dark,
Betwixt the gaunt-ribbed ruin, hast thou seen
The rose of peace ; Or in some donjon deep,
Rent by a giant in the blasted rock
And proof against his peers,—hast thou behold
Prone in the gloom, naked and shining sad
In her own light of loveliness, a fair
Daughter of Eve : Then as thou seest God
In some material likeness, less and more,

Thou hast seen Chamouni, 'mid sternest Alps
The gentlest valley ; bright meandering track
Of summer when she winds among the snows
From Land to Land.   Behold its fairest field
Beneath the bolt-scarred forehead of the hills
Low lying, like a heart of sweet desires,
Pulsing all day a living beauty deep
Into the sullen secrets of the rocks.
Tender as Love amid the Destinies
And Terrors ; whereabout the great heights stand
Down-gazing, like a solemn company
Of grey heads met together to look back
Upon a far fond memory of youth.
Northward and southward of my hut, from heaven
To earth, two gates of ice shut in the scene,
As tho' between twin icebergs a green sea
Had melted, and the summer sun and sky
Shone in the waters.   All the vale is flowers.
Take thy staff shod with iron, gird thy loins
For conflict.   Let us to the northern gate !
Is this a wood of pines ?   Are these but rocks,
Hurled by the winter tempest ?   Did a chance
O'erthrow these trunks—in the stern wont of war
Supine ?   Or was it here the Thunderer smote
The Giants—and the battered remnant stand
Astonied giving glory to the Heavens ?
Aye, these are pines ; but thou shalt turn and break
The hugest on thy knee, having once passed
Out of their umbrage, and in open day
Fronted the everlasting looks of them
Who sit beyond in council ; round whose feet
Are wrapped the shaggy forests, and whose beards,
Down from the great height unapproachable,
Descend upon their breasts.   There, being old,
All days and years they maunder on their thrones

Mountainous mutterings, or thro’ the vale
Roll the long roar from startled side to side
When whoso, lifting up his sudden voice,
A moment speaketh of his meditation,
And thinks again.   There shalt thou learn to stand
One in that company, and to commune
With them, saying, “Thou, oh Alp, and thou, and thou,
        thou,
And I.”   Nathless, proud equal, look thou take
Heed of thy peer, lest he perceive thee not,—
Lest the wind blow his garment, and the hem
Crush thee, or lest he stir, and the mere dust
In the eternal folds bury thee quick !
The forest now behind thee, at thy feet
The torrent, thrust thine head back as who seeks
The pole-star ; and above the mountains green,
And o’er the shepherd’s shealing,—less than nest
On tree-top—and o’er woods that are as moss,
Black on a ruin,—over the icy sea
—A billowy Sibir of ten thousand hills
As tho’ yon white rocks, bending evermore
So potently above the floods, begat
A likeness, and from out their yielding breasts
Compelled a brood of stone—o’er naked crags,—
Aye, above where the shyest roe unseen
Draws the thin breath, and marmot cannot pass
The inexorable famine,—over wilds
For ever dead, and snow, and upper snow,
And wastes above the snow, see nearer heaven
The base of a great pyramid, and rise
Slow to this peak, like a grey pinnacle
Of the towered earth piercing the cloudless skies.
To us how calm and lonely, tenantless
And silent as the still and empty air,
But to that height the seldom mountaineer

Looks from the extremest footing of some ridge
Incredible, three times beyond our ken,
And to his keen and upward-straining eyes
Round it midway the circling eagles sail,
As daws that round some thin and distant spire
On English hill, scarce seen thro' lucent air,
Are motes in the evening sun.
                              Now, if thou durst,
Drop from the Alp to lowest vale remote
Breathless ; nor be the first in that great fall.
So yon dark glacier from his native snows
Fell on the narrow valley, which beneath,
Like a poor foundered skiff, when some vast whale
In his unwieldy death-pang leaps and falls,
Is sunk and lost.   Grim with mortality,
War-stained he lies in heavy length, and bleeds,
A hill of death.   Behold aloft the seas
Whence he came down, unmelting seas of snow
Well-named, the ocean of a frozen world.
A marble storm in monumental rage,
Ploughed on the fragment of a shattered moon.
Passion at nought and strength still strong in vain,
A wrestling giant, spell-bound, but not dead.
As tho' the universal deluge passed
These confines, and when forty days were o'er
Knew the set time obedient and arose
In haste : but Winter lifted up his hand
And stayed the everlasting sign which strives
For ever to return.   Cold crested tides
And cataracts more white than wintry foam
Eternally in act of the great leap
That never may be ta'en, these fill the gorge
And rear upon the steep uplifted waves
Immovable, that proudly feign to go,—
And on the awful ramparts of the rock

Bend forward, as in motion—side by side
Mixed manifold, rank after mingling rank,
In all the throng of multitude, but each
Condign, and in a personality
Confest.　Nor from the valley seen as waves.
But as lone shepherd, on some battle hill,
At setting of a chill moon on the wane,
Beholds his heroes from their unknown graves
Snow-cold, with blades of ice, out of the night,
The peopled peopling night, o'er airy crag
Crowding unstaunched invasion, with consent
Of hands that point advance, and martial gaze
Of helmèd heads, silent, majestical,—
All ghosts !　Or as some great acropolis,
Above the wondering eyes of ancient men,
On sacred feast, a statuary host
Sent out her idols round the incandent hill,
And all her marble deities went by
In solemn march, tall, white, innumerable,
Each after each divine ; while far beneath,
Lone, like some shattered pillar of the skies,
Half-buried by his fall, headlong and prone,
The broken worship of a ruder race,
A Greater lay.　Or so methinks of old,
Below a mount of Jewry, Dagon fell
Before the Highest ; and in him subdued
From their high seats, fair bowers, dim haunts
　　beloved,
And temples of the abdicated earth,
Upon a day the great mythology
Came forth by legions to behold the sign.
Dethroned, discrowned, divestured ; with bare brows
Paler than men ; proud whispering as they pass,
In murmur of a thousand waterfalls,
While somewhat like the finger of the world

Pointeth above their heads into the heavens,
And crash as of avenging thunderbolts
Pursues them,—nor can haste the step of gods.
Low in the abject earth lies Chamouni,—
Low in the last profound, whose narrow deep
Seems from you midway and diminished peak—
So hunters say—who, clinging to the rock,
Dizzy look down—a gulph of mountain-mist,
Rainbowed, or if substantial, sunk and lost,
Drowned in the abyss of air, and lapsed below
Terrestrial, hopeless in a void of dreams.
Beheld as one should spy from upper wave
Of seas unsounded fathomless and dark,
Low, thro' mysterious waters infinite,
Illumined by a gleam, some jewelled mine
Emerald and ruby flashing dreamy gold,
Rent in the nether bed of the mid-main.
Nor less above yon midway crag the calm
Unventured summit, than if who descried
The deep-sea gulph, with sudden gaze revert,
Sees from his span of footing on the wave
Far in unearthly ether unassailed,
A great white cloud serene in sacred light
And happy skies.

                          Here, in the lowest vale,
Sit we beside the torrent, till the goats
Come tinkling home at eve, with pastoral horn
Slow down the winding way, plucking sweet grass
Amid the yellow pansies and harebells blue.
            "The milk is warm,
            The cakes are brown ;
            The flax is spun,
            The kine are dry,
            The bed is laid,

> The children sleep ;
> Come, husband, come,
> To home and me."

So sings the mother as she milks within
The chalet near thee; singing so for him
Whom every morn she sendeth forth alone
Into the waste of mountains, to return
At close of day as a returning soul
Out of the infinite ; lost in the whirl
Of clanging systems and the wilderness
Of all things, but to one remembered tryst,
One human heart and unforgotten cell,
True in its ceaseless self, and in its time
Restored.   But now the dusk which like a tarn
Lay long since in the hollows of the hills,
Swells from deep caves and tributary glens
Unnumbered, till the lower mountain tops
Are covered, and the dull and dead sea line
Rests tideless on a shore of sacred snow.
And now an unknown trouble has made cold
Those higher Alpine foreheads whence supreme
Over our darkness a serener day
Looked westward and to all that we saw not,
The glory and the loss.   For they do watch
The journey of the setting sun as one
Who when the weaker inmates of the house
Have sunk about his feet in dews and shades
Of sorrow, watches still with brow of light
And manly eye a brother on his way ;
But when the lessening face shines no return
Thro' distance slowly lengthening and sinks slow
Behind the hill-top, nor him, looking back,
The straining sense discerns, nor the far sound
Of wheels, stands fixed in sudden gloom profound,
And thoughts more stern than woe.

                         Over those heights
Untrod, nor to be trodden, let thy soul
Pass like a fleeting sunshine.   Let it glide
Over the summit, southward, and descend
Where, thro' black mountains, a great river of snow
Banked by two Alps, from the eternal source
Whiter than clouds between the awful shores
Shines to the valley.   Meantime we below
Tread the dark vale uplooking ; or sit long,
With hopeless upturned eyes, as one let down
Into the abyss of everlasting night,
From the impossible deep should gaze in vain
Up through the silent chaos to the skirts
Of ordered Nature.   What is he, unseen,
Who with the dreadful glacier as a sceptre
Touches the vale, and in his left hand holds
Yon rounded summit as an orb of state ?
Thou canst not see them now, but forth to meet
The sovereign symbol, venerable woods
Climb the huge steep where age and pride allow,
And send their lither progeny to scale
The bleaker rock, ambitious.   These, inured,
Attain the lower precipice, nor blench,
Storm-bred : but these fall back aghast in sight
Of everlasting Winter, where, snow-borne,
In his white realm, for ever white, he sits
Invisible to men ; and in his works
Gives argument of that which, seen, makes faint
Aspiring Nature, and his throne a mount
Not to be touched.   On either wilderness
A snow-land spreads along the level skies.
Now from the eastward midnight draweth nigh,
When all things rest from labour.   As she goes
Her vestments floating shut out moon and stars
Mysterious ; and she breathes before her face

Darkness where all is dark.　　Mute goeth she,
And silently on either hand unyokes
The willing mountains from beneath their load
Even now dispersing while the valley shakes,
And in his bed the sleeping peasant stirs,
And dreams of thunder.　　They, beheld no more,
Leave only to the cataracts, and thee,
The great snow baseless in mid-heaven, self-shown,
Out-stretched and equal, like supporting wings,
Or thro' the windy and tumultuous dark
Down the long glacier sounding to the vale.
There was a legend wild, whispered at eve,
Late round the dying watch-fires to awed men,
In those dead seasons whence our Danish sires,
Of the Great Arctic Ghost, the efficient power
And apparition of the frozen North,
The mystic swan of Norna, the dread bird
Of destiny, world wide, with roaring wings,
Flapping the ice-wind and the avalanche,
And white and terrible as polar snows.
By them unseen behold it ! thro' the night
Swooping from heaven, its head to earth, its neck
Down-streaming from the cloud ; above the cloud
Its great vans thro' a rolling dust of stars
Thunderous descending in a rush of fate.

AN EVEN-SONG.

In the spring twilight, in the coloured twilight
Whereto the latter primroses are stars,
And early nightingale
Letteth her love adown the tender wind,
That thro' the eglantine

In mixed delight the fragrant music bloweth
On to me,
Where in the twilight, in the coloured twilight,
I sit beside the thorn upon the hill.
The mavis sings upon the old oak tree
Sweet and strong,
Strong and sweet,
Soft, sweet, and strong,
And with his voice interpreteth the silence
Of the dim vale when Philomel is mute !
The dew lies like a light upon the grass,
The cloud is as a swan upon the sky,
The mist is as a brideweed on the moon.
The shadows new and sweet
Like maids unwonted in the dues of joy
Play with the meadow flowers,
And give with fearful fancies more and less,
And come, and go, and flit
A brief emotion in the moving air,
And now are stirred to flight, and now are kind,
Unset, uncertain, as the cheek of Love.
As tho' amid the eve
Stood Spring with fluttering breast,
And like a butterfly upon a flower,
Spreading and closing with delight's excess,
A-sudden fanned and shut her tinted wings.
In the spring twilight, in the coloured twilight,
Ere Hesper, eldest child of Night, run forth
On mountain-top to see
If Day hath left the dale,
And hears, well-pleased, the dove
From ancient elm and high
In murmuring dreams still bid the sun good-night.
And sound of lowing kine,
And echoes long and clear,

And herdsman's evening call,
And bells of penning folds,
Sweet and low ;
Oh maid, as fair as thou
Behold the young May moon !
Oh ! happy, happy maid,
With love as young as she
In the spring twilight, in the coloured twilight,
Meet, meet me, by the thorn upon the hill.

At the midsummer, at the high midsummer,
Deep in the darkness let me sit embowered
All alone ;
What time the children of the earth and heaven,
As of two houses whom a feud divides,
Meet in the mingling mystery of midnight,
And melting clouds sink low with woers' tears,
Felt but unseen, dropping a balm of joy
Whereto the love-touched leaves
Tremble and whisper thro' the gentle land,
The incense riseth and the incense falleth
And all the stolen hour is stirred with kisses,
And silent loves constrain the passionate time ;
Rich loves that as they list
Exchange and take and give
Unmeted mede and debts for ever due.
And sweets are mixed along the languid air
Like balmy breath of lovers warm and near,
And glowing faces meeting thro' the dark.
Hush ! for the world stands still
Held in mere joy, as nought ou earth would lose
The happy place and moment where it stood.
Hush ! o'er a stillness, still as Love's delight,
Hearts gushing, bosoms heaving, moving arms
Winding, unwinding ; lips that close and part

And love still ending and beginning ; hush !
Put back the dawn, O Phosphor !   Set again !
Fall like a sweet drop from the honeyed heavens !
Go down, and carried by a tender cloud !
The exquisite best moment of the night
Sinks down with thee.   This is the ecstasy !
It sheds, it sheds !   The night is filled with flowers,
——The viewless night, faint night, the yielding
    night,
The favouring night,—with flowers and happy rain !
As tho' to-morrow's blossoms spreading odours
As they float
Soft thro' the season, shy thro' the dark season,
Like a warm dew sank murmuring from the skies.

Fall, fall, fall,
Fall, fall, fall,
Oh orchard fruit fall from the fading tree,
Fall fruit of Autumn on the sullen sod,
Heavy and dead as clods into a grave.
Fall, fall, fall,
Fall, fall, fall,
Lone lingering rose thou knowest all must die !
Canst thou convince the breeze of spring, or blush
The summer thro' the cheeks of sallow day ?
Thou, sick with solitude, and blanched with tears ?
Fall, fall, fall,
Fall, fall, fall,
Sere leaf that quiverest thro' the sad still air,
Sere leaf that waverest down the sluggish wind,
Sere leaf that whirlest on the Autumn gust,
Free in the ghastly anarchy of death.
The sad still air which as an alkahest,
Potent and silent doth dissolve the year ;
The sluggish wind that as a red stream slow

With carnage welters dull, and steams with death ;
The sudden gust that like a headsman wild,
Uplifteth Beauty by her golden hair,
To show the world that she is dead indeed !
Fall, fall, fall,
Fall, fall, fall,
Fall twilight rain that dost not strive nor cry,
But chillest all the time with silent sorrow ;
And not a wind does violence, nor a plaint
Stirs the dank quiet of the latter leaves ;
But—as in speechless looks of him who stands,
Withered and wan by the wayside of Fate,
Timeless, unwelcome, all his better lot
Outlived, and the dear fashion of his day
And race forgotten, bended to his ill,
And lifting not the unavailing voice
Which no man heedeth—lorn and stillest tears
Grow in the fade eyes of the relict world.

Trim the lamp,
Pile the fire ;
Brim the cup,
Touch the strings ;
Sigh of love,
Sing of joy ;
Trill of maids,
Chant of men !

Oh the young,
And the fair ;
Oh the love,
And the wine ;
Log of Yule,
Log of Yule,
In thy glamour

They shine !
For an hour
We are gods,
And of all
Love hath given
Lacking none
From our world
See the sun
Of our days !

Round the forms
That to-day
Blushed with life
Meet and smile
All the shapes
Of the past
In the light
Glimmer pale.

Early loves,
Friends of yore,
Ancient eyes,
Voices old,
Where the blaze
Charms the air
By our hearth
Come again.

And the sounds
And the dreams
And the quick
And the dead
In spell-dance
Move round me,
In murmur
And maze.

Oh ye Loves !
Oh ye Days !
Oh ye Dead !
Oh ye Dreams !
Bar the door,
Bar the door,
With a shout,
Shut them in !

For all the outer world is rocked in war !
The powers of harm break faith, and in mad might
Yell for the rout and will not be denied !
Even now the hungry sea begins to wreck,
And the impatient storms, eager for ill,
Bide not the expected signal, but blow out
The lingering Light that flickered in the west.
To-day is dead an hour before his time !
Good spells are broken, and the shrieking night,
Down from the haunted and mysterious hills, [snows,
Comes black and shuddering, wrapped about with
Like a starved Ethiop sheeted from the grave.

ENGLISH BIRDS.

　　　　　Yonder pensive thrush
Singing his rhythmic cadence, and, below,
The blackbird, earnest in the flowering thorn,
Chanting his mellow prose as tho' he told
A wonted story, ever old and new !
The fitful chaffinch, like a bashful youth
That hurries forth his love in sudden speech
And blushing pause, the loud and cheerful wren,
The sparrow's chirp, the swallow on the wall—
The swallow that pours out her liquid joy
Upon the morning flood of happiness,

Wherein it falls with silver sound and sweet
As water into water ; these, and all
The warbling voices breathing of the South,
The slender treble of the tuneful year
With throbbing throats that chorus sunshine thro'
The vocal world, dainty, and soft, and low !
And high o'er all a languid noise of rooks,
Lost in bright air, circling in sunny calm,
Or cawing from the haunt of oaken green
The leafy rest of June !

NATURE THE POET'S TEACHER.

      Herein behold why Nature
Is the one Teacher whom the Poet needs,
For she alone can show him in her works
Consummate art, and that supreme excess
Which fashions her fair work until the bound
Of possible performance, and the verge
Of the wrapt heart's belief ; and while we say,
" Behold the final good !" sprinkles a dew,
And with divine complacence, passeth both.
Or having wrought her statue from a block
Infallible, with an unfailing hand
Quickens the faultless whole, and with a touch
Makes cold Perfection live.   With her he sees
Not only snow, but driven snow, nor driven snow
But on the sacred summit of an Alp
Immaculate, and on the whitest peak,
Whiter than white ; the flower not only fair,
But fragrant, and the light not only warm,
The fire not only bright ; the summer fruit
Sweet to the taste but sweeter to the eye,

And over all is tangible a bloom
That never can be touched.   She, only she,
In her least work, as in her greatest, shows
To his confessing eyes the unattained
And unattainable, and tho' his pride,
Stung to its strength, outstrain the furthest stretch
Of man, and bring the trophies of the world,
She, still unsatisfied, by Day and Night
Points upward, saying,—"Be ye perfect as
Your Father in the Heavens!"

———

BALDER TO AMY.

			Thou hast said well
'Tis Resurrection-day.   For I remember
Once in a sleep of childhood I looked forth
Thro' a wide summer window, on a still
And Garden-world.   Eden, as at the first,
I saw, and all the summers since the first,
Above it, like a golden silent sea,
Lay warm and sweet and slumb'rous, soaking deep
All things in honeyed light—flowers, fruits, and trees,
Which breathed their gums and amber, and let down
From their festooned fair tops that no wind stirred
Visible odours—and the tepid Lakes
And the dissolving Hills.   And far below,
Down thro' green warmth of the relaxed sod
To hidden secrets of the inner Earth
Slow sank incumbent, sinking, sinking Light.
'Twas Resurrection-morn.   Where I beheld
City had never stood, nor ways of men,
Nor place of funeral.   But the Dead came up
Like spring-Flowers, white and golden, thro' the
	ground,

Lifting a little earth, as snowdrops lift,
On their strange heads.   This morning, as I stood
Beside my open window, ere thou camest,
And looked upon the day, methought I saw
My childhood's dream.   Is it a dream ?   For thou
Art such a thing as one might think to see
Upon a footstone, sitting in the sun,
Beside a broken Grave !

   .   .   .   .

                      I do know this moment !
This is the very wind that long ago
In the first morning of sweet life we breathed
By the open gate of Love, when thou and I
Went happy in together, knowing not
The place, nor heeding if 'twere Earth or no.
We were so young, thou wert so pure, the woes
And weary ills that keep the gate of Love
Looked on us as on shapes concerning whom
They had no charge ; the guardians of the trees
Slept all, and with us the sublimer Fates
Dealt softly as with children.   Did we dream
A dream of years upon some flowery knoll,
And do we wake where we lay down?   Is this
The outer world ?   Is this the common day
Of all the living ?   Oh Amy ! my own child,
I could believe this fancy ; never since
I felt this wind upon me in my youth
Have I beheld thee as now.   Dost thou remember
The old days when at trysting-time thou camest
Forth down the winding valley to the stile
To meet me, and beside me all the sweet
Meandering way trod back in silent joy,
With downcast eyes that ever sought the ground,
But tell-tale smiles that could not choose but come

Me-ward ; quick smiles that every word of mine
Stirred up anew so often that they met
Like sudden roses caught in a warm wind,
And did provoke each other, ruffling sweets
In dear confusion, and in all the change
Of my swift fancy changing till they lay
Upon thee like the thousand lines of light
Upon the shimmering water that the west
Moves with a sigh ? So we past slowly on,
And so, fond gazing on thy silent face,
I poured the glorious wine of love into
A vase of crystal, where it blushed and shone
More fair. Sometimes I marvel when I think
Of those first days of love ; love that unknown
Knew not himself, and still went in and out
Among the happy inmates of the heart
As an unconscious prophet walks amid
His brethren ere his equal lips be touched
With the live coals of fire. I that so long
Spake, and we knew not that I spake of love
Because it filled my speech, and being all
Seemed nothing, I who that I saw it not
Never believed it present, nor remembered
That the sole face on which I cannot look
Is this men know for mine—how did I win thee ?
Canst tell me ?
  Amy.   I can sing a little song.—

The sun he riseth up on new year's day,
And looketh on the earth and goeth down ;
The earth she stirreth to be looked upon.
The faithful sun he riseth day by day,
And looketh on the earth and goeth down ;
The earth she trembleth to be looked upon.
The faithful sun he riseth day by day,

And looketh on the earth and goeth down ;
The earth she blusheth to be looked upon.
The faithful sun he riseth day by day,
And looketh on the earth and goeth down ;
The earth she smileth to be looked upon.
The faithful sun he riseth day by day,
And looketh on the earth and goeth down ;
The earth she sigheth to him from the south ;
The earth she stands before him all in flowers ;
The many-voiced earth, she calleth him ;
She singeth at his chamber that he rise,
And long time holdeth him lest he go down.

THE FLOWER AT EDEN-GATE.

There grew a lowly flower by Eden-gate
Among the thorns and thistles.   High the palm
Branched o'er her, and imperial by her side
Upstood the sunburnt Lily of the east.

The goodly gate swung oft, with many gods
Going and coming, and the spice-winds blew
Music and murmurings, and paradise
Welled over and enriched the outer wild.
Then the palm trembled fast-bound by the feet,
And the imperial Lily bowed her down
With yearning, but they could not enter in.

The lowly flower she looked up to the palm
And lily, and at eve was full of dews,
And hung her head and wept and said, " Ah these
Are tall and fair, and shall I enter in ? "

There came an angel to the gate at even,
A weary angel, with dishevelled hair ;
For he had wandered far, and as he went,
The blossoms of his crown fell one by one
Thro' many nights, and seemed a falling star

He saw the lovely flower by Eden-gate,
And cried, " Ah, pure and beautiful ! " and turned
And stooped to her and wound her in his hair,
And in his golden hair she entered in.

Husband ! I was the weed at Eden-gate,
I looked up to the lily and the palm
Above me, and I wept and said, "ah these
Are tall and fair, and shall I enter in ? "
And one came by me to the gate at even,
And stooped to me and wound me in his hair
And in his golden hair I entered in.

—

SONG OF THE SUN.

Earliest bird
Thou hearest me,
Me afar off
Thro' the dark.
Roll O days into the years, and O years into the
    ages, and O ages into the mystery of God !
Oh, Love, oh Life, and all ye jocund train
Virtues and Joys, my lusty Company,
Be loud around me ! Sing because I sing !
Call each to each as I call unto you !

Love calling unto Life
"Oh Life ! Oh Life !"
Life calling unto Love
" Oh Love ! Oh Love !"
" How beautiful oh Life !"
" How beautiful oh Love !"
I am the sun singing behind the mountains !
Thou heaven, that didst watch for me on the hills,
Sitting upon the hill-tops above the valley of beauty,
Thou hearest me afar off singing behind the mountains,
And hast let fall thy mourning, and thy bosom is pale.
Also blushes are on thy cheeks lest I see thee, oh thou
    most beautiful.
But I will see thee, O thou most beautiful !
Robe thee in purple, take thy clouds about thee,
Rise up, O queen, with gold upon thy brows,
Behold I reach thee forth my golden sceptre,
Behold I give thee morning as a garment,
Sit on thy hill, and I will touch thy hill,
And thou shalt sit upon a diamond throne,
And shalt be glorified before my world !
For I see thee, O thou most beautiful !

Quiet valley, valley deep and still,
Dost thou hear my voice behind the mountains ?
I will come gently as a father peepeth
Over the cot, over the cot of beauty,
So will I lift my face up over thee.

Love, love, love, how beautiful, oh love !
Art thou well-awakened, little flower ?
Are thine eyelids open, little flower ?
Are they cool with dew, O little flower ?

Hath the south touched thee ? Hath the fairy kissed
    thee ?
Wilt thou come forth, come forth, into my day ?

Ringdove, ringdove,
This is my golden finger
Between the upper branches of the pine !
Come forth, come forth, and sing into my day !

Butterfly, butterfly,
This is my golden finger,
I will feel for thee down among the roses,
Sweet in the roses, in the climbing roses,
And put thee from thy bed into my day !

Love, love, love, how beautiful, O love !

I will arise, I will awake the world !
They shall be glad because of me, I feel
The joy-light shining thro' their lids of sleep,
Like music from the hollow of the earth.

It is time,	It is time	It is time,
O ye leaves,	O ye streams,	O ye bells,
On the tree-tops	On the hill-tops	In the grey spire
Of morning ;	Of morning ;	Of morning ;
Laugh down	Run down	Ring down
The trees,	The hills,	The spire,
That the pastures,	That the valleys	That the hamlet
May wake !	May wake !	May wake !

Awake !
I am the sun, I am above the mountains,
My joy is on me, I will give you day !
I will spend day among you like a king !
Your water shall be wine because I reign !
I stave my golden vintage on the mountains,

And all your rushing rivers run with day !
I am the sun, I am above the mountains !
Arise, my hand is open, it is day !
Rise ! as men strike a bell and make it music,
So have I struck the earth and made it day !
Move, move, O world, on all your brazen hinges,
Send round the thunder of your golden wheels ;
Throng out, O millions, out, O shouting millions ;
Throng out, O millions, shouting, shouting day !
For as one blows a trumpet through the valleys,
So from my golden trumpet I blow day !

O earth, O flowers, O birds, O beasts, O men,
Day is proclaimed !   I called until I heard
The caverns echo !   Day is everywhere :
White-favoured day is sailing on the sea,
And, like a sudden harvest in the land,
The windy land is waving gold with day !
As for you whom I have awakened, do
As shall seem good in all your shining eyes,
Your eyes still wet with morning.   They shall dry,
And day shall fade.   But I have done my task :
Do yours !   And what is this that I have given,
And wherefore ? look ye to it !   As ye can,
Be wise and foolish to the end.   For me,
I, under all heavens, go forth praising God !

―――――

Balder.   Alas ! that one
Should use the days of summer but to live,
And breathe but as the needful element
The strange superfluous glory of the air !
Nor rather stand apart in awe beside
The untouched Time, and saying o'er and o'er
In love and wonder, " These are summer days."

.   .   .   .   .   .

         Under this ash, last spring,
I saw a sight more sweet than ever clown
Came on a-sudden in a fairy-ring
By summer moon.   A growth of primroses,
Thick as the stars by night, and like the stars
In constellations and in orbits due,
Shone round the central tree.   I could believe
Queen Flora, on a royal progress tired,
Halted beneath it, and her flowery court
Pitched their fair tents about her, or, well-pleased,
Sole, or by twins, in fragrant converse, lay
Upon the enchanted ground.

A Chanted Calendar.

First came the primrose,
On the bank high,
Like a maiden looking forth
From the window of a tower
When the battle rolls below,
So looked she,
And saw the storms go by.

Then came the wind-flower
In the valley left behind,
As a wounded maiden pale
With purple streaks of woe
When the battle has rolled by
Wanders to and fro,
So tottered she,
Dishevelled in the wind.

Then came the daisies,
On the first of May,
Like a bannered show's advance
While the crowd runs by the way,
With ten thousand flowers about them they came trooping
    through the fields.

As a happy people come,
So came they,
As a happy people come,
When the war has rolled away,
With dance and tabor, pipe and drum,
And all make holiday.

Then came the cowslip,
Like a dancer in the fair,
She spread her little mat of green,
And on it danced she.
With a fillet bound about her brow,
A fillet round her happy brow,
A golden fillet round her brow,
And rubies in her hair.

BEAUTY.

                    Loveliness
Is precious for its essence ; time and space
Make it nor near nor far nor old nor new,
Celestial nor terrestrial.   Seven snowdrops
Sister the pleiads, the primrose is kin
To Hesper, Hesper to the world to come !

For sovereign Beauty as divine is free ;
Herself perfection, in herself complete,
Or in the flowers of earth or stars of heaven.
Merely contained in the seven-coloured bow
Arching the globe, and still contained in each
Of all its raindrops.   This, my thought, I give
To thee, and am no poorer ; no, nor thou
Still giving, nor a singular of all
Who ever shall possess it, tho' my thought
Become the equal birthright of unborn
Nations of men, in every heart a whole.
There cannot be a dimple on the cheek
But all an everlasting soul hath smiled ;
Day is day to all the eyes on earth,
No less than day to mine.   Love strong as death
Measures eternity and fills a tear ;
And beauty universal may be touched
As at the lips in any single rose.
See how I turn toward the turf, as he
Who after a long pilgrimage once more
Beholds the face that was his desert dream,
Turning from heaven and earth bends over it,
And parts the happy tresses from her brow,
Counting her ringlets, and discoursing bliss
On every hint of beauty in the dear
Regained possession, oft and oft retraced,
So could I lie down in the summer grass
Content, and in the round of my fond arm
Enclose enough dominion, and all day
Do tender descant, owning one by one
Floweret and flower, and telling o'er and o'er
The changing sum of beauty, still repaid
In the unending task for ever new,
And in a love which first sees but the whole,
But when the whole is partially beloved

Doth feast the multitude upon the bread
Of one, endow the units with no less
Than all, and make each meanest integer
The total of my joy.   Yet I have stood
And clasped the earth as if she were a maid ;
And held her, bearing all her sparkling stars
Upon.her like a vase of Castalie
Upon a Greek girl's head, and made my boast
Of her, and as a lover let her fill
My feeding eyes !   Or I have hovered far
Upon the verge of all things, and beheld
The round globe as a fruit upon a tree,
The spangled tree that night by starry night
Stands o'er us, and have seen an angel pass,
Pluck it and cool his lips, and drop the hull
To chaos, and this earth, that I have loved
And worshipped, fall out of the universe
As unrespected as a dead leaf falls
From summer aspen, while the innumerous stars
Twinkled and quivered in the wind of God
Walking between the shade of fruited heavens
Untold as once between the river-trees
Of Eden.   But wherever I beheld
Or one or every one, the whole or part,
Some better thing that is not either or all
For ever putteth forth from all and each
A hand, and toucheth me, as he of old
Was touched in sleep ; and I as one in sleep
Know not how or where, but, having felt,
Believe, and serve the Invisible Unknown,
   Calling it Beauty.

Incompleteness.

Oh Earth, that every year
Conceivest and hast no power to bring forth,
And year by year beginnest a psalm unsung,
So as with thee is it with all of thine !
As one who in a crowd of recreant men
Begins a chant of freedom, and with brow
Lift to the glowing sun, sings the first stave
Triumphant, but no ring of bold refrain
Surrounds him pausing for the wonted shout,
And he looks down to pallid lips and eyes
And all the silent treason, and, undone,
Sinks on the sward, and hides his shamèd face ;
So ever looking to a golden time
At each new year, impatient, thou criest out
" There shall be ! "—and art silent, casting dust
Upon thine head.　Oh, season ever new,
Oh Spring that risest with us, sun by sun !
Whither thine hurrying stream, where thy full tide,
Thy neap excess, and overflow ?　What vale
Far off in heaven dost thou yearly flood
With rainbow waters worthy of thy well,
Ah fountain Arethuse ?　For never here
Thy consummation ; but what time we hail
Thine outleap, and the pulsing channels sing,
Somewhat beyond the verdurous verge drinks down
The sudden waters, leaving yellow sands
That autumn gathers, till the rock beneath
Shines in the frost of winter.

Where on earth
Is the unknown meridian of that day
Which to the Morn I met upon the east,

Should be as man to babe ?   Doth the young moon
Complete her promised light or multiply
Her beauty by her days ?
                              Where is that rose
Which he who gave its bud as hieroglyph
Of budding love would own the equal sign
Of love's full-flowered perfection ?

        .   .   .   .   .   .

                        Oh little child, girl-child,
Last daughter of the old manorial house
In the green village, thou who when the sun
Is rising, and above, below, around,
The dew-drops shine, as every bough and spray,
Blade, leaf, small petal and least acrospire,
Yea, the unbodied joyance of the air
Had eyes, and smiled to see him, comest forth
Into the morning as an element
Of such ethereal season duly sweet
And sweetly due, while singing birds and bees
Sound like the bubbling of that stream of day
Whereby thou, tripping, givest song for song !
Fair happy child, who goest at thy will
Into the sunny midst as a white bird
Into the crystal water that reflects
Spotless a spotless image, pure in pure,
And each unlessened still enhancing each,—
The image whitens the white wave, the wave
Adds the pure image to the floating snow ;—
Thou who art native to the good of all ;
For whom the unsullied fairness of the earth
Guards not herself, nor deprecating hands
Mystic arise out of the Beautiful
To put thee from the beauty ; who dost tread
The daisies like a morning-wind and spill
Dews from lithe buttercups that fill again

With drops of pleasure; Oh thou unknown essence!
So near the eyes, so distant from the heart,
When dost thou take our nature, and become
No more than we? Something within her looks
A strange light through her lashes, and a joy
Beyond our throb.   It cannot be that this
Abideth with her, for such bliss fulfilled
Thro' all the coming seasons that must yet
Accomplish woman, and increasing still
Within the ampler temple, were a sight
To breed rebellion in the universe,
Burn every world with jealousy of her's,
Summer this earth, and make the schooldame Nature
Break thro' the ill-assumed severity
Of her enforcèd aspect, with a cry
Be all the mother, catch thee to her heart,
Begin the golden ages, and in thee
Restore mankind.   Therefore, thou most fair child,
Here thou hast no completion.   In what hour
Of what set night wilt thou give up this ghost,
Exhaled as the last fragrance from a flower
Unchanged in hue?   Upon what destined morn
Shall she come down a stranger to the board
Where the same face and form shall take a place
Not hers, and answer to familiar names
That have no owner upon earth?   Of them
Who loved her is there one who shall be grave
With an unconscious sorrow, knowing nought,
But saying in himself, since such a day
My heart is poorer?   Is there one of all,
Who thinking of a blissful time gone by
That floats in on his day-dream, like sweet air
From heaven, sun-bright and full of golden sounds
Going and coming, at one happy voice
Among the choir, starting, shall cry "Ah whose?"

And muse, and pass his hand across his brow
Perplexed?   Will they be sodden with a spell,
Nor lift astonished eyes and hands to see
Her shining crescent fill no fuller moon
Than others?   Nor so much as droop a lid
Sighing, as when the pulsing heart of youth
In mere abundance of young life's excess
Beats an unknown approach that never comes,
And we look up expecting, and look down
With melancholy wisdom mildly sad,
Smiling moralities?

              They will behold,
And she shall grow and marry, breed and die,
Even as her mother, and of many none
Shall question her.   Nevertheless at last
Truth shall be justified.   Of them who deck
Her bier, or chant her thro' the pompous aisle,
Or load the blazoned marble with her broad
And gravid virtues, or in sable grief
Swell the dark progress winding long and slow
Stately to honourable tombs, no hand
Will write upon her coffin, " This is she
Who played among the roses."

   Amy.   Surely the Lord is cruel but to me,
And over bounteous to the race of men
With mercy taken from my single lot.

I am the dwarf of this great family,
The favoured lips do drink the wine of life,
And all the mingled lees fill up my fate.

I am a place where music music meets,
Putting it out ; by how much joy is loud,
I am the darker silence : all the lines
Of sorrow cross above my wretched head.

They are grown sour with sweetness, they are proud
With pleasure, they care not to keep awake
Even to be happy.   Like a slave they bid
Their bliss abide their time, and, like a slave,
It fans their happy faces while they sleep.

Ah Heaven ! they sleep upon the flowery banks,
And daylight flowers fill them with honey dreams,
And pleasured smiles do light their languid lips.

Ah Heaven ! they stand amid the fruited trees,
The golden-fruited trees, and every wind
Daubs the ripe fruit upon their sated lips.

Ah Heaven ! they lie beside the living stream,
And the superfluous stream o'er-wells his banks,
And laps sweet waters to their happy lips.

Where they do most enjoy my need is worst ;
The living cup they spill would save my life ;
The joy that wearies them would give me rest.

I lie down in the night but cannot sleep ;
I keep vain vigil for my plighted bliss ;
I strain after the fruit I may not touch,
And cannot reach the river tho' I die !

Balder.—Full many a time and oft
I have sat still thro' all a summer day,
And listened to its change as to a book
Read by untiring lips.   Thou wouldst have sworn
The day was like a field of buttercups,
Where every shining moment stood and smiled
Beside his golden likeness ; but not I !
I know the hours, and call them by their names,
As a shepherd his sheep.

LAUS DEO.

In the hall the coffin waits, and the idle armourer
  stands,   [hands.
At his belt the coffin nails, and the hammer in his
The bed of state is hung with crape—the grand old bed
    where she was wed—
And like an upright corpse she sitteth gazing dumbly at
    the bed.
Hour by hour her serving men enter by the curtained
    door,
And with steps of muffled woe pass breathless o'er the
    silent floor,
And marshal mutely round, and look from each to each
    with eye-lids red,
"Touch him not," she shrieked and cried, "he is but
    newly dead !"   [say,
"Oh, my own dear mistress," the ancient Nurse did
"Seven long days and seven long nights you have
    watched him where he lay."

" Seven long days and seven long nights," the hoary
    Steward said.
" Seven long days and seven long nights," groaned the
    Warrener grey,
" Seven," said the old Henchman, and bowed his aged
    head ;
"On your lives !" she shrieked and cried, " he is but
    newly dead ! '
       Then a father Priest they sought,
       The priest that taught her all she knew,
       And they told him of her loss.
       " For she is mild and sweet of will,
       She loved him, and his words are peace,
       And he shall heal her ill."
       But her watch she did not cease.
       He blest her where she sat distraught,
       And showed her holy cross,—
       The cross she kissed from year to year—
       But she neither saw nor heard ;
       And said he in her deaf ear
       All he had been wont to teach,
       All she had been fond to hear,
       Missalled prayer, and solemn speech,
       But she answered not a word.
Only when he turned to speak with those who wept
    about the bed,
"On your lives !" she shrieked and cried, "he is but
    newly dead !"   [tell,
Then how sadly he turned from her it were wonderful to
And he stood beside the death-bed as by one who
    slumbers well,
And he leaned o'er him who lay there, and in cautious
    whisper low,
" He is not dead, but sleepeth," said the Priest, and
    smoothed his brow.

"Sleepeth ?" said she looking up, and the sun rose in
    her face !
" He must be better than I thought, for the sleep is
    very sound."
" He is better," said the Priest, and called her maidens
    round.
With them came that ancient dame who nursed her
    when a child ;
" Oh Nurse," she sighed, " Oh Nurse," she cried, " Oh
    Nurse ! " and then she smiled,
        And then she wept ; with that they drew
        About her, as of old ;
        Her dying eyes were sweet and blue,
        Her trembling touch was cold ;
        But she said, " My maidens true
        No more weeping and well-away ;
        Let them kill the feast.
        I would be happy in my soul.
        " He is better," saith the Priest ;
        He did but sleep the weary day,
        And will waken whole.
        Carry me to his dear side,
        And let the halls be trim ;
        Whistly, whistly," said she,
        " I am wan with watching and wail,
        He must not wake to see me pale,
        Let me sleep with him.
        See you keep the tryst for me,
        I would rest till he awake
        And rise up like a bride.
        But whistly, whistly !' said she.
        " Yet rejoice your Lord doth live ;
        And for his dear sake
        Say Laus Domine."
        Silent they cast down their eyes,

And every breast a sob did rive,
She lifted her in wild surprise
And they dared not disobey.
“ Laus Deo,” said the Steward, hoary when her days were
        new,
“ Laus Deo,” said the Warrener, whiter than the warren
        snows ;
“ Laus Deo,” the bald Henchman, who had nursed her
        on his knee.
The old Nurse moved her lips in vain
And she stood among the train
Like a dead tree shaking dew.
Then the Priest he softly stept
Midway in the little band,
And he took the Lady's hand.
“ Laus Deo !” he said, aloud,
“ Laus Deo,” they said again,
Yet again, and yet again,
Humbly crossed and lowly bowed,
Till in wont and fear it rose
To the Sabbath strain.
But she neither turned her head
Nor “ whistly, whistly,” said she.
Her hands were folded as in grace,
We laid her with her ancient race
And all the village wept.

BALDER'S PORTRAIT OF AMY.

                              In her,
Nature's first thought was beauty ; she conceived
Her image sitting in her robe of white
Thinking of spring, and, at the fancy moved.

Smiling breathed softly, and did turn to make
The firstling snowdrop of the stainless year.
And, as the year arose, her fairer thought
Took substance, and, consummate in her care,
Grew with the growing year ; for at her will
Day after day past by, and passing dropt
Its own memorial flower, the better sign
Of all ; and night by night, when shades are deep,
And that mysterious sorrow is transact
Unseen, and there is weeping in the air,
She understanding all, midst common dews,
Caught the accepted tear that makes the hour
So holy.   Nor herself in greater deeds
Forgot the less, thro' each surpassing mood
In which with higher ecstasy she wrought
Abundant summer, whatsoe'er confessed
Her happier hand—elect and dedicate
Increased the secret store ; and over all
Frequent and fond with dainty change and wise—
As meet perfection of each part admits
Phœbus or Dian,—various balm of life
She poured from golden and from silver vase
Of sun and moon.   But when the year was grown,
(And sweet by warmer sweet to nuptial June
The flowery adolescence slowly filled,
Till in a passion of Roses all the time
Flushed, and around the glowing Heavens made suit)
And onward through the rank and buxom days,
'Tho' she ceased not to work and help the year
Great with the burden of the honeyed past,
And gave her good deliverance and great pomp
Of harvest, and in royal glory robed
Matron and mother, to her dearer hoard
She added nought, nor what her love had hid
Unclosed before the broad unclouded face

And heated welfare of the lusty world.
But when the destiny that haunts the proud
Did tardy judgment, and the prosperous year,
Struck in her young maternity, beheld
First born and last lie low, and wrapping wild
The early mists about her, on the ground
Amid her prostrate hopes disconsolate
Sat veiled : or standing forth with upstretched hands
And strange appealing eyes, and wildered face
Hectic with fate, looked like her spring-time self
Transfigured on some martyr pile of woe
Seen through the flame ; then Nature knew her hour,
And at conjunction of the setting signs
Opened her sacred Casket and took forth
Well-pleased : and of the lone and latter rose,
Pale autumn violets, and all hapless blooms
Did make in mournful fragrance sadly sweet
The mortal breath of beauty.

  . . . . . .

         Nature thus,
The Poet Nature, singing to herself—
Did make Her in sheer love, having delight
Of all her work, and doing all for joy. . . . . .

  . . . . . .

. . . . . Ah, was the very air
Ethereal round her, so that whoso breathed
Revived to his best nature and grew bright
For her sake, as a mote from dim to dim
Sails the sunbeam ?—What deity indwelt
Her still small voice, which was her perfect self
Audible—that most happy voice, which when
It rose to gladness made men rich and glad
Unminished, and receiving but to spend

Sweeter abundance with a lovelier will.
Gayer for gaiety, but of the gay
Still gayest, as bright sun o'er brightened fields
Seems brighter, gaining from the light he gives.
That voice which was to sorrow as its sigh,
And by the side of wonted circumstance
Went as the tinkle of Titania's feet,
Ringing the hour of day on fairy bells
Marriage or funeral.   Nor less blessed when
It fell into the bosom of the poor
Like gold and silver.   That dear voice which when
She sang her life, the charmed listener hearing,
Accepted for consummate loveliness
Till she was mute, and his divided soul
Returning to the eyes, her silent beauty
By the higher sense perceived, seemed insomuch
Diviner music.
                    Oft have I admired
When the poor wayfarer on whom she looked
Clothed in his tattered fortune did take rank
A moment in her smile, and could not ask
The alms his famine craved ; the passing thief
Had virtue in her service, and the clown
Grace to be hers.   The maimed who chanced to meet
Her far-off beauty on the way, aside
Drew into shadow till she passed, nor begged
Aught that might turn the light of her sweet face
On the too conscious fault ; and Lazarus
Covered his sores with deeper sense of ill.
Rude country-wives to whom in lane or mead
Happened her sweet regards, with honoured face
And thankful did obeisance going by
As owning bounty and a duty known
Unschooled ; the village children at the door-
Little two-year children—having gazed,

Ran to her as she passed and caught her skirt
And looking up laughed strange intelligence,
Abashed and pleased, in the mere act repaid,
And wiser than the three-score-years-and-ten
That chid the holy freedom, being purblind.
For they who saw her were as one who knows
A mystic sign and smiles with consciousness.
There is a soul unto the grosser sense
Of spoken language, an unuttered thought
Virgin and peerless, which no man hath said
Nor hath the hope to hear upon the earth,
Tho' it be dear as the unbodied dream
Of early love, familiar as the wife
Upon his breast, albeit untouched as maids
In Paradise.　In every human speech
No speaker but hath with him, undeclared,
This angel ; and doth bear about a thing
Too lovely for his lips, beloved unnamed.
As every heart upon its secret so,
The world did look on her !　Where'er she went
Nature, in dale or hill, in cot or grove,
Owned her, and in the shepherd or the lamb
Confest no less.　The Lamb which to her knee
Came fearless, unsuspicious of the grey
Grim guardian of the fold who harmed her not
Nor challenged her just right what-time she took
The lambkin willing, to her purer breast.
Thus or in haunts beloved or foreign fields
Her equal way was all among her own,
Unquestioned still, nor anywhere or new
Or strange.　We had a wonted bower, secluse,
Of honeysuckle wild in mossy dell
Facing the noon, and sheltered from the north
By denser shade ; flowery it was and deep,
And caught the flowing light as chaliced leaves

The sunset.   In the inner sanctities
Shy birds did nest, and all the summer through,
Entering, with tumult of distress I shook
The troubled verdure, but she came at will
And sat there ; and the birds went in and out
As tho' she were so merely beautiful
That nought betrayed her limits, and she mixed—
She, undistinguished—with the love-lit air
The fragrance and the summer joy that lived
In that green bower.
                    " So lovely in her rest
More lovely her awakened beauty played
The smiling pastime of her innocent life
Gracious and holy, wherein fairest thought
And fond performance thro' melodious hours
Rhymed like a gentle ballad.   All she did
Expressed her.   The mild lore and simple arts
She knew and loved might exercise unblamed
Chaste Flora's self or what pure essence warms
The happy difference of a morn of May.
Song and answering lute, and mute delight
Of pencilled touch, and nice dexterity
Of bending Eve in gardened Paradise
Were hers ; she had a faërie forestrie
Of birds, and bees, and summer flies ; she knew
Sweet mysteries of sunrise and sunset,
Of seasons, moons, and clouds.   But chief in joy
Her skill was among flowers, which in her hand
Took better hues, and fell under her looks
Into an ordered beauty as before
Their queen ; and when they crowned her, unaware
The butterfly did court the rose as still
Upon the blushing tree.   Yet more I loved
An art which of all others seemed the voice
And argument ; rare art, at better close

Of chosen day, worn like a jewel rare
To beautify the beauteous, and make bright
The twilight of some sacred festival
Of love and peace.   Her happy memory
Was many poesies, and when serene
Beneath the favouring shades and the first star,
She audibly remembered, they who heard
Believed the Muse no fable.   As that star
Unsullied from the skies, out of the shrine
Of her dear beauty beautifully came
The beautiful, untinged by any taint
Of mortal dwelling, neither flushed nor pale,
Pure in the naked loveliness of Heaven.
Such and so graced was she. . . .

   .   .   .   .

. . .   Loved and loving she would live,
No more accompanied than by what train
Is love's, and in the love-feast of her days
Served while she sat, or sat whileas she served !
To know where winding from the ancient tree
By the grey stile thro' copse and daisied dell,
In every mood of immemorial mind
The simple village went a thousand years ;
Or o'er the brook upon the stepping-stones
To follow unperplexed thro' bosky maze,
The feet of sorrow to her shyest lair ;
Or at the ruined cot, and down the dim
Deserted path, to watch under the dust
The unwonted grass rise slowly up and lift
The memory of the dead from off the earth ;
Or round the 'wildered garden to convince
The graceless moss of greed ; or from lone lane
At summer eve to trace some ancient track

A-field and learn what need or joy of life
Saw viewless landmarks in the devious way,
Her daily pleasaunce. ' But where men are met,
If unpropitious hap or lot unsought
Awhile constrained her, fate that did the wrong,
Jealous, allowed no other ; as a King
Seizing his bride, rapt from her native bowers
Circassian, in the amorous crime completes
His cruelty and makes the captive queen.
Not otherwise, and looking like a flower
Dropt in the city street—some blossom fair
That grew dew-nursed and lone green miles away—
Into the heedless crowd that knew her not
She came uncrowned, and they w'st not she came ;
Till simply sitting in the parlous midst
Her presence like a silent virtue spread
About her.   For a little while she sat
Unhonoured, but a consciousness disturbed
The spot, and as a holy influence
Did touch the unwilling people into awe,
Whom gentle observance and sweet respect
Disposed, till who partook her magic ring
Still or discursive, sole or sociable,
Each in his several function did denote
Her place.   Nor customary in mere use
Perfunctory, and rite of cap or knee,
The general homage ; but of some inborn
Content and central sanction in the soul,
Inmost and earlier than where creeds begin
Or doubts divide.   Men turned and asked not why,
Nor, seeing, marvelled that they turned ; but apt
Took reverent distance : nor, decorous, ceased
The fealty of regard.   With decent eyes
And with no louder sign nor needless bruit
Of the unuttered reason than what-time

On wintry day they face by mute consent
The seldom sun.   Thus she who came unknown
Into the stranger crowd with modest step
And eyes that rather would be ruled than rule,
Having no need of praise, nor hope of fame,
Nor conscience of dominion, did subdue
Its chaos to her nature, being divine ;
And merely present could no less than stir
The dull and grosser essence to revolve
About her, as by instinct and hid force
Of that well-ordered universe whereof
Its matter was a part.   Herself informed
The jarring elements, till, as her sway
No utter sign enforced, nor shows of power,
Nor but a golden sweet necessity
Sovereign, unseen, the subject heart gave like
Confession.   Not as they confess a queen
With sudden shout, but as two friends regard
A rising star, and speak not of it while
It fills their gaze.   The loud debate grew low,
What was unseemly chastened, and the fear
Of Beauty waking her moralities
Sent thro' adjusted limbs the long-forgot
Ambition to be fair.   Nor sex, nor rank,
Nor age, nor changed condition, did absolve
Her rule, which whatsoever was remote
From sin, the more saluted.   Everywhere
Babes smiled on her, and women on her face
Did look as women look in happy love.

So the world blessed her ; and another world,
Like spheres of cloud that interpenetrate
Till each is either, met and mixed with this.

And as the angel Earth that bears her Heaven
About her so that wheresoe'er in space
Her footstep stayeth we look up and say
That Heaven is there—SHE moved and made all times
And seasons equal ;—trod the mortal life
Immortally, and with her human tears
Bedewed the everlasting, till the Past
And Future lapsed into a golden Now
For ever best.   She was much like the moon
Seen in the day-time, that by day receives
Like joy with us, but when our night is dark,
Lit by the changeless sun we cannot see,
Shineth no less.   And she was like the moon,
Because the beams that brightened her passed o'er
Our dark heads, and we knew them not for light
Till they came back from hers ; and she was like
The moon, that whatsoe'er appeared her wane
Or crescent was no loss or gain in her
But in the changed beholder.   I, who saw
Her constant countenance, and had its orb
Still full on me with whom she rose and set,
Knew she had no lunation.   In herself
The elements of holiness were merged
In white completion, and all graces did
The part of each.   To man or Deity
Her sinless life had nought whereof to give
Of worse or better, for she was to God
As a smile to a face.   Ah, God of Beauty !
Where in this lifeless picture my poor hand
Hath done her wrong, forgive ; she was Thy smile,
How could I paint her?   That I dared essay
Her image and am innocent, I plead
Resistless intuition, which believes
Where knowledge fails, and powerless to define
Or to confound, still calls the face and smile

Not one, but twain, and contradicts the sense
Material, which beholding her, beholds
Essence not Effluence, nor Thine but Thee.

———

Amy. That I might die and be at rest, O God !
That I might die and sleep the sleep of peace !
That I might die and know the balm of death
Cool thro' my limbs and all my silenced heart !
O God, that I might die ! that I might die !

Death, Death, thou wilt not take me ? should I bring
Disquiet to thy kingdom ? Yesterday
Was pain, and had a yesterday of pain
Whereto it was to-morrow ; and pain, pain
This dark to-day, to-morrow's yesterday
And yesterday's to-morrow ; then why not
To-morrow ? and why less because with thee ?

I know the wanderer in the desert heat,
When the well faileth and the cruse is spent,
Sees with his eyes his great necessity,
And hears the murmur of his strong desire,
And speeds—to drearer wastes and deadlier sand.
If I am he, O Death, and thou my Thought
Hast lain so long before me cool and sweet,
And art the mirage of a wretched heart !

In what fair shape hast thou beguiled me not ?
O Death, in all this vision of the world
What have I seen, Betrayer, if not thee ?

Sometimes I climb, and thou upon the height
My mother waiting for her weary child
With outstretched circling arms and bosom bare !
Or I am falling in a draw-well deep
Red round with infinite depth of hateful eyes
And night-mare mocking faces, and below
Thou liest like a smile of love and peace.

Sometimes I am a maimèd captive, bound
To the swift chariot of the pitiless sun,
And thou art night that dost unloose my chain !

Or I a pilgrim at the gate of heaven,
Torn with the thorniest way, and thou, O Death,
A virgin angel met upon the verge,
And pitiful thou dost divesture me
And there of all my tattered earthly weeds
Spreadest a bed where I may sleep my last
Nor enter weary on the happy land.

Or I a floating vapour, white and wan,
Casting a shade and shedding doleful dews,
And thou a sunshine from a sun unseen
Dost touch me, passing, to a rarer change.
I float and sadden not the summer air
Nor shed a doleful dew nor cast a shade.

Or I am sailing on an ocean wild
And o'er the bark I bend me, fain to die,
And hopeless look into the sea ; and eyes
Shine up like drownèd jewels from the depths,
And somewhat riseth in the deep to me,
And in the waters a familiar face
And a hand waving to the mermaid-cells.

Touch me, O Death !   This moment let me sleep !
I can do all, O Death, but doubt in thee.
Touch me, O Death, lest I be wild with fear !
Aye, now thou art again as thou hast been.
Stay with me ; lay thine hand upon my brow,
Cool, cool ; bend o'er me ; let thy shadowy hair
Shut out the distance from my aching eyes.
Stand between me and the unsetting sun ;
Console the frailty of my feeble limbs
And task me with a burden I can bear !
I fling me on the shore ; I cannot try
The ocean of interminable life.
Hush me, and sing me to a better mind.
A little rest, a little rest, O Death,
Ere the great labour of the world to come !

———

Balder.   Like a sailing eagle old
Which with unwavering wings outspread and wide
Makes calm horizons in the slumbrous air
Of cloudless noon and fills the silent heaven
With the slow circulation of a course
More placid than repose, this shining still
And universal day revolves serene
Around me, hasting not and uncompelled.

.   .   .   .

                              Here where I sit
The sun must needs be sweet,—the bees sing in it,
And yon large fly—a hawk among his kind—
Still in the very level of mine eye
Keeps on the wing, with shining long delay
Or sudden flash of capture.

                              On the bank
The nodding moor-hen lands to preen her quills.
The trout hath left the alders of the pool
And basks.   Her beak the brooding king-fisher
Shows, breathless, at her callow hole above
The brook ; within the eddies of the brook
The water-mouse dissolves and reappears ;
Therefore 'tis halcyon weather.
                              The small flock
That lay but now, fleece upon panting fleece,
About the knees of yonder aged oak—
Their lusty lord upon a gnarled root
High in the cooler midst—descend and fill
The lengthening shade.   The weed that shuts at
      noon
Is closer than a sleeping infant's lid ;
And the pale evening rose hath not yet set
Her chalice for the dews ; therefore it is
That heavy hour of silent afternoon
When even grief can slumber and forget.
       .   .   .   .   .   .
                              Across
My doorway I perceive the gossamer
Drew silver bars behind me.   They have lost
The immaterial beauty of the morn,
When passing on the gleaming wind they seem
Rather effect than cause, the cutting sheen
Of somewhat on the eye too swift for sight,
Or hung across the early way appear
A shining prohibition in the air
No more.   But these are stiff as rods of glass,
And flat with drought.   Therefore since I went forth
None hath gone in or out.   .   .   .   .
          .   .   .   .   How the motes
In idle sunshine slowly circulate,

A little heaven of worlds as calm and sweet
As any stars above us.   Eh ! my breath
Sucks gulphs beneath the golden equipoise
And sets a viewless tide that bears away
Systems and suns.   Thou great astronomer,
Perplexed by some new motion, Who on high,
Beyond thy telescopic organ stands
Breathing ?

STRIVING AGAINST THE INEXORABLE.

I am as one
Who hearing music thro' the dark doth press
Straight towards the sound and comes upon a tower,
And feels along the impediment whereby
To pass it ; and the walls still put him back
And the containéd voice still calls and he
Still pressing to the sound still journeyeth round
His hid desire ; and now by ear led on
Draws nigh,—and now, when close pursuit should
    break
The skin of fleshed enjoyment, hears the voice
Fainter and fainter from the further cell.
And so unconscious treads a beaten ring
Following that moony voice that wanes and fills
And wanes, and at the worst again is new.
Till at the last, instructed by defeat,
Step by slow step he measures round the wall
The crescent sound, and at one loudest spot
Of proximate possession lays his siege,
And with his straining strength and bruised hands
Would force the unyielding Stone !

BALDER TO AMY.

What weary Angel exiled from the skies,
Her baby at her breast, with failing strength
Paused at this earth and left thee ? Thou wert not
Of us and being grown up shouldst have gone
Back to thine heaven ; or having business here
It should have been in some excepted task
Set out and sacred from the common lot.
If there be any still and vesper hour
More pure than all the day, thou shouldst have been
Its tutelar, to lead it in and out,
Versed in the duteous season and each rite
Of welcome and farewell.   This changeful earth
Should be to thee a garden where we take
Rare pleasaunce and in happy weather walk
But do not dwell.   Thou shouldst have dwelt afar
With everlasting Morning, going forth
With her and from her chaste urn unrebuked
—Dipping thy sinless hand—shouldst sprinkle dews
Or at the side of Spring, her handmaiden
Bearing her violets, what time she comes
Over the hills, descending shouldst have passed
Into this valley blessing it and me.
And shouldst have loved me only while the fields
Were sown, nor pitied me forlorn, nor heard
My vows, nor faithless to thy Goddess-queen
Forgot thy better duty, but have gone
When she went, singing o'er the southern slopes
Joyous beside her ; turning on the height
For my sake and in richer violet-beds
Betraying that thine hand relaxed with thought.
So thou shouldst still have left me and returned

With the pervading year, for ever young,
Till that sad season when thy tearful care
Found not the old man on the wonted hill
Nor by the thorn nor the memorial tree ;
And made a time of strange forget-me-nots
And melancholy flowers that love the rain
Setting the fairest banks with saddest blooms
And by a grassy mound in one deep dell
Beating thy breast let fall the store of spring,
So that to other vales the spring came late
Tarrying for thee.

.

THE MAGYAR'S NEW-YEAR-EVE.

(1859.)

By Temèsvar I hear the clarions call :
The year dies.   Let it die.   It lived in vain.
Gun booms to gun along the looming wall,
Another year advances o'er the plain.
The Despot hails it from his bannered keep :
Ah, Tyrant, is it well to break a bondsman's sleep ?

He might have dreamed, and solved the conscious throes
Of Time and Fate in some soft vision blest :
Sighed his thick breath in childhood's happy woes,
Or spent the starry tumult of the breast
On some dear dreamland maid, nor known how high
The blind heart beats to hours like this.   'Tis nigh !

Lo in the air a trouble and a strife ;
I feel the future.   Mighty days to come
Strain the strong leash a moment into Life :
Shapes beckon : voices clamour and are dumb :
And viewless nations charge upon the blast
That blows the spectral host to silence, and is past.

Hark, hark ! the great hour strikes !   The stroke peals
    " one ; "
Again ! again !   God !   Have the earth and sky

Stopped breathing?   Will it never end?   'Tis done.
The years are rent asunder with a cry,
The big world groans from all her gulphs and caves,
And sleeping Freedom stirs, and rocks the martyrs'
    graves.

Oh ye far Few, who, battle-worn and grey,
Watch from wild peaks the plains where once ye bled,
Oh ye who but in fortune less than they
Keep the lone vigil of the immortal Dead,
Behold !   And like a fire from steep to steep,
Draw, draw the dreadful swords whereon ye lean and
    weep !

And oh you great brave harvest, that, war-ploughed
And sown with men, a grateful country yields,
You bearded youth who, beardless, saw the proud
Ancestral glories of those smoking fields
That now beneath ten grassy years lie cold,
Rise ! Shew your children how your fathers fought of
    old !

But we are fettered, and a bondsman's ire,
Howe'er it flash, can only end in show'rs.
Who shall unlade these limbs ?   Alas, the fire
Of passion will not melt such chains as ours ;
We have but heated them in wrath of men
To harden them in women's tears.   What then ?

Less than both hands at once what Freeman gives
To Freedom ?   Stand up where the Tyrant stands,
Draw in one breath the strength of slavish lives,
Lift the twin justice of your loaded hands,

And with that double thunder in the veins
Launch on his fated head the vengeance of your chains

They hear ! I see them thro' dissolving night !
Like sudden woods they rise upon the hills !
The mountains stream with a descending sight,
The hollow ear of vacant landscape fills,
From side to side the living landscape warms,
To arms ! Yon bleeding cloud is spread ! Day breaks !
    To arms !

Aye, Tyrant, the day breaks. Look up and fear.
To arms ! A greater day than day is born !
To arms ! A larger light than light is near !
A blacker night than midnight foams with morn !
Arise, arise, my Country, from the flood !
Arise, thou god of day, and dye the east with blood !

LOVE.

TO A LITTLE GIRL.

(1862.)

WHEN we all lie still
Where churchyard pines their funeral vigil keep,
Thou shalt rise up early
While the dews are deep ;
Thee the earliest bird shall rouse
From thy maiden sleep,
Thy white bed in the old house
Where we all, in our day,
Lived and loved so cheerly.
And thou shalt take thy way
Where the nodding daffodil
Tells thee he is near ;
Where the lark above the corn
Sings him to thine ear ;
Where thine own oak, fondly grim,
Points to more than thou canst spy ;
And the beckoning beechen spray
Beckons, beckons thee to him,
Thee to him and him to thee ;
Him to thee, who, coy and slow,
Stealest through dim paths untrod
Step by step, with doubtful glance,
Taking witness quick and shy

Of each bud and herb and tree
If thou doest well or no.
Haste thee, haste thee, slow and coy !
What ! art doubting still, though even
The white tree that shakes with fear
When no other dreams of ill,
The girl-tree whom best thou knowest,
Waves the garlands of her joy,
And, by something more than chance,
Of all paths in one path only
The primroses where thou goest
Thicken to thy feet, as though
Thou already wert in heaven
And walking in the galaxy.
Do those stars no longer glisten
To thy steps, ah ! shivering maid,
That, where upper light doth fade
At yon gnarled and twisted gate,
Thou dost pause and tremble and so,
Listening stir, and stirring listen ?
Not a blossom will illume
That chill grove of cambering yew
Wherein Night seems to vegetate,
And, through bats and owls, a dew
Of darkness fills the mortal gloom.
Haste thee, haste thee, gaze not back !
Of all hours since thou wert born,
Now thou may'st not look forlorn ;
Though the blackening grove is dread,
Shall he plead in vain who pled
" To-morrow ? "   Through the tree-gloom lonely
One more shudder, and the track
Softens : this is upland sod,
Thou canst smell the mountain air,
What was heavy overhead

Lightens, the black whitens, the white brightens !
Ah, dear and fair,
Lo the dazzling east, and lo,
Someone tall against the sky
Coming, coming, like a god,
In the rising morn !
And when the lengthening days whose light we
    never saw
Have melted his sweet awe,
And thy fond fear is like a little hare,
Large-eyed and passionately afraid,
That peepeth from the covert of her rest
Into the narrow glade
Between two woods, and doth a moment dare
The sunshine, and leap back ; yet forth will fare
Again, and each time ventures further from the
    nest,
Till, having past the midst ere she be 'ware,
Bold with fear to be so much confest
She flees across the sun into the other shade ;
Flees as thou that didst so coyly draw
Near him and nearer, and art trembling there
Midway 'twixt giving all and nought,
In a moment, at a thought,
Bashful to panic, hidest on his breast ;
Once again beneath the hill
Where round our graves these funeral pines refuse
The clamorous morning, thou shalt rise up early
When we all lie still.
Thou shalt rise up early while
Down the chimney, ample and deep,
Dreaming swallows gurgle, and shrill
In window-nook the mossy wren
Chirps an answer cheerly,
Chirps and sinks to sleep.

In the crossed and corbelled bay
Of that ivied oriel, thou
Lovest at morn and eve to muse ;
But this once thou shalt not stay
To mark the forming earth, and how
Far and near, in equal grey
Of growing dawn, thy well-known land
Now to the strained gaze appears
The nebulous umbrage of itself, and now,
Ere one can say this or this,
Divides upon the sense into the world that is
As the slow suffusion that doth fill
Tender eyes with soft uncertainties,
Suddenly, we know not when,
Shapes to tears we understand ;
Such tears as blind thy eyes with light,
When thou shalt rise up, white from white.
In thy virgin bed
On that morn, and, by-and-by,
In thy bloom of maidenhead
Beam softly o'er the shadowy floor,
And softly down the ancient stairs,
And softly through the ancestral door,
And o'er the meadow by the house
Where thy small feet shall not rouse
From the grass those unrisen pray'rs,
The skylarks, though thy passing smile
Shall touch away the dews.
And thou shalt take thy way,
Ah whither ? Where is the dear tryst to day ?
Trembler, doth he wait for thee
By the ash or the beech-tree ?
With the lightest earliest breeze
The dodder in the hedge is quaking,
But the mighty ash is still a-slumber ;

All its tender multiplicity
Drooped with a common sleep, by twos and threes,
That triple into companies,
Which, in turn, do multiply
Each by each into an all
So various, so symmetrical,
That the membered trunk on high
Lifts a colour'd cloud that seems
The numberless result of number.
Now still as thy still sleep, soft as thy dreams,
They slumber ; but when morning bids
The world awake, the giant sleeper, waking,
Shall lift at once his shapely myriads up,
As thou at once upliftest thy two lids.
Ah, guileless eyes, from whom those lids unclose ;
Ah, happy, happy eyes ! if morning's beams
Awake the trees, how can they sleep in yours ?
Look up and see them start from their repose !
Yet nay, I think thou wouldst forbid them hear
What some one comes this morn to say ;
Therefore, sweet eyes, shine only on the ground,
Nor venture to look round,
Lest thou behold how subtly the flow'rs sigh
Among the whispering grasses tall,
And see thy secret pale the lily's cheeks,
Or redden on the daisy's lips,
Or tremble in the tremulous tear
Wherewith the warmer light of day fulfils
That frigid beauty of the wort whose stars
Look, thro' the summer darkness like the scars
Of those lunar arrows shot
From the white string of that silver bow
Wherewith, as we all wot,
Because it was a keepsake of her Greek,
Diana shooteth still on every moony night.

What is it, then, that this close buttercup
Is shutting down into a golden shrine?
What hath the wind betrayed to the wind-flow'r,
That, on either side, it so abjures
Thy passing beauty, by such votive hands
Point to point with praying finger-tips?
I know not how such secrets go astray,
Nor how so dear a mystery
Foreslipped the limits of its destined hour ;
Perhaps, the mustered spring, in whatsoe'er
Deep cavern of the earth, ere it come here,
It takes the flowery order of the year,
Heard the soft powers speak of this loveliness
That in due season should be done and said,
As if it were a part o' the white and red
Of summer ; or perchance some zephyr, willing
To sweeten the stol'n fragrance of a rose,
Caught one of thy breaths, and blew it
To the flow'rs that suck the evening air,
And in it some unspoken words of thine
Went thro' the floral beauty, and somewhere
Therein came to themselves, and made the fields
      aware.
Thus, or not thus, surely the cowslips knew it ;
Else wherefore did they press
Their march to this sole day, and long ago
Set their annual dances to it,
This day of all the days that summer yields?
Didst thou not mark how sure and slow
They came upon thee with exact emprise ?
First a golden stranger, meek and lone,
Then the vanward of a fairy host
Following the nightingales,
Bashful and bold, in sudden troops and bands,
Takes the willowy depths of all the dales,

And, on unsuspected nights,
Makes vantage-ground of mounts and heights
Till, ere one knew, a south wind blew,
And a fond invasion holds the fields !
Over the shadowy meadowy season, up and down
        from coast to coast,
A pigmy folk, a yellow-haired people stands,
Stands and hangs its head and smiles !
And art thou conscious that they smile, and why ?
That with such palpitating flight
Thou fleest toward the linden-aisles ?
Ah, yet a moment pause among
The lime-trees, where, from the rich arches o'er
        thee,
The nightingale still strews his falling song
As if the trees were shaken and dropt sweetness :
No heed ?   More speed ?   Ah, little feet,
Is the ground soaked with music that ye beat
Silver echoes thence, and keep
Such quick time and dainty unison
With the running cadence of the bird
That he hath not heard
A note to fright him or offend,
While down the tell-tale path from end to end
Such a ringing scale has run thro' his retreat ?
The limes are past, and ye speed on ;
Ah, little feet, so fond, so fleet,
Fleeter than ever—why this fleetness ?
Who is this ? a start, a cry !
A blind moment of alarms,
And the tryst is in his arms !
Fluttering, fluttering heart, confess
Truly, didst thou never guess
That he would be here before thee ?
Didst thou never dream that ere

The last glow-worm 'gan to dim,
Or the dear day-star to burn,
Or the elm-top rooks to talk,
Or the hedge-row nests to threep,
He was waiting for thee here?
Ah! ne'er so fair, ah! ne'er so dear,
For his love's sake pardon him,
Smile on him again, and turn
With him thro' the sweet-brier glade,
With him thro' the woodbine shade;
In the sweetbrier wilderness,
To his side, ah! closer creep,
In the honeysuckle walk
Let him make thee blush and weep,
While the wooing doves, unseen,
Move the air with fond ado,
And, lest the long morning shine
Show you to some vulgar eye,
To ye, passing side by side,
With a grace that copies thine,
Favouring trees their boughs incline;
While, where'er ye wander by,
Hawthorn and sweet eglantine
From among their laughing leaves
Stretch and pluck ye by the sleeves:
And all flow'rs the hedge doth hide
Sigh their fragrance after you;
And sly airs, with soft caresses,
Letting down thy golden tresses,
Marry those dear locks with his;
While from the rose-arch above thee,
Where the bowery gate uncloses,
Budded tendrils, lithe and green,
Loosen on the wind and lean
Each to each, and leaning kiss,

Kiss and redden into roses.
Oh, you Lovers, warm and living !
And ah, our graves, so deep and chill !
As ye stand in upper light
Murmuring love that never dies,
While your happy cheeks are burning,
Will ye feel a distant yearning ?
Will a sudden dim surprise
Lift up your happy eyes
From what you are taking and giving,
To where the pines their funeral vigil keep,
And we all lie still ?
Love on, plight on, we cannot hear or see.
Oh beautiful and young and happy ! ye
Have the rich earth's inheritance.
For you, for you, the music and the dance
That moves and plays for all who need it not,
That moved and played for us, who, thus forgot,
In the dark house where the heart cannot sing
Nor any pulse mete its own joyous measure,
See not the world, nor any pleasant thing ;
And ye, in your good time, have come into our
　　pleasure.
Ah, while the time is good, love on, plight on !
Leap from yourselves into the light of gladness !
The light, the light ! surely the light is sweet ?
And, if descending from those ecstasies,
Ye touch the common earth with wavering feet,
Your life is at your will ; whate'er betide,
We shall not check or chide.
The hand is dust that might restrain ;
The voice whose warning should distress ye
By any augury of doubt or sadness,
Can never speak again.
The angel that so many woo in vain

Descends, descends !   Ah, seize him ere he soar ;
Ah, seize him by the skirt or by the wing ;
What matter, so that, like the saint of yore,
Ye do not let him hence until he bless ye ?
In our youth we had our madness,
In the grave ye may be wise.
Love on, love on, for Love is all in all !
Manners, that make us and are made of us,
Who with the self-will of an infant king
Do fashion them that have our fashioning,
And make the shape of our correction ;
Virtue, that fruit whose substance ripens slow,
And in one semblance having past from crude
To sweet, rots slowly in the form of good ;
Joy, the involuntary light and glow
Of this electric frame mysterious,
That, radiant from our best activities,
Complexion their fine colours by our own ;
And Duty, the sun-flower of knowledge,—these
Change and may change with changing time and
    place :
But Love is for no planet and no race.
The summer of the heart is late or soon,
The fever in the blood is less or more ;
But while the moons of time shall fill and wane,
While there is earth below and heaven above,
Wherever man is true and woman fair,
Through all the circling cycles Love is Love !
And when the stars have flower'd and fall'n away,
And of this earthly ball
A little dust upon eternity
Is all that shall remain,
Love shall be Love : in that transcendent whole
Clear Nature from the swift euthanasy
Of her last change, transfigured, shall arise ;

And we, whose wonted eyes
Seek vainly the familiar universe,
Shall feel the living worlds in the immortal soul.
But nor of this,
Nor anything of Love except its bliss,
On that summer morning shalt thou know ;
Nor, in that moment's apotheosis
When, like the sudden sun
That, rising round and rayless, bursts in rays,
And is himself and all the heavens in one,
Love in the sun-burst of our own delight
Makes us for an instant infinite,
Owning no first or last, before or after,
Child of Love, shalt thou divine
That, years and years before thy day,
In the little Arcady
And planted Eden of thy line,
On such mornings such a maid
Lived and loved as thou art living and loving,
Through the flowery fields where thou art roving,
And in the favourite bowers and by the wonted
    ways,
Stepped the morning music with thy grace ;
Smiled the sunshine which thou with her face
Smilest ; so, with sweeter voice,
Helped the vernal birds rejoice,
Or, when passing envy stayed
Matins green and leafy virilays
Startled her sole self to hear,
Like a scared bird hushed for fear ;
Or, more frightened by my passionate praise,
Rippled the golden silence with shy laughter.
Yet I saw her standing there,
While my happy love I made,
Standing in her long fair hair,

And looking (so thou lookest now)
As when beneath an April bough
In an April meadow,
Light is netted into place
By a lesser light of shadow ;—
Standing by that tree where he
This morn of thine makes love to thee
Leaning to his half-embrace,
Leaning where, full well I know,
While slow day grows ripe to noon
Thou untired shalt still be leaning,
Still, entranced by Love's beguiling,
Listening, listening, smiling, smiling ,
Leaning by the tree—Ah me,
Leaning on the name I cut
In the bark which, while she tarried here,
Chased it with duteous silver year by year ;
But from the hour that heard her coffin shut
Blindly closed over the withered meaning,
Till argent vert and verdant argentric
Encharged each simple letter to a rune.
Ah me, ah me ! the very name
To which—another yet the same—
(The same, since all thy loveliness is she,
Another, since thou dost forget me)—
Thou answerest, as she answered me
When on summer morns she met me,
While the dews were deep,—
She whom earliest bird did rouse
From her maiden sleep,
From her bed in the old house,
Her white bed in the old house—
She whom bird arouseth never
From that sleep upon the hill
Where we all lie still.

For what is, was, will be.   Suns rise and set
And rise : year after year, as when we met,
In one brief season the epiphany
Of perfect life is shown, and is withdrawn ;
As maidens bloom and die : but Maidenhood for
      ever
Walks the eternal Spring in everlasting Dawn.

AN AUTUMN MOOD.

(1863.)

PILE the pyre, light the fire—there is fuel enough and to
    spare ;
You have fire enough and to spare with your madness
    and gladness ;
Burn the old year—it is dead, and dead, and done.
There is something under the sun that I cannot bear :
I cannot bear this sadness under the sun,
I cannot bear this sun upon all this sadness.
Here on this prophecy, here on this leafless log,
Log upon log, and leafless on leafless, I sit.
Yes, Beauty, I see thee ; yes, I see, but I will not rejoice.
Down, down, wild heart ! down, down, thou hungry dog
That dost but leap and gaze with a want thou canst not
    utter !
Down, down !   I know the ill, but where is the cure?
Moor and stubble and mist, stubble and mist and moor,
Here, on the turf that will feel the snows, a vanishing
    flutter
Of bells that are ringing farewells,
And overhead, from a branch that will soon be bare,
Is it a falling leaf that disturbs my blood like a voice?
Or is it an autumn bird that answers the evening light?
The evening light on stubble and moor and mist,
And pallid woods, and the pale sweet hamlets of dying
    men.

Oh, autumn bird ! I also will speak as I list.
Oh, woods ! oh, fields ! oh, trees ! oh, hill and glen !
You who have seen my glory, you who wist
How I have walked the mornings of delight—
Myself a morning, summer'd through and lit
With light and summer as the sunny dew
With sun : you saw me then—
You see me now ; oh, hear my heart and answer it.
Where is the Nevermore and the land of the Yesterdays?
    Aye,
Where are Youth and Joy, the dew and the honey-dew,
The day of the rose, and the night of the nightingale?
    Where—
Where are the sights and the sounds that shall ne'er and
    shall e'er
Come again?
Once more I have cried my cry, once more in vain
I have listen'd ; once more, for a moment, the ancient
    pain
Is less, though I know that the year is dead and done.
Once more I bear
Under the sun the sadness, over the sadness the sun.
Bear?   I have borne, I shall bear.   But what is a man
That his soul should be seen and heard in the trees and
    flow'rs of the field ;   [yield
Have I tinctured them mortal? or doth their mortality
Me like a fragrance of autumn?   Ah ! passion of Eve,
Ah ! Eve of my passion,—which is it that aches to com·
    plain ?
Oh, old old Minstrelsy, oh, wafty winds of Romaunt,
Blow me your harps.   My sick soul cannot weave
These gossamers of feeling that remain
To any string whereon its ill may grieve.
Blow me your harps—harp, wind-harp, dulcimer,
Citerne, bataunt,

And mandolin, and each string'd woe
Of the sweet olden world, and let them blow
By me, as in sea-streams the sea-gods see
The streaming, streaming hair
Of drownèd girls, and every sorrowy sin
O' the sea.
And so let them blow out the din
Of daylight, and blow in,
With legendary song
Of buried maids,
The evening shades.
And when the thronging harps, and all
The murmurings of wild wind-harps,
Are still ;
And shimmer of dim dulcimer,
And thrill of trill'd citerne,
And plaint of quaint bataunt, and throb of long
Long silent mandolin,
And every other sound that grieves,
Hath dropt into its colour on the leaves,
In the silence let me hear
The round and heavy tear
Of orchards fall.
And as I listen let the air unseen
Be stirr'd with words ;
Let the ripe husk of what is gape open and shed
What has been ;
Through click of gates and the games
Of the living village at play,
Let me hear forgotten names
Of ancient day.
Down like a drop of rain from the evening sky
Let somewhat be said ;
Up from the pool, like a bubble, let something reply,
In the tongue of the dead.

Through the swallows that fly their last
Round the grey spire of the past,
In the faded elms by the height,
Let the last hour of light
Strike, and the yellow chimes
Forget and remember
A dream of other times.
And above let the rocks be warm with the mystical day
        that is not
To-day or to-morrow ;
And from the nest in the rock let me hear the croon
Of orphan-doves that yearn
For the wings that will never return.
And below the rocks, on the grassy slopes and scárps,
Let the tender flowering flame of the exquisite crocus of
        sorrow
Sadden the green of the grass to the pathos of gentle
        September.
And below the slopes and scarps, where the strangled
        rill
Blackens to rot,
Let the unrest of the troublesome hour
Blossom on through the night, and the running flow'r
O' the fatuous fire flicker, and flicker and flare,
Through the aimless dark of disaster, the aimless light of
        despair.
And meantime, let the serious evening star
Contemplative, enlarge her slow pale-brow'd
Regard, until she shake
With tears, and sudden, snatch a hasty cloud
To hide whate'er in those pure realms afar
Is likest human sadness ; and, full-soon,
Let night begin to slake
The west ; and many-headed darkness peer
From every copse and brake ;

While from a cottage nigh,
Where the poor candle of dull Poverty
May barely serve to show
Her stony privilege of woe,
Or if, like her, it try
To leave the cabin'd precincts of its lot,
Steals trembling forth to struggle and expire ;
A milkless babe that shall not see the morn
Starves to the fretted ear,
With lullaby and lullaby,
And rocking shadow to and fro
Athwart the lattice low ;
And from yon western ridge, black as the bier
Of day, let a faint, far-off horn,
Mourning across the ravish'd fields forlorn,
Sound like a streak of sunset seen through the grief of the
      moon.
And, further yet, from the slant of the seaward plain,
The bleating and lowing of many-voicèd flocks and herds,
Forced from their fields, mix on the morning breeze
With sob of seas,
Till the long-rising wind be high,
And, from the distant main,
A gale sweep up the vale, and on the gale a wail
Of shipwreck fill and fail,
Fail and fill, fill and fail, like a sinking, sinking sail
In the rain !
But ere all this to us let the dim smoke rise !
To us from the nearest field, from the nearest pyre
Of stubbled corn, let the dim smoke rise ; and let
The fire that loosens the stubble corn
Loose the soul like smoke, and let tears in the eyes
Confuse the passionate sense till the heart forget
Whether we be the world, or whether the fading world be
We.

ON A
RECENTLY FINISHED STATUE.

1854.

SAID Sculptor to immaculate marble—" Show
Thine essence ; into necessary space
Most pure, describe thine unshaped Purity !"
And lo this Image !   As a bubble blown,
Swiftly her charms, dilating, went through all
The zones of sphered Perfection, till the stone
Smiled as to speak. Some coming thought half-shown
Forms on her parting lips, so that her face
Is as a white flow'r whence a drop of dew,
White with the fragrant flow'r, inclines to fall.
" Oh Everlasting Silence keep her so !
Immortalise this moment, lest she grow
To such a living substance as can die !"
He cried.   Consent Eternal heard his cry.

THE CONVALESCENT TO HER PHYSICIAN.

FRIEND, by whose cancelling hand did Fate forgive
Her debtor, and rescribe her stern award,
Oh with that happier light wherein I live
May all thine after years be sunned and starred !
May God, to Whom my daily bliss I give
In tribute, add it to thy day's reward,
And mine uncurrent joy may'st thou receive
Celestial sterling !   Aye and thou shalt thrive
Even by my vanished woes : for as the sea
Renders its griefs to Heaven, which fall in rains
Of sweeter plenty on the happy plains,
So have my tears exhaled ; and may it be
That from the favouring skies my lifted pains
Descend, oh friend, in blessings upon thee !

ON THE

DEATH OF MRS. BROWNING.

WHICH of the Angels sang so well in Heaven
That the approving Archon of the quire
Cried, " Come up hither !" and he, going higher,
Carried a note out of the choral seven ;
Whereat that cherub to whom choice is given
Among the singers that on earth aspire
Beckoned thee from us, and thou, and thy lyre
Sudden ascended out of sight ?   Yet even
In Heaven thou weepest !   Well, true wife, to weep !
Thy voice doth so betray that sweet offence
That no new call should more exalt thee hence
But for thy harp.   Ah lend it, and such grace
Shall still advance thy neighbour that thou keep
Thy seat, and at thy side a vacant place.

*.

TO 1862.

(Written late in December 1861, *after the death of Prince Albert, and in prospect of war with America.)*

OH worst of years, by what signs shall we know
So dire an advent ?   Let thy New-Year's-day
Be night.   At the east gate let the sun lay
His crown : as thro' a temple hung with woe
Unkinged by mortal sorrow let him go
Down the black noon, whose wan astrology
Peoples the skyey windows with dismay,
To that dark charnel in the west where lo !
The mobled Moon !   For so, at the dread van
Of wars like ours, the great humanity
In things not human should be wrought and wrung
Into our sight, and creatures without tongue
By the dumb passion of a visible cry
Confess the coming agony of Man.

TO 1862.

HARK ! a far gun, like all war's guns in one,
Booms.   At that sign, from the new monument
Of him who held the plough whereto he bent
His royal sword, and meekly laboured on,
Till when the verdict of mankind had gone
Against our peace, he, waiving our consent,
Carried the appeal to higher courts, and went
Himself to plead—She whom he loved and won,
The Queen of Earth and Sea,—her unrisen head
Bowed in a sorrowy cloud—takes her slow way
To her great throne, and, lifting up her day
Upon her land, and to that flag unfurl'd
Where wave the honour and the chastity
Of all our men and maidens living and dead,
Points westward, and thus breaks the silence of the
    world.

A QUEEN'S SPEECH.

"SINCE it is War, my England, and nor I
On you nor you on me have drawn down one
Drop of this bloody guilt, God's Will be done,
Here upon earth in woe, in bliss on high !
Peace is but mortal and to live must die,
And, like that other creature of the sun,
Must die in fire.   Therefore, my English, on !
And burn it young again with victory !
For me, in all your joys I have been first,
And in this woe my place I still shall keep,
I am the earliest widow that must weep,
My children the first orphans.   The divine
Event of all God knows : but come the worst
It cannot leave your homes more dark than mine."

TO A FRIEND IN BEREAVEMENT.

No comfort, nay, no comfort.   Yet would I
In Sorrow's cause with Sorrow intercede.
Burst not the great heart,—this is all I plead—
Ah sentence it to suffer, not to die.
"Comfort?"   If Jesus wept at Bethany,
—That doze and nap of Death—how may we bleed
Who watch the long sleep that is sleep indeed!
Pointing to Heaven I but remind you why
On earth you still must mourn.   He who, being bold
For life-to-come, is false to the past sweet
Of Mortal life, hath killed the world above.
For why to live again if not to meet?
And why to meet if not to meet in love?
And why in love if not in that dear love of old?

JOHN BOHUN MARTIN.

(CAPTAIN OF "THE LONDON.")

KEEPING his word, the promised Roman kept
Enough of worded breath to live till now.
Our Regulus was free of plighted vow
Or tacit debt : skies fell, seas leapt, storms swept ;
Death yawned : with a mere step he might have stept
To life.   But the House-master would know how
To do the master's honours ; and did know,
And did them to the hour of rest, and slept
The last of all his house.   Oh, thou heart's-core
Of Truth, how will the nations sentence thee?
Hark ! as loud Europe cries "Could man do more?"
Great England lifts her head from her distress,
And answers " But could Englishman do less?"
Ah, England ! goddess of the years to be !

FLORENCE, *February* 1866.

TO TOCHTERCHEN.

As one doth touch a flower wherein the dew
Trembles to fall, as one unplaits the ply
Of morning gossamer, so tenderly
My spirit touches thine.   Yet, daughter true
And fair, great Launcelot's mighty nerve and thew
Best clove a king or caught a butterfly,
(Since each extreme is perfect mastery
—Accurate cause repaid in the fine due
Of just effect—) and, child, it should be so
With Love.   The same that nicely plundereth
The honeyed zephyrs for thy cates and wine
Should train thee with the tasks of toil and woe,
Or hold thee against adverse life and death,
Or give thee from my breast to dearer arms than mine.

FRAGMENT OF A SLEEP-SONG. *

SISTER Simplicitie,
Sing, sing a song to me,
Sing me to sleep.
Some legend low and long,
Slow as the summer song
Of the dull Deep.

Some legend long and low,
Whose equal ebb and flow
To and fro creep
On the dim marge of grey
'Tween the soul's night and day,
Washing "awake" away
Into "asleep."

Some legend low and long,
Never so weak or strong
As to let go
While it can hold this heart
Withouten sigh or smart,
Or as to hold this heart
When it sighs " No."

* This and the following fragments were found in MS. after
the death of the writer.

Some long low swaying song,
As the swayed shadow long
Sways to and fro
Where, thro' the crowing cocks,
And by the swinging clocks,
Some weary mother rocks
Some weary woe.

Sing up and down to me
Like a dream-boat at sea,
So, and still so,
Float through the "then" and "when,"
Rising from when to then,
Sinking from then to when
While the waves go.

Low and high, high and low,
Now and then, then and now,
Now, now;
And when the now is then, and when the
    then is now,
And when the low is high, and when the
    high is low,
Low, low;
Let me float, let the boat
Go, go;
Let me glide, let me slide
Slow, slow;
Gliding boat, sliding boat,
Slow, slow;
Glide away, slide away
So, so.

BALLAD.

OH Ladye fair, oh Ladye fair and mine,
Where'er thou be,
Canst thou divine
The Love that hungers thus in me?
The secret cell where lone I lie and sigh for thee?
Long, long I wait, but shall I wait in vain?
How long the Summer waited for the Rose!

Ah say, oh say I shall not wait in vain!
How long, ah fairest! must I keep
The vigil of unsleeping eyes?
Summer's sighs avail,
Summer that sang himself to sleep,
Summer that piping in a grove all day
Played out his lovelorn soul upon the nightingale,
Oh songs more blest than mine, ah happier sighs!

For at rich midnight all the bells
Of all the valley-lilies rang a tune
Like moonlight up and down the dells,
And June
As a naked maiden thro' the shades
Slipt thro' the woods and took her throne.

By this the east is red and white,
The queen of months is seen and known,
Like flocks of doves that soar and fall,

Like butterflies that hover and alight,
Like tears of ecstacy when tear on tear
From both wild eyes rains thro' the wreathèd hands,
The blush of morning drops upon the lands,
The Rose, the Rose is here !
And rapture, rapture crowns the passion of the year.

Hark, hark,
Something stirs the arching green,
Thro' the verdurous aisles the doves are cooing,
And the birds of smaller quire,
As fairies that do run and sing
Before the bridal of their queen,
Flittering and fondly twittering,
Lead thro' the languid air the sick delight of wooing.

Sure thro' the distance dim I see the morn again !
Leaves that meet and part the hues of dawn disclose.
Has she heard my woes?
Has she pitied all my pain?
'Tis she ! 'tis she !
As Summer waited for the Rose
I shall not wait in vain !
As June soft slipping warms the purple Dark,
So thou slippest thro' the shades to me,
So throbs my throbbing heart its thickening throbs
    to thee.

LORD ROBERT.

TALL and young and light of tongue,
Gallantly riding by wood and lea,
He was ware of a maiden fair
And turned and whispered, " Remember me."
(Oh Lord Robert, Lord Robert, Lord Robert,
Oh Lord Robert, 'tis I, 'tis I ;
Under their feet where the cross-roads meet
Dost thou think I can lie and lie,
Lord Robert, Lord Robert, Lord Robert?)

Day by day she walks that way
Never hoping by wood or lea
To be ware of the stranger gay
Who turned and whispered, " Remember me."
(Oh Lord Robert, Lord Robert, Lord Robert,
Oh Lord Robert, 'tis I, 'tis I ;
Under their feet where the cross-roads meet
Dost thou think I can lie and lie,
Lord Robert, Lord Robert, Lord Robert?)

Chance for chance he rides that way,
And again by wood or by lea
He was ware of the maiden fair,
And again he whispered, " Remember me."
(Oh Lord Robert, Lord Robert, Lord Robert,
Oh Lord Robert, 'tis I, 'tis I ;

Under their feet where the cross-roads meet
Dost thou think I can lie and lie,
Lord Robert, Lord Robert, Lord Robert ?)

Chance for chance that way rode he,
And again where he was ware,
Debonnair to that maiden fair
He turned and said " You remember me."
(Oh Lord Robert, Lord Robert, Lord Robert,
Oh Lord Robert, 'tis I, 'tis I ;
Under their feet where the cross roads meet
Dost thou think I can lie and lie,
Lord Robert, Lord Robert, Lord Robert ?)

Chance for chance on a summer-day,
Meeting her still by wood and lea,
He leaped gay from his gallant grey
And said, " I see you remember me."
(Oh Lord Robert, Lord Robert, Lord Robert,
Oh Lord Robert, 'tis I, 'tis I ;
Under their feet where the cross-roads meet
Dost thou think I can lie and lie,
Lord Robert, Lord Robert, Lord Robert ?)

Chance for chance when they hap'd to meet
He pressed on her lip, he breathed in her ear,
Dear, dear words and kisses sweet,
Words and kisses too sweet, too dear.
(Oh Lord Robert, Lord Robert, Lord Robert,
Oh Lord Robert, 'tis I, 'tis I ;
Under their feet where the cross-roads meet,
Dost thou think I can lie and lie,
Lord Robert, Lord Robert, Lord Robert ?)

When the morn enchants the east,
When the south is dazed with noon,
When the eve weeps to the west,
When the night beguiles the moon,
The maid moon that sat so lowly,
Sat so lowly with bended head,
Sat so lowly and rose so slowly,
Rose so slowly and walked so lowly,
Ever, ever, with bended head,
Till the black, black hour of the starless sky,
The black, black hour and the dark, dark bed,
And live maids weep as they turn in their sleep,
Weep in their sleep, and know not why,
And the white owls shriek and the dead men croon.

Now all ye gentlemen, grand and gay,
When you meet a maid by wood or lea,
Sir Knight, I pray, ride on thy way,
Nor turn and whisper, " Remember me."
Lest you drink no wine so strong or fine
But out of the cup, like a shell of the sea,
Thou shalt learn how slaves from their wormy graves
Can do that bidding, " Remember me."
(Oh Lord Robert, Lord Robert, Lord Robert,
Oh Lord Robert, 'tis I, 'tis I ;
Under their feet where the cross-roads meet
Dost thou think I can lie and lie,
Lord Robert, Lord Robert, Lord Robert ?)

Lest never in hall when the knights stand tall
And the goblets flash and the ladies shine,
And thou risest up the king of them all,
To drink to wassail and woman and wine,
Risest up with thy jewelled cup,

But out of the cup, like the sea in a shell,
A voice thou hast known by hill and wood,
A voice, a voice thou hast known too well !
And the cold wine boils on the lip like blood,
And the blood streams cold to the heart like wine,
Cold and hot to the heart like wine.
(Oh Lord Robert, Lord Robert, Lord Robert,
Oh Lord Robert, 'tis I, 'tis I ;
Under their feet where the cross-roads meet
Do you think I can lie and lie,
Lord Robert, Lord Robert, Lord Robert ?)

FRAGMENT OF BALLAD.

How shall I sing? the thing I crave
To say is speechless as a Lover's trance.
How shall I give to thee
What even now is all so wholly thine
That but by losing thee in me
Or me in thee it never can be mine?

As a sliding wave of sliding sea
Before my following hand doth dance
Ever and ever onward to the shore,
And breaks and is a thousand things at once,
And from the moment's multiplicity
Takes itself up again into a wave :

So all I feel and see
Breaks to the thousand-fold of Fate and Chance,
But from the moment's multiplicity
Takes itself up into the thought of thee.

SNOW-DROPS.

Fragment of a Poem that was to have described what the *sight hears* and the *hearing sees* in some of the natural facts of Spring. (Barton End, 1874.)

HAVE you heard the Snow-drops ringing
Their bells to themselves?
Smaller and whiter than the singing
Of any fairy elves
Who follow Mab their Queen
When she is winging
On a moth across the night
And calls them all
With a far-twinkling call
Like the tiniest ray of tiniest starlight
That ever was seen?

Far and near, high and low,
Don't you hear the little bells go?
Not in the big winds that blow
The roaring beeches to and fro,
Not in the lower rivers
Of the breeze
Below the trees,
When the stiff bracken shines,
And the thin bent quivers,
And the limp green waves to and fro,
You shall hear the little bells go,

But in the jets and rivulets
That sputter from the melting snows
When against the mighty bole
Of a beech they dash and swirl
And twist and twirl,
The licking leaves throw
A thousand airy drops invisible
Down the strong perpendicular
To where the snowdrops are ;
Tiny drops that fall and meet,
And swift and sweet
Run dim viewless course of fitful force,
Like an airy waterfall
You shall hear the little bells go
All the tiny snow-bells swinging,
Tiny chauntlets high and low.

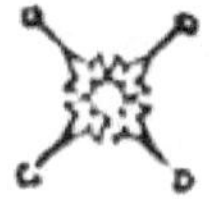

NEW YEAR'S EVE.

As when at twelve o'clock
Strong January opes the gates of Life
And we that were so cabined and so dark
Within the round tower of the rounded year
Feel the far Spring blown in on us and look
Straight to the primroses, and with the swallow
Skim thro' the dawns of daffodils and up
To bluebell skies, and from the bluebell skies,
Like a wild hawk upon a flight of doves,
Swoop upon June and Paradise, and on
Beyond the bounds of Eden to an Earth
Boss'd with great purples of new-clustered wine
Betwixt the tented harvests red and gold,
And so into a cloud, and know no more——

THE WALTER SCOTT PRESS, NEWCASTLE-ON-TYNE.

THE CANTERBURY POETS.

EDITED BY WILLIAM SHARP. 1/- VOLS., SQUARE 8VO.
PHOTOGRAVURE EDITION, 2/-.

Christian Year.	Irish Minstrelsy.
Coleridge.	Milton's Paradise Lost.
Longfellow.	Jacobite Ballads.
Campbell.	Australian Ballads.
Shelley.	Moore's Poems.
Wordsworth.	Border Ballads.
Blake.	Song-Tide.
Whittier.	Odes of Horace.
Poe.	Ossian.
Chatterton.	Fairy Music.
Burns. Poems.	Southey.
Burns. Songs.	Chaucer.
Marlowe.	Golden Treasury.
Keats.	Poems of Wild Life.
Herbert.	Paradise Regained.
Victor Hugo.	Crabbe.
Cowper.	Dora Greenwell.
Shakespeare: Songs, etc.	Goethe's Faust.
Emerson.	American Sonnets.
Sonnets of this Century.	Landor's Poems.
Whitman.	Greek Anthology.
Scott. Marmion, etc.	Hunt and Hood.
Scott. Lady of the Lake, etc.	Humorous Poems.
Praed.	Lytton's Plays.
Hogg.	Great Odes.
Goldsmith.	Owen Meredith's Poems.
Mackay's Love Letters.	Imitation of Christ.
Spenser.	Toby's Birthday Book.
Children of the Poets.	Painter-Poets.
Ben Jonson.	Women-Poets.
Byron (2 Vols.).	Love Lyrics.
Sonnets of Europe.	American Humor. Verse.
Allan Ramsay.	Scottish Minor Poets.
Sydney Dobell.	Cavalier Lyrists.
Pope.	German Ballads.
Heine.	Songs of Beranger.
Beaumont and Fletcher.	Poems by Roden Noel.
Bowles, Lamb, etc.	Songs of Freedom.
Sea Music.	Canadian Poems.
Early English Poetry.	Modern Scottish Poets.
Herrick.	Poems of Nature.
Ballades and Rondeaus.	Cradle Songs.

London : WALTER SCOTT, LIMITED, Paternoster Square.

THE SCOTT LIBRARY.

Cloth, uncut edges, gilt top.   Price 1/6 per volume.

ALREADY ISSUED.

Romance of King Arthur.

Thoreau's Walden.

Thoreau's Week.

Thoreau's Essays.

Confessions of an English
Opium-Eater.

Landor's Conversations.

Plutarch's Lives.

Browne's Religio Medici.

Essays and Letters of
P. B. Shelley.

Prose Writings of Swift.

My Study Windows.

Lowell's Essays on the
English Poets.

The Biglow Papers.

Great English Painters.

Lord Byron's Letters.

Essays by Leigh Hunt.

Longfellow's Prose.

Great Musical Composers

Marcus Aurelius.

Epictetus.

Seneca's Morals.

Whitman's Specimen
Days in America.

Whitman's Democratic
Vistas.

White's Natural History.

Captain Singleton.

Essays by Mazzini.

Prose Writings of Heine.

Reynolds' Discourses.

The Lover: Papers of
Steele and Addison.

Burns's Letters.

Volsunga Saga.

Sartor Resartus.

Writings of Emerson.

Life of Lord Herbert.

English Prose.
The Pillars of Society.
Fairy and Folk Tales.
Essays of Dr. Johnson.
Essays of Wm. Hazlitt.
Landor's Pentameron, &c.
Poe's Tales and Essays
Vicar of Wakefield.
Political Orations.
Holmes's Autocrat.
Holmes's Poet.
Holmes's Professor.
Chesterfield's Letters.
Stories from Carleton.
Jane Eyre.
Elizabethan England.
Davis's Writings.
Spence's Anecdotes.
More's Utopia.
Sadi's Gulistan.
English Folk Tales.
Northern Studies.
Famous Reviews.
Aristotle's Ethics.
Landor's Aspasia.
Tacitus.
Essays of Elia.
Balzac.
De Musset's Comedies.
Darwin's Coral-Reefs.

Sheridan's Plays.
Our Village.
Humphrey's Clock, &c.
Tales from Wonderland.
Douglas Jerrold.
Rights of Woman.
Athenian Oracle.
Essays of Sainte-Beuve.
Selections from Plato.
Heine's Travel Sketches.
Maid of Orleans.
Sydney Smith.
The New Spirit.
Marvellous Adventures.
  (From he Morte d'Arthur.)
Helps's Essays.
Montaigne's Essays.
Luck of Barry Lyndon
William Tell.
Carlyle's German Essays.
Lamb's Essays.
Wordsworth's Prose.
Leopardi's Dialogues.
Inspector-General (Gogol)
Bacon's Essays.
Prose of Milton.
Plato's Republic.
Passages from Froissart.
Prose of Coleridge.
Heine in Art and Letters
Essays of De Quincey.

New Series of Critical Biographies.

Edited by ERIC ROBERTSON and FRANK T. MARZIALS.

GREAT WRITERS.

Cloth, Gilt Top, Price 1s. 6d.

ALREADY ISSUED—

LIFE OF LONGFELLOW. By Prof. E. S. ROBERTSON.

LIFE OF COLERIDGE. By HALL CAINE.

LIFE OF DICKENS. By FRANK T. MARZIALS.

LIFE OF D. G. ROSSETTI. By JOSEPH KNIGHT.

LIFE OF SAMUEL JOHNSON. By Col. F. GRANT.

LIFE OF DARWIN. By G. T. BETTANY.

CHARLOTTE BRONTE. By AUGUSTINE BIRRELL.

LIFE OF CARLYLE. By RICHARD GARNETT, LLD.

LIFE OF ADAM SMITH. By R. B. HALDANE, M.P.

LIFE OF KEATS. By W. M. ROSSETTI.

LIFE OF SHELLEY. By WILLIAM SHARP.

LIFE OF GOLDSMITH. By AUSTIN DOBSON.

LIFE OF SCOTT. By Professor YONGE.

LIFE OF BURNS. By Professor BLACKIE.

LIFE OF VICTOR HUGO. By FRANK T. MARZIALS.

LIFE OF EMERSON. By RICHARD GARNETT, LL.D.

LIFE OF GOETHE. By JAMES SIME.

LIFE OF CONGREVE. By EDMUND GOSSE.

LIFE OF BUNYAN. By Canon VENABLES.

GREAT WRITERS—continued.

LIFE OF CRABBE. By T. E. KEBBEL, M.A.

LIFE OF HEINE. By WILLIAM SHARP.

LIFE OF MILL. By W. L. COURTNEY.

LIFE OF SCHILLER. By H. W. NEVINSON.

LIFE OF CAPTAIN MARRYAT. By DAVID HANNAY.

LIFE OF LESSING. By T. W. ROLLESTON.

LIFE OF MILTON. By RICHARD GARNETT.

LIFE OF GEORGE ELIOT. By OSCAR BROWNING.

LIFE OF BALZAC. By FREDERICK WEDMORE.

LIFE OF JANE AUSTEN. By GOLDWIN SMITH.

LIFE OF BROWNING. By WILLIAM SHARP.

LIFE OF BYRON. By Hon. RODEN NOEL.

LIFE OF HAWTHORNE. By MONCURE CONWAY.

LIFE OF SCHOPENHAUER. By Professor WALLACE.

LIFE OF SHERIDAN. By LLOYD SANDERS.

LIFE OF THACKERAY. By HERMAN MERIVALE and
   FRANK T. MARZIALS.

LIFE OF CERVANTES. By H. E. WATTS.

LIFE OF VOLTAIRE. By FRANCIS ESPINASSE.

LIFE OF LEIGH HUNT. By COSMO MONKHOUSE.

LIFE OF WHITTIER. By W. J. LINTON.

LIFE OF RENAN. By FRANCIS ESPINASSE.

Bibliography to each, by J. P. ANDERSON, British Museum.

LIBRARY EDITION OF "GREAT WRITERS."

Printed on large paper of extra quality, in handsome binding,
Demy 8vo, price 2s. 6d. per volume.

London : WALTER SCOTT, LIMITED, Paternoster Square.

LIBRARY OF HUMOUR.

Cloth Elegant, Large Crown 8vo.   Price 3/6 each.

VOLUMES ALREADY ISSUED.

THE HUMOUR OF FRANCE. Translated, with an Introduction and Notes, by Elizabeth Lee. With numerous Illustrations by Paul Frénzeny.

THE HUMOUR OF GERMANY. Translated, with an Introduction and Notes, by Hans Müller-Casenov. With numerous Illustrations by C. E. Brock.

THE HUMOUR OF ITALY. Translated, with an Introduction and Notes, by A. Werner. With 50 Illustrations by Arturo Faldi.

THE HUMOUR OF AMERICA. Edited, with an Introduction and Notes, by J. Barr (of the *Detroit Free Press*). With numerous Illustrations by C. E. Brock.

THE HUMOUR OF HOLLAND. Translated, with an Introduction and Notes, by A. Werner. With numerous Illustrations by Dudley Hardy.

THE HUMOUR OF IRELAND. Selected by D. J. O'Donoghue. With numerous Illustrations by Oliver Paque.

THE HUMOUR OF SPAIN. Translated, with an Introduction and Notes, by S. Taylor. With numerous Illustrations by H. R. Millar.

THE HUMOUR OF RUSSIA. Translated, with Notes, by E. L. Boole, and an Introduction by Stepniak. With 50 Illustrations by Paul Frénzeny.

IN PREPARATION.

THE HUMOUR OF JAPAN. Translated, with an Introduction, by A. M. With Illustrations by George Bigot (from Drawings made in Japan).

London: WALTER SCOTT, LIMITED, Paternoster Square.

BOOKS OF FAIRY TALES.

Crown 8vo, Cloth Elegant, Price 3s. 6d. per vol.

ENGLISH FAIRY AND OTHER FOLK TALES.

Selected and Edited, with an Introduction,
By EDWIN SIDNEY HARTLAND.

With 12 Full-Page Illustrations by CHARLES E. BROCK.

SCOTTISH FAIRY AND FOLK TALES.

Selected and Edited, with an Introduction,
By SIR GEORGE DOUGLAS, BART.

With 12 Full-Page Illustrations by JAMES TORRANCE.

IRISH FAIRY AND FOLK TALES.

Selected and Edited, with an Introduction,
By W. B. YEATS.

With 12 Full-Page Illustrations by JAMES TORRANCE.

London : WALTER SCOTT, LIMITED, Paternoster Square.

NEW EDITION IN NEW BINDING.

In the new edition there are added about forty reproductions in fac-simile of autographs of distinguished singers and instrumentalists, including Sarasate, Joachim, Sir Charles Hallé, Paderewsky, Stavenhagen, Henschel, Trebelli, Miss Macintyre, Jean Gérardy, etc.

Quarto, cloth elegant, gilt edges, emblematic design on cover, 6s. May also be had in a variety of Fancy Bindings.

THE

MUSIC OF THE POETS:

A MUSICIANS' BIRTHDAY BOOK.

EDITED BY ELEONORE D'ESTERRE KEELING.

THIS is a unique Birthday Book. Against each date are given the names of musicians whose birthday it is, together with a verse-quotation appropriate to the character of their different compositions or performances. A special feature of the book consists in the reproduction in fac-simile of autographs, and autographic music, of living composers. Three sonnets by Mr. Theodore Watts, on the "Fausts" of Berlioz, Schumann, and Gounod, have been written specially for this volume. It is illustrated with designs of various musical instruments, etc.; autographs of Rubenstein, Dvorák, Greig, Mackenzie, Villiers Stanford, etc., etc.

London : WALTER SCOTT, LIMITED, Paternoster Square.

COMPACT AND PRACTICAL.

In Limp Cloth; for the Pocket. Price One Shilling.

THE EUROPEAN
CONVERSATION BOOKS.

FRENCH.   ITALIAN.
SPANISH.   GERMAN.
NORWEGIAN.

CONTENTS.

Hints to Travellers—Everyday Expressions—Arriving at and Leaving a Railway Station — Custom House Enquiries—In a Train—At a Buffet and Restaurant—At an Hotel—Paying an Hotel Bill—Enquiries in a Town—On Board Ship—Embarking and Disembarking —Excursion by Carriage—Enquiries as to Diligences—Enquiries as to Boats—Engaging Apartments—Washing List and Days of Week — Restaurant Vocabulary — Telegrams and Letters, etc., etc.

The contents of these little handbooks are so arranged as to permit direct and immediate reference. All dialogues or enquiries not considered absolutely essential have been purposely excluded, nothing being introduced which might confuse the traveller rather than assist him. A few hints are given in the introduction which will be found valuable to those unaccustomed to foreign travel.

London · WALTER SCOTT, LIMITED, Paternoster Square.

Crown 8vo, Cloth, 3s. 6d.   Half Morocco, 6s. 6d.

THE
CONTEMPORARY SCIENCE SERIES.

EDITED BY HAVELOCK ELLIS.

Illustrated Vols. between 300 and 400 pp. each.

EVOLUTION OF SEX. By Prof. GEDDES and THOMSON.
ELECTRICITY IN MODERN LIFE. G. W. DE TUNZELMANN.
THE ORIGIN OF THE ARYANS. By Dr. ISAAC TAYLOR.
PHYSIOGNOMY AND EXPRESSION. By P. MANTEGAZZA.
EVOLUTION AND DISEASE. By J. B. SUTTON.
THE VILLAGE COMMUNITY. BY G. L. GOMME.
THE CRIMINAL. By HAVELOCK ELLIS.
SANITY AND INSANITY. BY Dr. C. MERCIER.
HYPNOTISM. By Dr. ALBERT MOLL (Berlin).
MANUAL TRAINING. By Dr. WOODWARD (St. Louis, Mo.).
THE SCIENCE OF FAIRY TALES. By E. S. HARTLAND.
PRIMITIVE FOLK. By ELIE RECLUS.
THE EVOLUTION OF MARRIAGE. BY LETOURNEAU.
BACTERIA AND THEIR PRODUCTS. By Dr. WOODHEAD.
EDUCATION AND HEREDITY. By J. M. GUYAU.
THE MAN OF GENIUS. By Prof. LOMBROSO.
THE GRAMMAR OF SCIENCE. By Prof. KARL PEARSON.
PROPERTY : ITS ORIGIN. By CH. LETOURNEAU.
VOLCANOES, PAST AND PRESENT. By Prof. E. HULL.
PUBLIC HEALTH PROBLEMS. By Dr. J. F. J. SYKES
MODERN METEOROLOGY. By FRANK WALDO, Ph.D.
THE GERM-PLASM. By Professor WEISMANN. **6s.**
THE INDUSTRIES OF ANIMALS. By F. HOUSSAY.
MAN AND WOMAN. By HAVELOCK ELLIS. **6s.**
THE EVOLUTION OF MODERN CAPITALISM. By JOHN
    A. HOBSON, M.A.
APPARITIONS AND THOUGHT-TRANSFERENCE. By
    FRANK PODMORE, M.A.
AN INTRODUCTION TO COMPARATIVE PSYCHOLOGY.
    By Prof. C. LLOYD MORGAN. **6s.**
THE ORIGINS OF INVENTION. O. T. MASON, A.M., Ph.D.

LONDON : WALTER SCOTT, LIMITED, PATERNOSTER SQUARE.

"BOOKLETS"

By COUNT LEO TOLSTOY

NEW EDITIONS, REVISED.

Small 12mo, Cloth, with Embossed Design on Cover, each containing Two Stories by Count Tolstoï, and Two Drawings by H. R. Millar. In Box, price 2s. each.

VOLUME I. CONTAINS—
WHERE LOVE IS, THERE GOD IS ALSO.
THE GODSON.

VOLUME II. CONTAINS—
WHAT MEN LIVE BY.
WHAT SHALL IT PROFIT A MAN?

VOLUME III. CONTAINS—
THE TWO PILGRIMS.
IF YOU NEGLECT THE FIRE, YOU DON'T PUT IT OUT.

VOLUME IV. CONTAINS –
MASTER AND MAN.

VOLUME V. CONTAINS –
THE THREE PARABLES.
IVAN THE FOOL.

London : WALTER SCOTT, LIMITED, Paternoster Square.

Crown 8vo, Cloth Elegant, in Box, Price 2s. 6d.

THE CULT OF BEAUTY:

A MANUAL OF PERSONAL HYGIENE.

BY C. J. S. THOMPSON.

CONTENTS—

CHAPTER I.—THE SKIN.

CHAPTER II.—THE HANDS.

CHAPTER III.—THE FEET.

CHAPTER IV.—THE HAIR.

CHAPTER V.—THE TEETH.

CHAPTER VI.—THE NOSE.

CHAPTER VII.—THE EYE.

CHAPTER VIII.—THE EAR.

"'Quackery,' says Mr. Thompson, 'was never more rampant than it is to-day' with regard to 'aids in beautifying the person.' His little book is based on purely hygienic principles, and comprises recipes for toilet purposes which he warrants are 'practical and harmless.' These are virtues in any book of health and beauty, and Mr. Thompson's advice and guidance are, we find, not wanting in soundness and common-sense."— *Saturday Review.*

London: WALTER SCOTT, LIMITED, Paternoster Square.

www.ingramcontent.com/pod-product-compliance
Lightning Source LLC
Chambersburg PA
CBHW032006120726
47902CB00014B/1367